Dance With Me

ALLISON A. ANDREWS

ABOUT THE AUTHOR

Allison A. Andrews is a romance author, wife, and mum based in
Brisbane, Australia.
A lifelong book lover with a vivid imagination, she turned her
passion for storytelling into swoon-worthy novels filled with men
who don't need to be taught how to be human, strong women,
and unforgettable stories.

www.aawpublishing.com

ALSO BY ALLISON A. ANDREWS & ANTOINETTE W. MAY

Order of the Dragon Trilogy (Paranormal Romance)

#1 Illusions

#2 Blood Memories

#3 Phoenix Rising

Circle of Friends Series (Contemporary Romance)

The Winning Ticket

Chasing Horizons

Dance With Me

Pieces of Us

Calgary Mounties

(Contemporary Hockey Romance)

On Thin Ice

Melt The Ice

Coming Home For Christmas Anthology

From Snow to Surf (Circle of Friends and Calgary Mounties

Crossover)

Dark Desires (Contemporary Spicy Romance)

(Writing as Antoinette W. May)

Reckless (Intro Novella)

Ravage

Ruin

CONTENTS

WANT A SNEAK PEEK
OF PIECES OF US?

For Linda. For being the most caring mother-in-law a woman could ever hope for. Eleven years was not long enough to have you in my life but I hope you're watching over us all with a smile and know that we are okay.

Song List

Intrusive Thoughts - Natalie Jane

Tattoos - Citizen Soldier

My Mouth (la la la) - ISHAN

SNAP - Rosa Linn

Love Me Now - Ziggy Alberts

I'll Be Good - Jaymes Young

Unsteady - X Ambassadors

How Do I Say Goodbye - Dean Lewis

Teeth - 5 Seconds Of Summer

Cheap Thrills - Sia

Emotionless - Ashley Kutcher

The Hunter - Adam Jensen

I'm Not Okay - Citizen Soldier

Loved Us More - Munn

abcdefu (angrier) - GAYLE

Like You Mean It - Steven Rodriguez

Something In The Orange - Summer Rios

Perfectly Imperfect - Declan J Donovan

Lose Control - Teddy Swims

Hurt Myself - Ekoh, Nate Vickers

People Watching - Taylor Acorn

Heavy - Citizen Soldier, SkyDxddy

CONTENT/TRIGGER WARNING

Please note some themes within this novel may cause distress. See below for a list of potential triggers.

- Loved one with a terminal illness - dealing with grief
- Mention of previous passing of a loved one.
- Loss of a parent
- Parental estrangement

1

I HATE WEDDINGS

NEW FARM PARK on a sunny Brisbane winter afternoon has long been one of my favourite places. Mind you, I'm not usually dressed quite so formally when I'm here.

"You ready, T?" My best friend Kylie grins at me, her long brown hair cascading over one shoulder in expertly styled soft waves.

My own long, red hair has been tamed into a similar style, but it doesn't have quite the same effect as it does on Kylie. Probably because Kylie is stunning. Her floor length, single shoulder emerald green dress skims her gorgeous curves, making her tanned skin and green eyes stand out even more. While I am pretty sure my fat rolls are sticking out of the back of my identical dress, and my pale skin is basically glowing, as usual. How is it possible that Kylie now lives in one of the coldest cities in Canada but can still maintain a tan, while I live in Brisbane, the capital of one of the hottest states in Australia, and I still look like a ghost? Having spent over a decade trying not to compare myself to my friends, I've always struggled with my weight and appearance, so it's near impossible not to feel like the ugly-step sister. Especially in circumstances like this one where I'm wearing the exact same clothes as two of them and don't look even half as good. Behind her, our friend Morgan smooths the skirt of her own dress, looking just as stunning, with her blonde hair styled the same as ours. She's always had the supermodel look going for her, but add in professional hair and make-up, and it's a wonder her husband can concentrate on anything else today.

You know what? I hate weddings.

As a twenty-seven-year-old woman, I know I'm not meant to say that. But when you're the perpetually single one at every wedding you've been to, the over the top displays of devoted love just serve as a constant reminder that all of your friends are happily shacking up while you're adrift in a sea of shitty tinder dates.

Growing up, I looked to my future with rose-tinted glasses. But over time, the tint darkened. Every guy I was interested in had inevitably lusted after one of my friends or my older sister, and I became like the main character in that movie *The Duff*. Relegated to friend status while they pumped me for information on whether the true objects of their affections were single and if they'd ever be interested in dating the *nice* guy. I was lucky to be surrounded by a tight knit group of friends that included my sister, Annelisa, and her boyfriend, Will, who was like an older brother to me. Then she up and left him brokenhearted, and I was once again cast aside, avoided by the one guy who had seemed like he would never treat me like the others had.

I've been single for pretty much my entire life. Except for a brief three-month relationship in my early twenties with a guy who was on the rebound and eventually realised he'd rather be single like the rest of his mates than shackled to the woman who was ready to finally be in a committed relationship. I have never had a one-night stand, so I've slept with exactly one guy... At twenty-seven... Let that sink in for a moment. My dildo gets far more action than I'm willing to admit.

So yeah, I hate weddings.

And the hardest part about this particular wedding is that the bride, Bri, is one of my best friends, which means I'm in the damn bridal party. So I have had to paste on a smile for the last several hours while we've posed for the usual pre-wedding photos, and helped Bri get into her beautiful dress. The torture is now about to continue while I walk down the aisle with Kylie, and her brother, Will. Yep, the same Will who essentially ignored me after my sister abandoned him.

He's now standing near the faux flower wall that hides us from view of the wedding guests, watching us both patiently while we gather our bouquets and do the last make-up and hair checks and wait for our turn to head down the aisle on the other side.

When the music starts, Morgan and her husband, Chris, take the first steps out past the wall, heading towards the groom - the last member of our circle of friends, Jake - who is waiting at the temporary altar next to the rose garden. Bri's Mum is a few steps behind them, holding the lead of Bri and Jake's little dog, Maddie, who is their ring bearer. Although my mood isn't particularly stellar right now, I have to admit that is freaking adorable.

Making sure my expertly crafted fake smile is firmly in place, I nod towards Kylie. "Yep, let's go."

With a final look back at Bri, who gives us a nervous smile, we take our places on either side of Will, each slipping a hand in the crook of his elbows before stepping around the wall.

Will and I have reached an understanding. We pretend there are no issues between us when we're with the group, and I completely ignore him the rest of the time. He tried to apologise for how he treated me in the wake of the break-up with Annelisa, however it was a case of too little, too late for me. But because we've been putting on such a good show of being fine, Bri and Jake hadn't thought it would be an issue to have the two of us walking down the aisle together on their big day.

At least Kylie is here to draw the attention off my tight, fake smile.

The three of us reach the altar, and Kylie and I join Morgan, while Will moves to stand with Chris and Jake. All three men are extremely attractive. Each one of them is tall with varying shades of brown hair, and the black suits definitely work for them. The nervous groom is staring intently at the flower wall, waiting for the love of his life to appear with her father. The look of anticipation on his handsome face sets off a feeling of envy that I immediately force myself to squash down. No use dreaming about something that just doesn't seem like it is going to happen for me.

Despite my anti-wedding sentiment, I have to admit that my best friend is an absolutely stunning bride, and I hold my breath while I watch Jake's face transform once Bri steps into view. I've known the two of them my entire life, and aside from Chris and Morgan, I can't imagine two people more perfect for each other. For years, I watched, mostly silent, while they danced around each other, but I'd like to think that my encouragement helped Bri to finally make the move to go from friends to lovers. And it was all worth it to see the look of pure love on both their faces right now.

Once Bri arrives in front of Jake, it's hard to imagine a more beautiful couple. Wearing a simple cream, figure-hugging lace dress, with her long blonde hair styled into a sleek bun behind her right ear, Bri is the picture-perfect bride, straight from the pages of a bridal magazine. Coupled with Jake's brown hair, tanned skin and blue eyes, the pair of them are basically Barbie and Ken brought to life.

There isn't a dry eye amongst us by the time the ceremony is over, and everyone applauds when they are declared husband and wife. Their kiss is full of emotion, which has me feeling both thrilled for them as well sad for myself that I've never had someone look at me like they are looking at each other.

. . .

Several hours later, once we make it through the photos and are finally at the reception, I can feel the cracks in my mask of happiness starting to show.

They've booked out the function room at one of the luxury hotels in the city, and it's expertly decorated with tropical plants and flowers, fitting in with Bri's love of gardens. Everything is perfect, but I'm reaching my limit.

"You okay?" Kylie asks, taking a seat next to me at the bridal table.

"Yeah, I'm good." I smile at her, but obviously something on my face gives me away.

She cocks her head to the side. "What's going on?"

"Nothing. I'm fine, I promise." I reach out and squeeze her hand.

"You two look gorgeous." Kylie's boyfriend, Seth, slides in beside her.

Kylie grins at him. "Thanks, babe. You look pretty hot yourself."

The tall Canadian definitely looks good in a suit. Well, he looks good in anything, really. Kylie and I met him and his best friend, Lincoln, on an under-thirties tour around Europe two years ago, and it was pretty much love at first sight for the two of them.

Bri and Jake had timed their wedding so that it was in the hockey off-season, which meant Seth, the captain of the Calgary Mounties NHL team, could come with Kylie, and it's great to see them both together. It's been hard, having my best friend move to the other side of the world, but seeing her so happy makes it worth it.

It also just makes me wonder if it will ever be my turn to have someone make me feel the same way.

After making it through dinner, the speeches and the first dance, once everyone has entered party mode, I finally have the chance to step away unnoticed for a little while.

Slipping into the decadent bathroom, I stand in front of the mirror, staring at my reflection for a moment, wishing that the person staring back at me looked different. Even with professional hair and makeup, it can't make me love myself like I'm supposed to. Years of being surrounded by women who may as well be super models has given me a healthy dose of low self esteem, something that I am working on. But it's not easy, and I wish I could meet someone who I wasn't worried wanted to be with one of my friends or sister instead.

One of Jake and Bri's friends from Stanthorpe stumbles drunkenly out of one of the stalls, and I turn, ready to catch her if she falls.

"Oh hey! You're one of the bridesmaids!" she declares, and I stifle a laugh while I nod. "Which one of those fucking hot groomsmen are you going to be hooking up with tonight?"

Too shocked to hold the laugh in this time, it comes out in a splutter. "Um, definitely neither of them. One is married and the other is my sister's ex."

"Oh, well, better not let all the fancy hair and makeup go to waste. Plenty of other guys at this wedding for you to get laid," she continues babbling on while she washes her hands, before touching up her lipstick.

"Yeah, I don't think that's going to be happening. Been a very long time since any guy was looking at me for a tumble between the sheets."

She pauses, the lipstick hovering over her lips while she looks at me in the mirror.

"Honey, that's all the more reason to wake those lady parts up and rip the suit off of one of the single men out there. I plan on going home very satisfied after the trip to the city, once I work out which one is coming back to my hotel room."

She shoots me a cheeky grin before heading back out to the

party, and I shake my head, wishing I had even half her level of confidence.

Sighing, I push the door open and pass the hotel bar on the way back into the ballroom. I pause at the doorway, watching my friends dancing away happily. Even Will is smiling, although I'm aware he is probably feeling just as lonely as I am amongst the many happy couples.

A lump forms in my throat, and I can't seem to make myself cross the threshold. I've had enough of playing pretend today.

Turning, I head back the way I've just come, and find myself standing at the door of the bar. I've never been much of a drinker, but after a day of too much lovey-dovey fun, I could go for a cocktail right now. The sweeter, the better.

I take a seat at the long bar, looking around for the bartender. The room is almost completely empty, aside from a couple sitting in a corner booth with their heads together, and a rather attractive guy with wavy reddish-brown hair about my age sitting at the other end of the bar, scrolling on his phone with a beer in front of him.

The bartender appears from the door leading out the back and smiles at me. "What can I get you?"

I glance at the cocktail menu before closing it. "Can I have a pina colada, please?"

She nods and gets started on putting together the fruity drink.

"They not serving cocktails in that posh wedding?" I look over to see that the guy on his own has moved closer, standing just a few stools down with his beer in hand.

Up close, it's hard not to notice how hot he is. He's wearing a blue button-up shirt with the sleeves rolled to his elbows and a pair of dark blue jeans. His short beard, cut close to his jawline, seems to be something that I find attractive, based on how dry my mouth has just become. I'm going to put my body's reaction down to the fact that it has been far too long since I've had sex. Usually I'm pretty oblivious, but right now, my lady parts have woken right up and are doing a little dance while I hold his gaze.

Clearing my throat, I shrug a little. "Maybe they are. I didn't check. Just needed a bit of a break."

"Not a fan of weddings?" He sits down on the stool beside me.

"Not so much. But when it's your best friends, you gotta put on the big smiles and be happy for them." I wave my hand over my dress.

"Ah, let me guess. Maid of honour?"

I shake my head. "No, thankfully. Her sister took that joyful job. But I got to walk down the aisle with my sister's ex-boyfriend, so that was fun." The bartender places the drink in front of me, and I wave my phone over the bank machine to pay.

He tilts his beer towards me, the universal sign to cheers him. I tap my glass to his and take a sip.

"Sounds like you've had a hell of a day." He rests both arms against the edge of the bar.

"It wasn't so bad," I concede, feeling a little guilty about how bitter I sound. "I'm glad it all went well for them. They are the sort of couple who deserve only good things. Just hard being the single one at every wedding." It must be something about him being a complete stranger that has me speaking so candidly, but it feels good not to be pretending for a change.

"I get it. I haven't really been to many weddings, but I was single at all of them. It's hard watching everyone else live their lives when yours feels like it's standing still." He's put into words what I haven't been able to say out loud for a few years now.

"Yep," I reply, the P making a popping sound, while I stare at the drink in my hand.

"Want a drinking mate?" he asks.

I turn to look at him, running my eyes over his face. He seems genuinely interested in talking to me, which sets off a swarm of butterflies in my stomach.

Attempting to appear casual, I shrug. "Sure... Why not?"

2

WHAT'S YOUR STORY?

AIDEN

My day started out pretty boring. I only arrived in Brisbane yesterday, and until I find a place to live, this luxury hotel, that my father is paying for, is home. I've never felt comfortable in places like this, so I spent most of the day wandering around the city, trying to get acquainted with my new home. It's definitely smaller than London, where my mother moved us when I was ten, and before that, we lived in Sydney.

Good old Dad wasn't in the picture much. Pretty sure the posho hotel room and the new job is his way of trying to make up for a childhood of not giving a toss and leaving the hard work up to Mum.

I get the sense that the redhead sitting next to me at the bar has some issues of her own, and it feels good to have someone to talk to after a few weeks of being alone. After Mum's death, I kind of hid from the world. But this move is a fresh start. So why not have a drink with a beautiful woman and see if, at the very least, I can make a new friend?

Although, I'll be honest, the attraction I'm feeling towards her is definitely less about my desire to be friends and more about wondering how her plump lips would feel against mine.

"So. You know why I'm hanging out looking all sad in a bar. What's your story?" She downs the rest of her drink and waves her hand at the bartender to order another.

"Just having a drink before bed." I don't feel much like getting into my stuff right now, and I can tell she needs to talk.

"Must be a nice bed if this is where you're staying," she replies.

I can't tell if she's aware of how suggestive that comment is, but I decide not to bite. There's something about her that tells me she's not the type to jump into bed with someone straight away, and I'm not really sure I want to go down that path again, either. I'd put my years of one night stands and friends with benefits behind me a while ago.

"It's a nice bed. But the company in the bar beats my lonely bed right now."

She pauses in the process of lifting her second cocktail to her lips and lifts an eyebrow. "Wow, that was smooth. Guys don't normally use lines like that on me unless my friends are around."

I blink, digesting that bit of information. "What do you mean?"

She shrugs. "I don't normally get hit on unless my very attractive friends are around. Like, supermodel hot. I'm usually the stepping stone to the pretty ones."

"Um... I don't quite know what to do with that... Does that seriously happen?" I ask.

"All. The. Time." She takes another mouthful of her cocktail.

If I knew her better, I'd suggest she slows down, but I get the feeling that would probably piss her off. Knowing she's in the bridal party from next door, I at least know where to go to get her friends if she gets messy.

Instead, I shake my head. "Well, I'm sorry to hear that. Cause you are a very beautiful woman, and no one deserves to feel like they aren't someone's first choice."

Who would overlook this woman? With the type of figure that gives you something to hold on to, she's got curves for days. I've always had a thing for redheads, and right now, I can't remember finding any of the ones before as attractive as I do this one.

She puts her drink down on the bar and turns in her seat to face me, her pretty green eyes twinkling with amusement. "You obviously know all the right words to say to a woman."

I laugh, probably a little bitterly. "Not usually. I haven't spent much time around a woman one on one for a while. Unless you count my best friend, which I don't." And I haven't slept with anyone since the last time Sarah, the best friend in question, and I hooked up a year ago.

She tilts her head to the side and studies me. "Why's that?"

I take a sip of beer while I consider how much to say. "I've been busy with family stuff the last few years. Kind of ate into my socialising time."

"That sounds lousy, I'm sorry."

I shrug. "It is what it is. But I'm here with you now, so I'm glad to say things are looking up."

She snorts and shakes her head. "So many pretty lines. Obviously, the time away did nothing to your pickup lines." She sticks out her hand. "I'm Tara, by the way."

I take her hand. "Aiden." Just to lean into the suave persona I've got going, I lift it to my lips and kiss the back of it.

She throws her head back and laughs. But she doesn't pull her hand away, so I continue to hold it. I don't even know what my goal is here, but I will happily keep making her laugh like that. It's better than the bitterness that was in her tone earlier.

"So, Aiden. Is that an English accent I detect?"

I nod. "It is. Although, I'm Australian. I just like to pull out the accent to see if it wins me any points with the ladies." I grin.

She raises an eyebrow. "Really?"

I laugh. "No. I mean, I am Aussie, but we moved to London when I was a kid, so I picked up the accent. Only been back for a day, so it's going to take me a while to shake it."

"Well, keep that up and you'll be reeling in the ladies."

I squeeze her hand. "Promise?"

Her breath hitches a little, and she looks down at our hands. "Oh yeah, definitely."

"There you are!" Tara jumps, whirling around when a pretty brunette wearing the same dress as her appears behind us. "We've been looking for you."

Tara holds up her phone. "You could have just messaged."

"I couldn't find my phone. I think I left it back in the bridal suite. Who's this?" Her friend turns, running her interested gaze over me.

"Aiden." I put my hand out, and she shakes it, her grip firm.

"Kylie. Nice to meet you."

Is this one of the friends she was talking about earlier? She's very attractive, but no more so than Tara. They both have similar curvy builds, but while Kylie is tanned with brown hair, Tara has flawless cream skin and deep red hair. Both beautiful in their own way, and Tara is definitely more my type.

"I'm done for the night. Just going to finish up my drink and head up to my room," Tara says, drawing her friend's attention back to her.

"You sure you're good?" Kylie asks, placing a hand on Tara's shoulder.

"Yep. I'm good, I promise."

The two women hold each other's gazes for a few beats, before Kylie nods and looks back at me. "It was nice to meet you, Aiden."

"You too, Kylie."

She turns to leave, shooting a cheeky grin over her shoulder at Tara. "Don't do anything I wouldn't do, T."

Tara turns bright red, and Kylie heads back towards the door of the bar, joining the tall, well-built man who is waiting for her. Judging by the way she slides her arm around his waist, I assume he's her boyfriend or husband. He nods towards me, and I nod back. A silent communication where he's letting me know he's watching me... And I let him know I get it.

"So, is that one of the girlfriends you mentioned earlier? The ones men use you to get closer to?"

She wrinkles her nose. "Yeah. She's one of my best friends, and probably the most outgoing person I've ever met."

"Well, I mean, she's beautiful, but you're just as stunning, if not more so."

She rolls her eyes. "You're just saying that."

I shake my head. "No, I'm really not. Just don't tell that wall of a boyfriend of hers I said that."

She laughs again, her eyes twinkling. "Seth is a lover, not a fighter. Well, at least, off the ice."

"What do you mean, off the ice? He does meth?" I raise my eyebrows and look back towards the door that her friends left through.

She keels over, laughing hard. "Oh, God, no. I didn't even realise how that sounded. He's an ice hockey player. Like, a famous one. In Canada."

I nod slowly. "Well, I guess that explains his size. If anyone feels inadequate around here, it should be me, if that's the sort of men you're used to hanging around."

"Believe me, you have nothing to feel inadequate about."

I smile, moving to hold her hand again. "Is that right?"

She blushes a little while she looks down, keeping her hand still while I trace a circle on the back of it with my thumb.

She clears her throat and brings her gaze to mine. The heat behind that gaze is enough to scorch me. "Yes. That's right."

We continue to watch each other for a few more heartbeats.

"Another drink?" I ask, my voice coming out a little rough.

She nods slowly. "Yes please."

I look at the bartender and nod, and she organises both our drinks.

It's been a long time since I've been this close to such a beautiful woman that I felt this sort of chemistry with, and I'm interested to see where the rest of the night takes us.

3
YOU LOOK A BIT PALE

TARA

Sunlight pours through the window of my hotel room. Opening my eyes, slowly, I blink, trying to clear my blurred vision, before clamping a hand over them when unbearable pain stabs my brain.

Groaning, I roll over, and gasp when I see a shirtless man lying beside me.

Oh my god... What happened last night?

Aiden's chest rises and falls steadily while he continues to sleep. Lifting the sheet that covers me very slowly, I see that I'm wearing what I assume is his shirt. And only that shirt.

Shit... Where are my undies?

The soft cotton brushes across my braless chest when I sit up, trying to keep my movements slow to stop the stabbing pain behind my eyes from growing any worse. Keeping my eyes on Aiden, I slide out of bed and tiptoe into the bathroom of what I now realise must be his hotel room.

Fighting back the wave of nausea that hits me while I go to the bathroom, I wash my hands and take in my reflection. My face is smeared with make-up, although my false lashes seem to be staying put, which is impressive.

I have no memory of anything after about the sixth cocktail, and my state of undress has me very concerned that I did something last night that my sober self will regret. Opening the door, I silently gather my things, keeping my eyes on the gorgeous man sleeping soundly on the bed, trying not to be distracted by the very impressive abs on display. The sheet covers him from his hips down, and it's hard not to stare at the V that taunts me, begging me to look a little lower. Something I adamantly refuse to do, even though it takes every ounce of my self control.

Stepping back into the bathroom, I pull my bridesmaids dress back on as quickly as I can, struggling for a moment to get the zip back up on my own. Checking to make sure I have my phone and room key in my little handbag, I ease my way back into the bedroom to find Aiden still fast asleep. While I envy his ability to sleep so soundly, right now I'm incredibly grateful, as it gives me a chance to make a fast getaway without any awkward conversation.

Out in the empty hallway, I'm unsure what floor I'm on, so I'm grateful that the layout seems to be the same as the one my room is on as I make a beeline for the elevators. My racing heart doesn't slow until the elevator doors close, and I breathe a sigh of relief. Just wish I'd made it back to my own room instead of apparently sleeping with a random stranger.

Checking my phone for the first time, I see that I've got an hour before we're all scheduled to meet for brunch. Plenty of time to throw up and then get ready, with no one having to know what I've been up to.

I can't believe I've finally slept with someone after four years of forced celibacy and I don't even fricking remember if it was any good or not.

. . .

"Where'd you end up last night?" Morgan asks when I take a seat next to her at brunch.

Jake and Bri had arranged for us all to stay in the hotel where the wedding had been, wanting everyone together so that we could make an entire weekend out of the celebrations. At the time, I'd thought it was a waste of money, given how close I live, but now that I'm feeling so crap, I'm glad they'd splashed a little cash, so that I didn't have to go far to meet everyone.

I'd not had the energy to do much with my appearance, so my hair is piled on top of my head in a messy bun, and I haven't got a stitch of make up on. Turns out, I needed more time to throw up than I'd thought. I'm just grateful we hadn't decided to have breakfast at the hotel, or I'd be looking over my shoulder for Aiden. Not that he'd recognise me, as I definitely no longer look as good as last night.

"Just had a few drinks in the bar and then went up to bed."

Not a lie. We just won't discuss whose bed.

Chris eyes me from across the table. "You okay? You look a bit pale."

"Just had a bit more to drink than usual. I'll be okay after I have a cup of tea and some toast."

I hope.

Aside from a night in Amsterdam when I tried my first - and only - edible, I've never had a hangover before. If this is what they all feel like, I have no idea why anyone would do this more than once.

"Tara met a guy last night," Kylie says with a grin, and I kick her under the table. "Ow. What?"

I glare at her. "We were just talking."

"I know. I didn't say you did anything with him." She bends slightly to rub her leg while raising any eyebrow.

Seth clears his throat beside her, and she shoots him a look before glancing back at me. She narrows her eyes, but doesn't say anything further.

I'm almost grateful when Will takes a seat on the other side of me. Almost.

Great, as if this could get any more awkward.

Finally, the newlyweds join us, and a server appears to take our orders.

"What do we say? Mimosas for the table?" Morgan says, looking around while the others nod, and I have to fight the urge to vomit at the mere thought of any more alcohol right now.

It's clear that I'm the only one who drank way too much last night.

Thankfully, Kylie also says no, as she doesn't drink, so I'm not the only one not touching alcohol this morning.

I order a camomile tea and Vegemite on toast, something that raises a few eyebrows. Out for brunch and I order the most boring thing on the menu, but I don't care. Vegemite on toast has always been my go to when I feel sick.

"So, you guys are here for a few more days?" Chris asks Seth and Kylie.

"Yeah, just til Wednesday. We're crashing at the apartment, then heading up north for a few weeks. We'll be back before we head back to Calgary, though."

"The apartment" is how everyone refers to the one that Jake won a few years ago, a gorgeous penthouse in Kangaroo Point, and where I currently live. It's basically a half-way house for everyone in the group who lives out of town, but I get the main bedroom and ensuite, so it doesn't worry me all that much. It's nice to have company occasionally. Jake and Bri used to come once a month or so, but lately it's been more like the occasional weekend stay every two or three months. And Kylie only comes home once, maybe twice, a year, so I live alone most of the time. In a fancy four-bedroom apartment. It gets lonely sometimes, but it's worked out well. I pay next to nothing in rent, which has helped me to save for my own place. I'm not sure when that will be, but it's nice to have the option there for one day soon.

"You're back at work tomorrow, right T?" Kylie asks, and I realise I've blanked out on the conversation the others were having.

"Um, no, Tuesday. I figured I'd probably need tomorrow to sleep in."

"How are things at work, anyway?" Chris asks.

We used to work together, but he left a year ago to go to a bigger insurance brokerage.

"John just retired. I know the clients better than anyone, so I've been hoping to take on the role myself. I'm ready to move out of personal lines."

Chris nods. "They'd be stupid not to hand the portfolio to you."

The server arrives with our drinks, and I take a sip of my tea. "That's my thoughts as well, but it's David's call, so who knows?"

Chris winces. "Yeah, that will be interesting. Still no female brokers?"

"Nope." I shake my head, before realising that's a stupid idea with the mother of all hangovers.

My boss isn't exactly known for his strong sense of equality in the workplace. He's old school, been in the industry since his father brought him in right out of high school forty years ago. All the brokers in the office are men, while most of the assistant brokers and support staff are women. It is something that has pissed off quite a lot of us over the years, but I'm determined to break that ridiculous stereotype.

The rest of brunch is uneventful, and I'm so ready to go home and try to recover from everything that happened last night. But home won't be a sanctuary today. Not with two of the happy couples staying there.

As we're all finishing up, my phone buzzes on the table between myself and Will. Looking down, I spy my sister's name on the screen, showing an incoming message. I glance at Will and swallow hard when I see his eyes trained on the screen. I slide the phone off the table and grip it in my hand. As much as I resent him for how he treated me when she left, I don't want to cause him any pain. And Annelisa... Well, just the mere mention of her name causes Will pain.

I tilt the phone away so that Will can't see the screen, even though he's making an obvious effort to look anywhere else but at me.

ANNELISA

Hey. You good for our chat tonight?

TARA

Can't. It's a full house at the apartment. The wedding was last night, remember?

ANNELISA

Right. I forgot. Guess it'll be next week then.

Annelisa and I have a standing monthly chat on the last Sunday night of each month. Well, Sunday night for me, but it's early morning for her in London. On the nights when I have people staying at the apartment though... Well, I guess that's the consequences of her actions, when she abandoned everyone for what is still an unknown reason.

4

YOU GET AN OFFICE

AIDEN

Waking up in an empty bed on Sunday morning definitely wasn't on my bingo card for the day before I start a new job. Not when I'd fallen asleep next to a beautiful woman the night before.

We'd had a really good time on Saturday night, but it wasn't until Tara stood up to head to bed that the alcohol hit her, and she slumped to the floor.

I hadn't wanted to leave her alone in the hotel bar while I found one of her friends, so I'd sent the bartender in, but the wedding had cleared out. Seems we'd been talking far longer than either of us had realised. I gave the bartender my details and let her know I was going to get her sobered up upstairs. But as soon as we'd gotten into my room, she woke up and started stripping off her clothes, seemingly unaware of my presence, even though I'd carried her up here.

My solution? Pull one of my shirts over her head and put her to bed with a glass of water and the bin beside her.

When I'd woken up to find her gone, the lonely feeling I'd been struggling with for the past two days had sunk in again. The

21

first person I'd gotten to know in this new city, and she ghosted me. I'd hoped to get to know her a bit better. Maybe get her number and see if she'd be interested in catching up once I'm more settled here. Instead, I'm alone once more in this luxury hotel room, a constant reminder that I don't know anyone aside from my father in this town.

"Aiden, come in." My step-mother, Lisa, stands aside to let me in the door when I arrive at the home she shares with my father and younger half-siblings.

"Hi Lisa. It's nice to meet you."

She's two decades younger than my father. Closer to my age than his. And my half-siblings are three-year-old twins, Daisy and Mitchell. Weird being twenty-nine with siblings who are young enough to be your own children. But that's how my old man rolls. After his brief relationship with my mother, all the women afterwards were younger. I wonder if Lisa realises she'll probably be traded in for a younger model in a few years?

Best not to mention anything to her.

This is my first time meeting her and the twins. Dad had invited me over for dinner. An olive branch, I guess. Or maybe it was Lisa's idea, and he thought he better make it look like we were one big, happy family. Either way, it's awkward as hell.

"Come on in. Your father is in the lounge room with the kids." Lisa leads the way through their house, and I try not to stare at everything while I follow behind.

Much like the hotel, it's obvious, just from the hallway alone, that my father isn't afraid to splash the cash around. The house is huge, and it's hard not to feel resentful when I look at this and compare it to the two-bedroom flat I lived in with Mum in Clapham growing up. While it was her choice to move us back to her home in London, he certainly didn't bother to send her much money to raise his eldest child.

"Ah, Aiden. There you are." David Sanderson, aka dear old dad, rises to his feet from where he was sitting on the couch, watching what looks like some Disney movie, with two tiny versions of himself sitting on either side.

"Hi Dad." I nod, sliding my hands into my pockets, not sure what else to do with them.

He comes to stand in front of me, his arms outstretched, and for a moment, I have no idea what he's expecting from me. Hugging him just seems strange, as I haven't seen him in person in almost fifteen years.

"I'm glad you could come. How's the hotel?" he asks, letting his arms drop when it's obvious I'm not onboard with the hug thing.

I shrug. "Fine. I'll start looking for a place this week."

"However long it takes, that's not a problem. Stay there as long as you need." He heads into the kitchen with Lisa and grabs some wine glasses. "Let's go out to the deck and chat for a bit til dinner."

Nothing sounds less appealing than idle chit-chat with a man I barely know.

I follow him out and watch quietly while he pours us both a glass of red wine. The fact that he didn't even ask if I drink wine, or red wine, at that, speaks volumes to the type of man he is. And I'm not the slightest bit surprised.

Why did I come here again? Right, because I am not qualified for anything and I need a job.

"Are you looking forward to starting tomorrow?" he asks.

I take a seat across from him. "Yeah. I've been doing the reading for the course, and I had my exam last Friday, so it'll be good to get some on the ground knowledge."

I decide not to tell him that I needed to refer to the books far more than I probably should have. Insurance seems unnecessarily complicated.

"Oh good. Well, you're in good hands with your assistant. She's been with the company for years and knows all the clients, so it should be a smooth transition. She knows her stuff, too, and she'll be able to fill in any blanks you have while you learn the industry more."

"If she's so good, how come she's my assistant? Shouldn't it be the other way around?" I ask, trying not to let my dislike of the wine show on my face when I take a sip.

"Well... To be honest, the thought never occurred to me. The role was open, and it seemed like the perfect time to bring you onboard, now that things have changed for you," he replies, glossing over the reason things have changed for me.

We lapse into silence, and I can tell this is just as uncomfortable for him as it is for me. Eventually, Lisa calls out that dinner is ready, and it's a relief to have the twins as a distraction. Getting them fed is clearly a two person job, and I have to keep reminding myself that they are my brother and sister. I'd been an only child for twenty-six years, and suddenly having toddlers as siblings is a rather large adjustment. When Mitchell dumps his dinner bowl on top of Daisy's head, I take that as my queue to start clearing the table. Lisa smiles at me, the relief in her eyes obvious, when I take her plate and head into the kitchen.

"I'm going to head back to the hotel and have an early night. Big day tomorrow, and all," I say after I've loaded the dishwasher and head back out onto the deck.

The tiny terrorists are running in circles, chasing the dog, and it's all a bit too chaotic for my jetlagged brain at this point.

"Oh, of course. Well, we should try to make this a regular thing." Dad looks a little put out, but I don't particularly care.

"Sure." I try to make my reply sound enthusiastic, but it's hard to override years of resentment in just one evening.

I order an Uber and feel a wave of relief once I slide into the backseat and am on the way back to the hotel. I'd thought I'd be okay with my father, but it's becoming painfully obvious that the issues I've been running from for years are well and truly still present.

Grabbing a beer from the mini-bar in my room, I pull out my phone and message my best friend.

AIDEN

Hey, are you around?

SARAH

I'm just out at brunch with Simon and his friends. Is everything okay? I can call you in a few hours?

Fighting off the wave of loneliness that has overtaken me, I try not to feel resentful that she's out with her new boyfriend while I'm stuck on the other side of the world feeling miserable.

AIDEN

No, it's okay, just wanted to say hi. Have fun at brunch.

I toss my phone on the other side of the bed, face down, and drain the rest of my beer.

Guess I'll just go to bed then.

After a night of barely any sleep because of a combination of jetlag and nerves about starting a new job, I impulsively shave off my beard, deciding I need a fresh start. Afterwards, I get dressed in my suit and walk the few blocks to my new office. Sanderson and Chambers Insurance Brokers is apparently one of the largest brokerages in Australia, with offices in every capital city. Two of Dad's brothers work out of the Sydney office, where he worked when he met my mother, but for over a decade, he's been the Sanderson in the Brisbane office. And now, I guess I am, too.

It's my first time working in an office, or working anywhere important, really, so the stop for a coffee is required. Not just to acquire caffeine, but also as an excuse to delay the inevitable a little longer.

The fear that I'm going to completely choke when it comes to this new job is causing my stomach to twist into knots, and, not for the first time, I wonder what the hell I'm doing here. I don't even care about insurance, but I need an income.

Steeling myself, I catch one of the many lifts up to the top floor and step out, making my way to the reception desk.

"Hi. I'm Aiden Sanderson."

The young blonde woman behind the desk blinks at me a few times, as if in a trance, before jumping to her feet. "Oh, of course! Mr Sanderson said to expect you and to bring you right back as soon as you arrived." She bustles off down the corridor, turning to beckon me to follow when I stay where I am.

He makes his staff call him Mr Sanderson? Yeah, that tracks.

It's like my feet don't want to move, and I have to force myself to trail after her. Once we go through the wood panelled corridor, I step out into a sea of desks. Even though it's not yet nine am, most desks are already occupied, and the sound of multiple people talking on the phone fills my ears. We weave our way through to the glassed offices along the back wall, and the woman knocks on the office door that has my father's name written on it. Through the glass door, he looks up from his notebook, nodding when he sees me.

"Go on in," she says, looking me up and down before turning back and returning to where we'd come from.

Thrown by the blatant ogling from the receptionist, I stand outside the door for a beat longer before shaking my head and heading inside.

"You made it." Dad rises to his feet, and I nod.

"Yes, sir."

"Let's get you settled in your office. Your assistant is away today, apparently. I hadn't realised she had put in for leave, but I'll get one of the others to get you sorted with everything. Won't be much for you to do until you get all the IT stuff sorted, anyway."

He leads the way back out into the sea of desks, and I notice a few people watching us with interest. Guess it's pretty rare for the boss to be showing the new hire around.

Once we enter the empty office two doors down, I look around with interest. "Wait... I get my own office? I assumed I'd be out there with everyone else."

"No. You're a Sanderson. You get an office."

I'm not entirely sure this is such a good idea. The last thing I want to do is walk into this place and make it seem like I'm being jetted in over the heads of more qualified people just because I'm the boss's son. But then again... that's exactly what's happening.

This is going to be a long day.

5
HE'S HOT

HONESTLY, if hangovers last this long, why do people do this to themselves?

I'm so grateful that I took Monday off work, because the hangover from my cocktail binge on Saturday night took two days to fully go away. Having to be social with everyone in the apartment also didn't help. Although at least having them there was a nice distraction from thinking about how I finally had sex and can't even remember it. I try not to feel guilty about how I snuck out of Aiden's room, but he probably wouldn't have wanted me to hang around, anyway. A guy that good looking probably has women throwing themselves at him all the time and is well practiced in the art of one-night-stands.

"Alright, I'm off to work," I say, passing Seth and Kylie in the kitchen on Tuesday morning.

Jake and Bri headed home to Stanthorpe yesterday. They aren't going on their honeymoon for a few months, and Jake needed to get back to his electrician's business.

"Have a good day, honey. Don't work too hard," Kylie calls back with a grin, shutting the fridge with her arms full of food.

It always makes me jealous of how much she can eat without putting on a single kilo, while all I have to do is look at food and my hips expand.

She's dressed in one of Seth's Mounties jersey's and a tiny pair of shorts. She clearly hadn't bothered to brush her hair, but somehow that just makes her look effortlessly hotter.

Seth nods at me from where he stands in front of the stove, even less chatty than usual when it's first thing in the morning. Wearing a white shirt and a pair of athletic shorts, if he wasn't Canadian, I'd be asking him if he was cold, but Kylie has assured me that this is basically summer weather in Calgary.

"Have a good day, guys." I let myself out of the apartment and put my headphones on, sighing when I hear Seth's deep voice say something on the other side of the door and Kylie's infectious laugh in reply.

Finally getting some time to myself, even if it is just for the twenty minutes to get to work, is just what I need right now. I love my friends, but being constantly surrounded by happy couples can be draining.

Stepping outside my building, I stop and inhale deeply, enjoying the feeling of the Brisbane winter air surrounding me. A slight bite to the air does nothing to take away the beauty of the clear blue sky and the sun beaming down.

I begin my regular walk down to the Brisbane River and cross the bridge from Kangaroo Point into the CBD. It's the only exercise I do, despite Kylie trying to get me to join her for so many activities over the years. I just don't enjoy exercise like she does. But walking has long been my go to, and the walk along the river has become a balm for my troubles.

This morning, though, I spend the walk going over my pitch to David about promoting me to take over John's now vacant role.

I've been working there for five years, and for the last two, I was the main contact for all of John's portfolio while he focussed on his golf handicap, just showing up for the sales pitch and leaving all the actual work to me. I've more than earned this, and David has got to give me a chance. I hope...

I walk into the lobby of the building where our office is and grab a hot chocolate before heading up to the top floor.

"Hey Tara. How was the wedding?" Celeste, our receptionist, asks when I nod to her.

"It was good. How was your weekend?" I ask, stopping next to her desk, and she launches into a detailed description of the busy weekend she had with her boyfriend, which included multiple nightclubs and liquid lunches.

She's a lovely girl, but at almost ten years younger than me, conversations with her always make me feel old.

"Have you seen the new broker yet? He's hot." Celeste's voice drops to a dramatic whisper.

"Um, no? I didn't realise we were getting a new broker. What department are they in?" I ask, silently praying she doesn't say mine.

"He's taking John's job. He's David's son."

Fan-fucking-tastic.

I didn't even have an opportunity to interview for the role. Probably wasn't even considered an option.

My anger must show on my face, cause Celeste sits back, her expression wary. "Didn't you know?"

"Nope," I reply, taking a mouthful of my drink and willing myself to get my emotions in check before I meet the son of the boss. "Is he in yet?"

"He just arrived a few minutes ago. I can't believe David didn't tell you." Celeste's eyes are wide, and I'm sure within minutes of me heading to my desk, she'll be straight into the other side of the office to gossip about it with the admin staff.

Determined not to give any of the mean girls in the admin team ammunition, I paste on a smile and shrug. "Guess it slipped his mind. I better go introduce myself. See you later."

I head towards my desk and resist the urge to slam my bag down. Taking a fortifying breath, I look over at John's old office. The blinds on the internal glass wall are open, and I can see a man standing with his back to me, looking out the window. Despite my disappointment at the situation, I can't help but notice how well he fills out the suit. From behind anyway.

Then I mentally kick myself. *No, Tara, do not check out the boss's son's butt. We hate him, remember?*

I sit down and get my laptop out of my bag, connecting it to the multiple screens on my desk. Firing it up, I get to work opening all the programs I'll need for the day. The amount of programs it takes to do this job is a little ridiculous, but I'm old hat at all of this now.

My phone rings just as I'm connecting my ear piece, and I look down, recognising the number of one of John's biggest clients.

"Good morning Dayna, how are you?" I answer, knowing that the personal touch is the key to this woman's heart.

"Oh Tara, darling, it's been a horrible night. We had a break in at the Paddington location, and they've taken all the equipment. I've spent the last hour calling patients to cancel appointments, but we're booked for weeks. I need this sorted ASAP."

I start taking notes, asking all the usual questions and assure her that I will get the claim lodged immediately. She hangs up, and I sigh.

This is why I should have that job. I know the clients, and they all trust me. Instead, I'm doomed to continue being nothing more than the assistant broker.

Grabbing my left over dinner from my handbag, I head towards the lunchroom. I'm searching for a free space in the fridge when I'm startled by voices on the other side of the open fridge door.

"I can't believe David didn't even tell her," Felicity, one of the senior admin staff, says.

"Well, it's not like she was going to get the role. As if he'd put her in front of clients. She isn't exactly 'client facing' material. I mean, you've seen her wardrobe." I recognise Amber's voice.

I look down at my black pants and loose-fitting white business shirt while I ignore the sting behind their words. They are two of the worst instigators in the admin team, who thrive on drama.

Oh, and they are massive bitches.

I slam the fridge door, giving them the fakest smile possible while they both stare at me. I don't bother to say anything before brushing past them both, ignoring the laughter once I've exited the room.

I head to the bathroom and lock myself in the closest stall, willing myself not to cry. Between the catty conversation and the bitterness of disappointment, my emotions are fighting to take over, and I need to pull it together. This is not the type of office where it's safe to cry in the bathroom. The piranhas in the admin team will circle and use it to bring me down. The bullying in this place has definitely gotten worse in the last few months, and David does nothing about it. He's too afraid of the women that run this place. I had stayed off their radar mostly, but if I'm found crying in here, it would provide ammunition that they would gladly lob straight at me.

Why am I still working here?

Forcing myself to take a deep breath, I head back out and splash water on my face at the sink before remembering I'd actually put make up on this morning. Thankfully, there's no serious damage done, and I thank the gods for waterproof mascara. The must have accessory of all women working in this industry when surrounded by men who refuse to see their potential.

Leaving the bathroom, I bypass my desk and head to the door of John's office. Well, I guess it's no longer John's office. I realise now that I don't even know this guy's name.

Knocking, I watch as he jumps and whirls around. And then we both freeze, staring at each other.

Neither of us moves for the longest time, each of us apparently lost for words.

"Tara?" His eyes are wide.

I swallow hard. "Aiden."

6

YOU'VE SEEN ME NAKED

AIDEN

When I turn around and find Tara standing in the doorway of my office, I wonder if I'm hallucinating.

She looks different. Gone is the professional makeup and fake lashes. The fitted bridesmaid dress that clung to her curves has been replaced by ill-fitting office attire, a white button-up shirt and black trousers that look pretty baggy on her. She's still gorgeous, but looks so different to the woman I spent time with two nights ago that I have to blink a few times to make sure it's definitely the same person.

"What are you doing here?" she asks, clinging to the door frame.

"I work here. Which, I'm guessing, you do too?" I move closer, and she puts her hand up, halting me in my tracks.

She steps in quickly and shuts the door behind her, reaching over and closing the blinds behind the glassed wall.

"You're David's son? The man who just swooped in and took John's job?"

I raise an eyebrow. "Uh, I'll cop to the David's son part, reluctantly. But I didn't swoop in and take anything. My dad told me he had a job for me, I came. That's it."

She scoffs and crosses her arms over her chest, glaring at me. "Nice try. So, what? You saw my photo on the company website and decided to hunt me down at the wedding to humiliate me before we have to work together, is that it?"

I gape at her for a moment, before finding my voice. "What the hell? No, that's not it. I had no idea who you were on Saturday night. No one told me my assistant's name yesterday, just that she'd show me the ropes and was the best in the company at her job." I tamp down the anger I can feel clawing at my throat, thrown by the accusation she threw my way.

"Of course I'm the best in the company at my job. I worked my butt off for it."

At this point, I have no idea what she's angry about anymore. That I got the job? That I spoke to her on Saturday night? That I'm breathing the same air as her? The list is endless, but also, not my fault.

"I don't know why you're so mad at me when you're the one who snuck out of bed on Sunday morning without a word."

Two can play at this game of righteous anger, love.

She glares at me, opening her mouth to respond, when a knock at the door startles us both. My father lets himself in without waiting for an invitation.

"Oh, Tara, fantastic. I see you've met Aiden." Dad shows no sign of recognising the tense atmosphere that he's walked into.

Tara straightens slightly, dropping her hands to her side. "Yes. I didn't realise you'd replaced John so quickly." There's an underlying animosity to her words that sails right over my father's head.

"Oh yes. I reached out to Aiden as soon as John let me know he was retiring. He was in London, so he needed time to pack up his life and move over."

Tara looks like she's fighting back tears, but if that's the case, it's definitely angry tears. I don't know who she's more pissed at, me or Dad, but I'd prefer to be left out of all of this.

"So you've known for months and didn't tell me?"

Dad looks confused. "Why would I need to tell you? It will be the same for you as it was when John was around."

And in that moment, I see that he's just as clueless as a boss as he is as a father. From the fleeting expression that passes across Tara's face, I can tell that she doesn't want things to be the same as they were under John. I also think that was a stretch on Dad's part. I have nowhere near the knowledge and experience that John had, as evidenced by my day yesterday when I was handed paperwork to read and it all meant nothing to me. I'm going to be relying on my assistant a lot, and seeing the unimpressed look on her face, I'm not looking forward to the moment when Tara realises that.

"I guess it would have been nice to be given a heads up, considering that I'm the one with the relationship with the clients," Tara says, practically vibrating as she holds herself back.

Yeah, this is not going to be fun.

After Dad continues to fumble through the conversation with Tara, she leaves with barely contained rage. I swallow hard when it's just Dad and me alone in my office.

"Why the hell didn't you say anything to her about me coming?" I ask, shaking my head.

"I didn't think about it. I don't understand why it's such a big deal, anyway," he replies, staring at the closed door, confusion written all over his face.

"You can't seriously be this naive, Dad. She clearly isn't happy, and I have to work with her. It puts me in a really shitty position."

"Nonsense. Tara will be fine. She's one of the most professional women in the office, never gets involved in any of the office politics and just gets on with it. She'll be fine."

I was wrong. Apparently, he is that naive.

. . .

An hour later, I bite the bullet and call Tara back into my office.

Needing to clear the air, I wave for her to take a seat on the other side of my desk, which she does, albeit reluctantly. I sit in my chair and suddenly have no idea what to do with my hands. This woman makes me nervous for reasons I can't quite work out.

"Look, I think we got off on the wrong foot earlier. I can tell you aren't happy about me being here, but I honestly had no idea who you were on Saturday night, I promise." I lean forward to rest my forearms on the desk and click the pen in my hand for something to do.

Tara stares at the pen, then back at my face, her jaw clenched. "Well, as you can imagine, it's put me in a really shit position. I never sleep with strangers, and the one time I do, it turns out he's my new direct superior."

I raise an eyebrow. "Just to be clear... When you say 'sleep with', are you... Do you think we had sex?" This has gone to a whole new level of inappropriate, and now I'm wondering if HR is about to bust the door down.

Tara's cheeks redden. "Well, I woke up in your bed wearing nothing but your shirt."

I let out a breath. "So you don't remember? Tara, I promise, all we did was sleep. I don't sleep with women who are too drunk to consent. I tried to find your friends after you'd passed out on me, but they must have all left after you told them you were going to bed. So I gave the bartender my details and told her I was going to get you sobered up enough to get you back to your room. But when I got you upstairs, you stripped your clothes off before I had a chance to give you a drink of water. My solution to that was to put you in one of my shirts and let you sleep it off. I was going to ask you to go for breakfast in the morning, but when I woke up, you were gone." I raise my hands in surrender.

She stares at me for a moment. "Somehow, that all makes me feel worse."

I laugh, dumbfounded. "So you'd prefer it if we'd slept together and now we have to work together?"

"No," she snaps. "But you've still seen me naked and we have to work together."

My automatic response is to offer to even the score, but I'm pretty sure that joke would fall flat here. And also, far too inappropriate for the office. Even though I'd really like to see her naked again.

I scrub my hand over my face. This is not going well. "Look. How about we both agree to forget about Saturday night and start fresh?"

She sits back in her chair and crosses her arms, considering me closely. She's quiet for so long, I wonder if she's about to tell me to get lost, but she finally nods.

"Fine."

She doesn't seem fine.

"Okay then," I reply warily. "I'm glad we could clear the air. Do you think you could run me through how things are done here?"

She raises an eyebrow. "What do you need me to show you?"

I want to say "Everything", but I suspect that way would lead to me getting a swift kick up the arse, or worse. So instead, I wave my hand towards the stack of papers on my desk that one of the admin team members brought in earlier. "Well, for starters, what am I meant to do with these?"

Tara looks at the stack of papers, reading through the note on top before looking back at me. "Did they not have you reviewing your renewals at your old office?"

"Uh, no. This is all new to me."

She stares at me, and I instantly know I've said the wrong thing.

"You've done this job before, right?"

Despite the warning voice in my head screaming at me to lie, I shake my head. If I lied, she'd eventually work it out anyway when she uses all the insurance jargon that everyone else is fluent in, but has sailed right over my head.

"No. I'm new to the industry."

Her mouth drops open. "You're kidding, right?"

"Fraid not," I reply, hoping my grin is enough to charm her.

Spoiler... it is not.

"So. Not only did your *father*," she says through gritted teeth, "not bother to tell me he was hiring someone else, but that someone else has no clue what they are doing, and I'm just expected to do all the work once again?" I try not to flinch at the venom in her voice. "Unbelievable," she adds under her breath.

I honestly miss the version of her I met on Saturday night. This one is scary and yet, still just as hot. There is something seriously wrong with me that I'm equal parts terrified and turned on right now.

She takes a deep breath. "Look, Aiden. I'm going to let you in on a secret. This place is like a vipers den, and your father has left you to fight to the death. There are plenty of assistants who would have killed for the chance to interview for this position, myself included. Add in that we have an admin team that makes the girls in *Mean Girls* look like innocent puppies, and it's basically a constant shit fight in this place. David is completely clueless because he chooses to be, but make no mistake, you're about to be eaten alive."

Fabulous.

"I had no idea. Honestly, this is all as much a shock to me as it is to you. Please, can we just work together? I might not have a clue what I'm doing, but I'm a fast learner. In the meantime, maybe we can share the role," I offer, practically begging at this point.

Her words have made it even harder to walk out of this office and interact with all the people I was already pretty sure weren't happy I was here. Having it confirmed is making me consider just getting on a plane and heading back to England. But there's nothing left for me there now, and I really need this job. At least for the foreseeable future.

"Even if you somehow convinced your father to let you share the role with a woman, I'd still be the one carrying the load." She sighs and shakes her head. "Look, it's done now. But you better work things out pretty quick. John may have slacked off in the last couple of years, but his shoes are pretty big ones to fill. His clients expect their broker to know the answers straight away. You've at least got your qualifications, right? Tell me David wasn't that stupid?"

I nod. "Yeah, he had me do all the tests last week."

"Well, that's something, I guess." She gets to her feet and points at the stack of papers again. "You need to review those, comparing them to last year's policies. You're not just looking at price, but need to see if any additional clauses have been added by the underwriters. Usually this is all done by email, so I don't know why they've printed it all off. Probably some sort of joke for the admin teams to get their kicks out of. I avoid them as much as possible, but if you don't want to be swimming in paperwork, I suggest you ask their manager to ensure that these are emailed to you from now on."

With that, she sweeps out of my office, leaving me staring at the papers with a sinking feeling.

This all just got so much harder.

7
STEP OUTSIDE OF
THAT COMFORT ZONE

TARA

AFTER TUESDAY'S BOMBSHELL, I spent the rest of the week fielding client calls and doing even more work than usual while Aiden tried to wrap his head around how to do the job that he is nowhere near qualified for.

"It's so insulting, Lis. I can't even begin to explain how difficult this week has been," I say, ranting to Annelisa on video chat while I get my dinner ready on Friday night.

"Well, maybe it's finally time to look for another job," my sister replies. "You've been there for years. Chris has left, so it's not like you're obligated to stay there or anything."

"Yeah, I guess. I just... I know the clients there, and even if I went somewhere else, there's no guarantee that things will be any better there." I sigh, stirring the wooden spoon through the chicken and stir-fry mix in the pan on the stove.

"You were never great with change, T. Might be time to step outside of that comfort zone."

"Not all of us have the luxury of running away from their normal lives," I snap back, instantly regretting my words.

Annelisa is quiet for a few moments. "Are you okay? I've noticed you haven't been yourself the last few times we've talked," she finally says.

I don't know how to answer that without opening up the little box that I've shoved into the back of my mind, marked *do not touch*. The one I've filled with all the hurt and anger I've been feeling for years, ever since Annelisa left, but refuse to address. Avoidance has long been my preferred way of coping. Something that I learned from my sister. Given that Annelisa is a large source of my hurt and anger, I just don't have the energy to unpack it all after the week I've had.

"I'm fine," I reply.

"Well, what are you going to do about the situation?"

"I don't know. Let's talk about something else. How are things with you?" I pour the sauce into my mix and keep stirring. There's a pause, and I glance over at the screen to see her watching me with a concerned look on her face. "Seriously, Lis, enough about me."

"Fine. Things with me are okay. Nothing exciting happening here. I'm on a deadline at the moment so I've been in the writing cave all week."

My sister is a very successful romance author, and as her number one fan, I'm eagerly awaiting her next book just as much as the rest of her fan base.

"Well, that's exciting. When's this one coming out?"

"In eight months." She doesn't sound happy about it.

"Why does that sound like you think that's a bad thing?" I turn the stove off and serve myself a portion before moving the pan off the stove while my sister sighs.

"I've been struggling with ideas. First time I've had writers block in a while."

She's had two books out since she left Will, and I've noticed a distinct change in her voice. I bite my tongue, not wanting to point out the obvious. That maybe the reason she's struggling to think about romantic interludes is because she set her own love life on fire. It's been more than three years and she still hasn't told me what happened, only that she needed to get away from everything. Will has been equally tightlipped, according to Kylie. It's been a source of frustration for all of us, but we can't force the pair of them to open up about it. We just get to sit back and deal with the fallout.

"Well, I'm sure you'll work through it. Maybe you need to get out and about more over there. Have you met anyone yet?" I take a mouthful of my dinner and chew quietly while I wait for Annelisa to reply.

"I've been out with my flatmates a few times. Meeting someone hasn't really been on my radar though."

Because you left your heart back here.

Out loud, I say, "Maybe you just need to go on a holiday or something. You're so close to everything over there, and yet you've barely left London."

"To tire of London is to tire of life," Annelisa poorly quotes Samuel Johnson at me.

I roll my eyes. "I'd believe that if you'd actually seen more of London than your local grocery store and the Indian restaurant down the road."

"Yeah, yeah." She waves me off. "Have you been to see Mum lately?"

"I'm having lunch with her tomorrow. Have you been in contact with her?" I ask, leveling her with a pointed look.

"I spoke to her on the weekend, so you can skip the lecture I know you were about to give me."

"Good. You have a lot of people who miss you, Lis. Maybe it wouldn't kill you to reach out to a few of them."

She's quiet again for a while, biting her lip. "How was the wedding?" she finally asks.

I detect a slight wobble in her voice.

"It was beautiful, of course. It was perfect for them. They had the ceremony at New Farm Park, right near the rose garden." I leave off the obvious 'you should have been there' that hangs in the air.

Not every conversation between us needs to be laying on the guilt over the events of three years ago.

"And Will was one of Jake's groomsmen?"

I hesitate for a moment. She *never* asks about Will. She has actively avoided saying his name.

Having her ask now throws me off balance.

"Of course. And Chris."

"Of course... Was he okay?" The question sounds like it causes her physical pain to ask.

"Lis... I don't really feel comfortable talking to you about Will. It's a bit of a sore point for me."

That's the closest I've ever come to letting her know how her leaving has affected my relationship with Will.

"Sure. Sorry. Anyway, I should probably go. Need to write at least five thousand words today to stay on track."

I allow her to run away, exhausted by the whole situation yet again.

Once we end the call, I turn on the TV for the sole purpose of filling the quiet apartment with sound other than the noise from my own thoughts.

My thoughts aren't a great place to be these days. I've been off-kilter for months, with my anger towards Annelisa growing steadily stronger. Although I'm not sure why it's all affecting me more now than it used to. It's not like anything has changed recently. Because nothing ever really changes in my life.

"How are you, darling?" Mum greets me with a hug and kiss when I join her at the table she had reserved for us at her favourite cafe in South Bank.

The view of the river is the perfect backdrop for a boozy lunch, as she called it when she invited me to meet her. Mind you, her idea of a boozy lunch is pretty tame compared to others, and I know both of us will be well under the limit to drive home afterwards.

Stella Richards is as much of a lightweight as her two daughters.

We chat while we scan the menu, before giving our orders to the server and settling down with the glass of wine we both ordered.

"So. I do have an ulterior motive for getting you here today."

I raise an eyebrow at my mother's confession. We don't often catch up, as she is off travelling most of the time, taking full advantage of early retirement and an empty nest, but I hadn't detected anything suspicious when she'd extended the invitation to lunch.

"Okay... Hit me with it." I put my glass down.

"Your father." My face immediately contorts into a scowl, but Mum continues. "He reached out."

"How nice for him. Did you tell him to fuck off?"

"No, I did not, in fact, tell him to fuck off," Mum replies, giving me a pointed look. "He wants to talk to you and Annelisa."

"Good for him. He can want to talk to us both all he likes. I can't speak for Lis but... Actually, no, I can speak for Lis, because I know she is even less likely to speak to him than I am. I'm not interested in anything he has to say."

Ever since he walked out on our family twelve years ago, Annelisa and I have refused all contact with our father. Getting your assistant, who is half your age, pregnant while married with two teenage daughters at home is a sign of a pretty shitty human, as far as we're concerned.

"Tara." Mum reaches across the table and takes my hand. "He's sick."

That makes me pause, and I study her closely. "Sick how?"

"He has late stage kidney disease. It seems he has been sick for quite some time, but it's gotten worse." Sadness flickers across my mother's features, and I can feel a tightness in my chest.

"Is he dying?" I ask, glad that I'm sitting down.

Mum hesitates for a moment. "It doesn't look promising," she finally replies.

I stare out the window, watching a City-Cat ferry go past while I process this information. "I don't know what to say..."

Mum squeezes my hand, bringing my focus back to her. "I think you should talk to him. I know you and your sister were both hurt, but he's still your father."

I nod, feeling numb. "I'll think about it. Please don't say anything to him yet. I need to get my head around this."

Mum nods slowly. "Of course. But try not to leave it too long. You never know when things can change."

In other words, your father is going to be dead soon, Tara. Don't let him die without saying goodbye.

Our food finally arrives, but it may as well be ash in my mouth now. "Have you told Lis yet?"

"Not yet. I thought you would be the better one to tell first."

I'm not sure how my sister is going to take this news, so I nod. Was probably the right call. Annelisa holds grudges even worse than me, and I'm not sure dying will be enough of a reason for her to speak to him after all this time.

Lunch concludes on a much more sombre note than how it started. I go home to my empty apartment, wishing I had someone that I could talk this all over with. Someone who could offer me a different perspective and a hug.

Not for the first time, I envy my two best friends for the partners they've found. If this was Bri or Kylie, they would have an amazing guy who would support them through it. But as always, I have no one, not even a pet.

And that reminder makes it all hurt even more.

8

WE'VE GOT A FEW PERKS

AIDEN

WHEN ONE OF the other brokers invited me out for a drink on Saturday night, I was almost embarrassed at how quickly I jumped to say yes. Not knowing anyone in town other than my father and a very hostile assistant has made it hard to feel at home here, and I'm desperate to start making friends and put down roots.

I'd hoped when I met Tara last weekend that she would be the first new friend I'd made, but this week has shown me that is very unlikely. She's been professional, but the tension in the air around us is thick, and I don't see any way past the armour she's built up around herself.

"So. How was the first week?" Damien takes a seat across from me on the other bar stool at our high table.

"Not great. Dad really threw me in the deep end, I'm not gonna lie."

"Yeah, tell me about it. It's not the greatest feeling when you're the newbie in the office. But just give me a yell if you need any help." He taps his beer bottle to mine and takes a swig.

"Thanks, man. I think I need all the help I can get. I took my first client call yesterday and legitimately thought I was going to have a panic attack. Tara was watching me like a hawk the whole time and my hands were sweating."

It had not been a pleasant experience.

"Yeah. Tara is fantastic at her job, but you don't want to get on her bad side. She has a very low bullshit tolerance. I learned that the hard way." Damien rubs the back of his neck.

"Why? What did you do to piss her off?" It makes me feel marginally better to see that I'm not the only one who has endured her wrath.

"I fucked up something on the system when I was making a change to a clients policy and she damn near tore me to shreds. It took me months to get back into her good books. If I hadn't seen her outside of work with my friend Chris, I'd think she was a pretty horrible person, but she's actually really nice. Just has to put up with a lot of shit at the office, I guess."

"Who's Chris?" I ask, trying not to seem overly interested.

I don't know why, but the mention of another guy around Tara makes me feel weird. Must be the beer.

"He used to work with us. Another broker. He and Tara went to school together, and he got her the job. But he left last year."

For some reason, his answer doesn't make me feel any better.

I nod. "So the place is all about who you know, not what you know?"

Damien shrugs. "Basically. Although Tara already knew her stuff before she started with us. To be honest, I'm surprised she's still a broking assistant. She knows more than most of the brokers in the office. Everyone goes to her with the tough ones."

"Yeah, I get the distinct impression that she was after my job when she thought it was up for grabs." I pick at the label on my beer bottle.

"Just give her time. She'll warm up to you. She's not like the bitches in the admin team. Those are the ones you really need to watch out for." Damien shudders.

"Starting to really question my choice to come here." I shake my head with a bitter laugh.

Damien grins. "It's not all bad. We've got a few perks. The company does some pretty good social activities, and we've got a few conferences coming up. Will be a good way for you to network and meet some new people."

"Yeah, Dad mentioned something about Singapore to me the other day. Wasn't sure if I'd be going, though."

"Oh, you'll be going. No way David isn't going to send his son. He's not above playing favourites, that one."

I laugh again, but there's no humour in it. "I definitely don't think we have to worry about me being his favourite."

Damien cocks his head to the side. "I sense that there is a story to tell behind that statement."

Realising I need to tread lightly, I just shrug. "Nah, it's fine. Just didn't have a lot to do with him growing up, living in London and all. We barely know each other, truth be told."

Damien's girlfriend, Vanessa, joins us eventually, and the three of us chat for a few hours. They live nearby to the pub in Kangaroo Point and mentioned it's popular with people our age who have outgrown the nightclub scene but haven't quite hit the bowls club phase. I don't know what the bowls club phase looks like, but I definitely won't be hitting the clubs of my own free will, so I'm grateful for their choice of location.

"You should look around this area for an apartment. It's close enough to the city for you, but less of the traffic chaos in the CBD," Vanessa says.

"Yeah, I'm going to check out a few places this week. Starting to feel a bit claustrophobic inside that hotel room."

"I get that. Hotels are okay for holidays, but they definitely aren't made for long-term accommodation," Damien replies. "We lived in one for a few weeks when we moved up from Sydney and it sucked."

"Did you guys find it hard to meet people here? It seems like everyone sticks with the friends they've known since school and it's hard for people to make friends when they're new to the city."

"It wasn't easy at first. But we got into rock climbing not long after we arrived, and that's where we managed to find the people we see all the time now. Is there anything you enjoy doing? Maybe that might be the way to go?" Vanessa asks, finishing her glass of wine.

"Back when I had time to do stuff in London, I sort of fell into the latin dancing scene when my friend Sarah dragged me along to a class for a bit of a laugh. I ended up really enjoying it though. Maybe I can see what it's like around here," I reply, trying to think of any other hobbies.

My life the last few years had been centred on Mum, so my own interests had become a low priority. It's been so long, I can barely remember what I enjoyed doing before everything went to shit.

"That's perfect!" Vanessa claps her hands together, grinning. "Friday nights, I've walked past this open air gathering up near the casino. It's all people dancing, and a DJ plays latin music. I think it's on every week. You should totally check it out."

"That does sound good. I'll go have a look on Friday, I guess. Although, I'll be worried about seeming like some creepy guy hanging around on my own."

"Nah, there's plenty of people milling around. From what I could tell, if you are a guy who can dance, you'll be sweet." Vanessa grins. "Hell, with your looks, you'd probably be fine even if you couldn't dance."

I laugh, taken aback by her frank assessment.

Damien rolls his eyes. "Vanessa has never had a problem with telling things how she sees them."

"What? He's hot. Don't worry, baby, you're still the only man for me." She gives him a quick kiss on the cheek before heading to the bar to get us another round.

"She's definitely not shy," I tell Damien, and he laughs.

"Definitely not. One of the many things I love about that woman."

I feel a pang in my chest. It's hard not to be envious when I see others settled down in relationships. Maybe one day soon, I'll find someone who puts the same smile on my face.

I push aside the thought of Tara in that moment. No good can come from that situation, but I can't help but wonder how different things would have gone last weekend if she hadn't snuck out.

And we didn't work together.

9
FINE WITH MY BOOKS

TWO WEEKS AFTER THE WEDDING, I realise that, other than going to work and that one meal with my mother, I have barely left the house. I still haven't contacted Dad, stewing in years of resentment and finding it difficult to muster up the energy to do anything more than read a book.

"This isn't healthy, Tara. I'm worried about you." Kylie's voice carries through the kitchen while I bang around, searching for my favourite bowl to serve myself the noodles I made for dinner.

She and Seth arrived in Cairns four days ago, having gone on a bit of an outback adventure first. They're having a holiday before they have to head back to Calgary for the start of the hockey season. She's been blowing up my phone with photos of gorgeous beaches on deserted islands. When you've got a millionaire NHL player for a boyfriend, apparently it's normal to get private helicopter rides around the various islands on the Great Barrier Reef.

Not that I'm jealous at all.

"I'm fine. I've just been busy with work," I reply.

"Well... Maybe it's time for a new job? Especially now that you have to work with a guy who you almost slept with." I'd cracked and told her about my humiliating moment with Aiden, figuring I needed to tell at least one person.

"Almost slept with is a bit of a stretch. Apparently, I just stripped all my clothes off in front of him." I shudder at the memory of that embarrassing conversation. "Besides, I've worked too hard to give up now." I finally find the bowl, piling it high with noodles, meat, and vegetables before moving to the couch.

At this point, I'm surprised there isn't a dent from where my butt has been sitting every night.

"In that case, you still need to find other things to do outside of working your butt off. I'm serious, T. I can tell you've withdrawn from the world. Don't make me come back and kick your butt out of the house." Kylie tends to get a little bossy when she's worried.

It's good to know she cares, but we both handle life in very different ways. While she is confident and direct, I've always been more reserved. A door mat, if you will. The only people I've ever stood my ground with are my close friends and family, and even then, it's selective. I'd surprised myself when I nearly blew up at Aiden that first day. But since then, I've just quietly simmered while handling even more of the workload while he bumbles his way through. The attraction I'd felt for him that first day is still burning away in the back of my mind, making me even angrier, which isn't helping the situation.

"There's nothing else I want to do. I'm fine here with my books."

"Tara, you are a breath away from turning into a recluse. Maybe you need to get a pet or something." I can almost hear the wheels in her brain turning. "Yeah, actually, now that I think about it, I think that's exactly what you need. Get a dog. It'll force you to get out of the house."

She might be onto something there. I fell in love with Bri's little dog, Maddie, but I think a cat would be better suited to my lifestyle.

"You're right. Maybe I'll go check out the rescue places in the next few weeks."

"Really?" Kylie's tone of voice goes up a notch. "I thought that would be a much harder sell. Are you just saying that to get me off the phone?"

I laugh. "No. It's actually a good idea. I've been considering getting a pet for a while."

"Oh yay! Well, send me photos when you start looking. I need a furry pet fix."

We end the conversation soon after, as Kylie needs to get ready for dinner out somewhere, and I'm once again sitting alone in the quiet apartment.

Maybe there's something to Kylie's insistence that I get out more. When we lived together, my social calendar was always full. But as I've gotten older and the people in my life have paired up and disappeared into coupledom, it's become a lot harder to find people to do things with. So I stopped trying, instead retreating into a book to escape the loneliness. Perhaps it's time to find something else to do with my personal life and stop living like a hermit.

I turn on the TV to have some noise around me, scrolling through social media on my phone while I finish my dinner.

Almost as though the device can read my thoughts, an ad pops up, advertising a new latin dance school that's opening up nearby in a few weeks. I'd done a couple of classes a few years ago with Kylie and had had a tonne of fun. But then we went on our holiday and we just never went back after we returned to Brisbane. When she moved to Canada, I was even less inclined to go on my own, and I'd forgotten all about it. But maybe this could be the thing I do to get myself out and about more.

I guess it couldn't hurt to try it.

My finger hovers over the sign up button, but my nerves get the better of me and I close the app, picking up my book instead.

The next morning, I jump online and start researching which pet rescues are the most reputable. Settling on my decision to get a cat, I start searching for kittens, and soon discover that there are so many that need good homes. While I'm still deciding, I spend a couple of happy hours ordering all the cat paraphernalia a kitten could ever need, figuring I can't back out once I've spent all this money.

Now that I've set my mind to it, I can hardly wait to bring my new little fur child home. I can't believe it's taken me this long, but I'm happy with my decision, and it feels good to have something to look forward to again.

While I'm on a mission of dragging myself out of the pit of apathy I've fallen into, I pull up the page for dance classes again, impulsively signing up and paying for a term of Thursday night salsa classes starting in two weeks.

As an afterthought, and before I can think about it too hard, I reactivate my dating profile on the god forsaken app that Kylie made me download a year ago. I'd swiftly deleted it when a fifty-year-old man with the name TooHotTooHandle tried to match with me, followed by about three more, getting steadily older. It was traumatising but I think I can deal with sifting through the crappy ones now in order to try to escape the loneliness. And the only guy I've come close to getting naked with in recent years is my incredibly hot, annoying boss. So it's not like I can just wait for someone to come along organically. And I need something to help me stop thinking about Aiden and how fucking good he looked without a shirt on, so dating apps it is.

And if it doesn't work, at least I'll have started collecting the cats I need to claim crazy cat lady status.

Hello new life, I embrace you with open arms.

Now I just have to work out how to go about stepping back into the shoes of my teenage self and find it inside me to contact my father and reopen that box I'd long shoved into the back of my mind when I cut him out of my life.

Wish that was easy to work out.

10

DEALING WITH THIS
AS A TEAM NOW

AIDEN

Monday morning of my third week arrives, and I'm still not feeling any more confident about my abilities as an insurance broker as I was when I started. I feel like I've read every article ever written on underwriting, risk management and claims settlements, and all I've learned is that this industry is going to bore me to tears.

At least I've found a place to live. After drinks with Damien and Vanessa, I'd centred my search area around Kangaroo Point, New Farm and Newstead. After a few dumps, I'd found the perfect fully furnished one-bedroom flat in Kangaroo Point, and am moving in on the weekend. It's only a twenty-minute walk to work and right up the road from the pub they'd taken me to.

Things sort of feel like they're starting to fall into place. Now if I could just get my assistant to stop hating me, that would be perfect.

"Dayna Melrose is on the phone." Tara's clipped voice comes through on the intercom, and I look through the glass in my office to see her watching me from her desk.

Although she's made it more than clear that any feelings

between us previously are gone on her side, I'm still finding it difficult to push past my deep attraction to her. Especially with the sexy, pissed off look that flashes across her face when I reply.

"Okay. And remind me of who she is, again?" I've been struggling to keep track of all the clients in the large portfolio I've been handed.

It seems like John didn't really have a specific client base, so I've been dealing with everything from medical practices to high end retail stores. Not exactly the easiest way to learn the ropes.

Tara sighs. I'm growing tired of the sound of it, but I can't really blame her, even though the sound of it makes me want to tear my hair out. Or bend her over my knee... You know, a completely appropriate reaction to the sound of your assistant sighing.

"She's your biggest client. They had a break-in a few weeks ago and they are dealing with the claims assessors."

"Right... What am I meant to do?" I wonder at what point I'm going to get the hang of this.

"Be her insurance broker," Tara replies, attitude practically rolling off her and slamming into me through the glass.

The roll of her eyes makes me both want to laugh and also punch something. This woman definitely has the ability to get under my skin, unlike anyone else I've met before.

"Ha bloody ha. I meant, what is my role now that the claims assessor is involved, if she's been dealing with them in person? Doesn't feel like I have anything to offer at this point."

Another sigh. I grip my pen in both hands and resist the urge to snap it in half.

"Dayna is the type of client who expects her hand to be held through everything. Just give her assurances that you're handling it. Maybe make an appointment to go out and see her."

Bloody hell. The idea of actually going and seeing a client already fills me with dread. I honestly don't know what I was thinking when I accepted this job from Dad. I am so far out of my depth that the prospect of getting a job washing dishes sounds far more appealing than fronting up to this client's place of work and pretending I have any right to manage arranging insurance for said business.

"Fine," I say through gritted teeth. "Put her through."

I manage to bumble my way through the call, although I'm not entirely sure how much faith Dayna has in my abilities by the end of it. We arrange for me to attend the practice when the assessor is going out on Wednesday, and I can feel my palms sweating already at the thought.

When I hang up, I call Tara in to my office.

"You're coming with me to a meeting with Dayna and the assessor on Wednesday."

Tara raises an eyebrow, crossing her arms and leaning against the door frame. "And why is that?"

I mirror her, crossing my arms and leaning back in my chair, affecting an air of arrogance that I don't come even close to feeling. "Because you have a relationship with the client and that will put her at ease."

"I've never met any of the clients in person."

I drop the attitude. "Really? Why?"

She shrugs. "That was John's thing. I dealt with all the actual work. He did the client facing stuff, went out and checked their businesses out, then brought me the information to get the cover sorted. I only talk to the clients on the phone."

I nod. "Right. Well, that's changing now. We're dealing with this as a team from now on," I say, putting my metaphorical foot down.

A glimmer of excitement shows on her face before she shuts it down. "So I guess I deal with the clients in person now too, as well as do all the background work. What is it you'll be doing?"

While I can understand her annoyance, I'm getting really fucking tired of the constant attitude.

"Look, I get it," I bite back. "You hate me and the fact that I got this job. But I'm out of my depth here and have admitted that. You say you want to move up the ranks, and I'm giving you the chance to get that experience. I am more than willing to learn the background stuff as well, so that you're not the one shouldering it all by yourself. But you gotta meet me halfway here."

She cocks her head to the side. "I don't hate you, Aiden."

"Could have fooled me, with all the sighs and snarky comments." I raise an eyebrow, and am pleased to see she seems at least a little ashamed about it, dipping her head while pushing her hair back behind her ear.

It's been driving me crazy that my initial attraction to her still remains. Hell, I'm pretty sure I'm a masochist, because the meaner she is, the fitter I find her. It's disconcerting, and I really think I need to speak to someone about this. Probably a professional.

She doesn't reply, and I shake my head, my turn to sigh now. "So you're going to be coming with me to client appointments now, and when we get back from each one, you'll run me through what needs to be done. Okay?" I sound far more sure than I actually am, but fake it til you make it is a real thing.

She nods slowly, her expression wary, before turning and heading back to her desk.

I let out a breath and lean back into my chair. Bloody hell, I really hope we can get this all behind us soon, because I'd like to see the nice version of Tara that I met that first night.

"So, how are you settling in?" Felicity slides in across the table from me in the office canteen.

This is the first time she's spoken to me since I met her on the first day, and I'm not entirely sure why I'm receiving her attention now. I usually head out of the office for lunch, but had been so busy that I'd run out of time, so just snagged a sandwich from the ones left over from some client meeting Dad had earlier.

I shrug while I chew the bite of the rather disappointing sandwich, swallowing before answering. "Fine, I guess."

She's an attractive woman with very shiny blonde hair that she wears pulled back into a severe ponytail, and perfect makeup. It's clear she spends a lot of time on her appearance before work each day, and I am yet to see her wear the same outfit twice. I know plenty of guys who would drool after her. But from what I've heard about the admin team from several others, I'm wary of letting my guard down around any of them. Besides, my brain space is taken up by one annoyingly attractive, curvy redhead.

"A few of us are going out for drinks on Friday. You should join us."

My desire to make new friends wars with my self-preservation instincts.

"Who's going?" I ask, taking a sip of my coffee, before pulling a face.

The coffee in the canteen is awful, but I forget every time.

"Besides me, you mean?" she says, smiling while fluttering her eyelashes a little.

"Well, seeing as you were the one mentioning it, I figured that was a given." I smile back, but her flirting is wasted on me.

"Claire, Matilda, me and a few of the assistant brokers." She shrugs, spearing her salad with a fork and bringing it to her mouth.

"Is Tara going?" I don't know if I want her to say yes or no.

"Pfft, as if. Tara never comes out with us. We're not exactly her crowd."

Ah, and there's the bitchy side I'd been warned about.

"In what way?" I ask, feeling a little protective of my prickly assistant.

"Well, you know... We're clearly very different people." She waves down her body, the implication clear.

I raise an eyebrow. "Maybe so. Have you ever actually asked her to go out with you all, though?"

"She doesn't socialise with anyone here, except for a few of the other assistant brokers. She keeps to herself. I don't think she likes fun."

I've got to wonder if Felicity is self aware enough to know how bitchy she sounds. I'm going to guess not, though. She doesn't seem like self reflection is high on her list of qualities.

"Well, thank you for the invitation, but I'll have to pass this time. I'm moving over the weekend so need to have an early night." She doesn't need to know that all I'll be doing is moving my suitcase across the river. "Maybe next time, though."

I ball up the wrapper of my sandwich and toss it in the bin on my way out. Deciding I deserve a better coffee than what I just attempted to drink, I head back down to the lobby and order a flat white on almond milk, adding a hot chocolate to my order at the last minute. When I return to the office, I weave my way back through the sea of desks and place the hot chocolate in front of Tara while she stares at her screen, eating her lunch at her desk like I've seen her do every day. I keep walking, saying nothing, but when I take a seat at my desk, I glance up and see her drinking it with a little smile.

Maybe I can get past that icy exterior after all.

By the time Friday night rolls around, I feel like I've just barely survived. While I've taken to buying Tara a daily hot chocolate, I've still yet to feel like she completely warmed to me. We'd been to two client meetings together, and I can tell she's itching to take the lead, but I know I need to still try and do the role I was hired for, even though she is clearly far more capable. When she was showing me the quoting systems, it was all very overwhelming. But I'm determined to no longer look like a complete idiot, so I've been trying to work it out mostly on my own. I decide not to let Tara in on how many times I've had to ask Damien to give me the rundown when she's not around.

After yet another sad dinner while sitting on the bed in my

hotel room, I down my last beer and decide to check out the free dancing event that Vanessa had told me about. At least if I'm out and about, I won't feel quite so alone.

Wandering through the Queen Street Mall, I find myself watching all the different people milling around. There are the office workers out having Friday night drinks, dressed more casually than they usually would be the rest of the week. Families with young children wander around, checking out the various street entertainers set up at different points, as well as couples out on dates. And university students walking from the city campus to the public transport hub with an innate coolness to them while they ignore everyone else, wearing their massive headphones and bored expressions.

When I reach the top of the mall, I hear the music pumping, and it calls to my soul. My gaze falls on the crowd at the base of the building facing the old casino, a heritage building that is dwarfed by the tall buildings surrounding it, including the new casino that I'm told is a recent edition to the city skyline. I like the look of the older one better.

My feet carry me closer of their own accord. I had long forgotten about my love of the latin dance community, and the fast pace of salsa in particular. A reggaeton song is playing, providing the beat for the dancers whose feet are moving so fast. While I can spot a few beginners in the crowd, staring down at their feet while they try to follow the basic salsa steps, it's the experienced dancers I'm drawn to. I'd had no idea that this community existed here, and I'm excited at the idea of getting amongst the dancers and letting the music flow through me.

But after years away from it, tonight all I'll be doing is watching and trying to find a place here.

Taking a seat at the open-air bar next to the unofficial dance floor, I order a beer and scan the crowd. While I'm admiring a few couples who are performing complicated footwork, a woman appears in front of me, with flyers in her hand.

"Hey. Are you interested in learning how to do this yourself?" she asks, thrusting one of the flyers in front of me.

"Uh, sure," I reply, taken aback slightly.

I wasn't quite ready to talk to anyone yet.

"We're a new dance school, starting next week. We've got casual classes as well as set terms. You should check us out. We always need more good-looking young men." She winks and moves along to accost some other unsuspecting spectators, leaving me staring down at the flyer.

Why not? This would be the perfect way to meet others to dance with, and I might finally find some friends outside of work and my father's new family.

11

GROWN UP SO MUCH

TARA

AFTER YET ANOTHER quiet weekend at home, Monday arrives, and I find myself sitting at a small cafeteria at the hospital, staring into the face of a man I haven't seen since I was fifteen years old.

Dad looks much older, like the past twelve years have been particularly unkind to him. I want to say that it's karma, but even I'm not that awful. His once round, cheerful face is gaunt, and he's hooked up to various bags of fluid attached to a pole on wheels. A nurse had wheeled him down here five minutes after I arrived. I'd purposely scheduled this catch up before work so that I had an excuse to bail early, but now I'm thinking I should have gone up to his room instead of meeting for coffee. He doesn't look like he should be out of bed.

He runs his gaze over me, his eyes filling with tears, and it takes all my willpower to remain here, instead of running for the hills. I don't think I can do this. I'm not built to handle this sort of emotional turmoil.

"You've grown up so much," he says finally, his voice catching.

I don't really have a response to that, so I just nod. I doubt anyone looks the same after twelve years, regardless of age. But the last time he saw me, I was an awkward teenager with braces.

"Your little sisters look just like you," he continues, oblivious to the fact that mentioning his other family might not go down well.

I grip the arm of the metal chair I'm sitting in and grit my teeth. "That's nice."

"And Annelisa? Is she well?"

I nod. "Yes. She lives in London now."

"Oh. Your mother didn't mention that when we spoke." His smile drops away, and he looks even older.

"She's been there for a couple of years," I reply with a shrug.

"Is she still with Will? Those two were inseparable."

The fact he can remember Will is surprising, as they'd only been together a few months before Dad blew up our family unit.

"No. She left him when she moved."

He must sense my reluctance to go into any further detail about Annelisa's life, as he shifts the questions back to me.

"And you? You must be beating men off with a stick. Anyone special?"

Why is that always the first question people ask? Like having a significant other is the most important thing once you reach a certain age?

"Nope. Just me. I'm about to get a cat." I don't know why I added that part.

Guess I really wanted him to know that I'm *that* kind of single.

"Oh. That's nice." He clears his throat while reaching forward to pick up the glass of water I'd poured for him.

His hand shakes a little, and I find my heart softening slightly. "So, how are Jo and the girls?"

Although I've refused contact with him, I know he married the assistant he knocked up and they have two girls together.

"Good. Jordan is eleven and Piper is seven. Both little redheads, like you and Lis."

I swallow hard. "Guess you got your do-over, then." I can't stop the words as they fall out of my mouth.

Dad winces, drawing in a sharp breath. "It was never like that, Tara. I never wanted things to happen the way they did. I never wanted to lose you girls. And Jordan and Piper aren't replacements for you. Not a day has gone by where I haven't missed you both with all my heart."

I'm quiet for a moment. "Do they know about us?"

"Yes. When they were younger, they used to beg to meet you both. The idea that they had two sisters that they never met was something neither of them could understand. They've seen photos, though." He pauses, cocking his head to the side. "Would you like to meet them?"

A lump forms in my throat. "I don't know. I'll have to think about it. It's all a lot."

"Of course. I understand."

I don't think I can handle much more.

I look at my phone and am relieved to have an excuse to leave. "I should get going. I need to get to work."

Dad nods, but I can see the sadness in his eyes. "Right. You must be very important there. Your mum mentioned you've been there for a few years."

I shrug. "Not that important. I'm just an assistant broker."

"If there's one thing I know about you, Tara, it's that you're not 'just' anything. I'm sure you run that place."

I resist the obvious retort, holding back the urge to say 'well, you don't know me, do you'. Because it was my choice not to have any contact with this man, and now he's dying. It's obvious that he won't be leaving this place, and the reality of that is hard to deal with.

I get to my feet, grabbing my handbag. "I'll get a nurse to come and get you. I'll..." I take a deep breath. "I'll try to come back soon, okay?"

"I would really like that, baby girl."

Hearing his favourite term for me, I feel something inside of me split open, and I can't speak, so I nod and all but flee the cafeteria. I ask the front desk to call up to have someone come and get him, and hop into a cab, feeling like a coward.

I know as soon as I sit down at my desk that I should have called in sick. My plan to use work as an excuse to leave has backfired on me, and now I have to spend the rest of the day trying to act like I didn't just have the hardest conversation of my life.

Doing my best to avoid breaking down in the office, I go through the motions of my usual morning routine, firing up my laptop and opening all the programs before heading to the lunchroom to put my food in the fridge.

"Morning Tara. How was your weekend?" Celeste asks, looking up briefly from where she's busy making several hot drinks.

"Fine, thanks. Yours?" I manage to reply, hearing the rasp in my voice and wincing.

Thankfully, Celeste doesn't notice and starts prattling on about her weekend. I pretend to listen, making all the appropriate noises, before escaping as soon as it's polite to do so.

I know I'm on the verge of a breakdown, and I look over towards Aiden's office. The absence of any hot chocolate on my desk tells me he hasn't arrived yet. The blinds behind the glass wall are closed, but I can see through the open door that it's empty, so I duck inside, closing the door behind me just as the tears start to flow.

Struggling to breathe, I begin to sob, doubling over before leaning against the wall and sliding to the floor. I haven't cried like this in years. Not since Dad first left, and it's like I'm right back in my childhood bedroom. Memories of that time come flooding back, making me cry harder as I remember that awful night. Lis and I had come home from school to find Mum in a heap on the floor, crying so hard she could barely tell us that Dad had packed up and left. When Will had arrived, he'd given me a massive hug while I cried in his arms. He'd then disappeared into Annelisa's room, and I was all alone in my room. Until Kylie arrived, alerted by an SOS text from her brother. I'd never been more grateful for her presence, having only met her a few short months beforehand. But she'd blazed into mine and Bri's lives, and made those awful early days of my parents' divorce so much easier to deal with. She and Will were a blessing to my family, along with their parents.

But now they are both off living their own lives, and I'm sitting on the floor of my boss's office trying to keep the broken parts of myself together while dealing with the reality that I will never get back the years where I cut him out of my life. That he grew a whole new family while Mum, Annelisa and I had to piece ours back together.

And I can't even be mad at him.

Because he's dying.

12

NOT THE FIRST PERSON
TO CRY IN THIS OFFICE

AIDEN

AFTER MOVING into my new flat on the weekend, I'd severely miscalculated the time it would take me to get to work. I'd gotten used to my five-minute walk from the hotel, so now I'm running late for work. Which wouldn't be such a big deal if Tara wasn't always in super early and I'm paranoid about giving her even more reasons to resent my existence.

I still take a detour via the coffee shop downstairs, figuring I could at least appease her with hot chocolate. But when I get upstairs, I find her desk empty. Her computer and hand bag are here, so I figure she's in the canteen. Depositing her hot chocolate on the desk, I head for my office, surprised to find the blinds and door closed. But that's nothing compared to the surprise I feel when I open the door to find Tara sitting on the floor near the window, her forehead resting on her knees while she sobs.

"Tara? What's wrong?" I ask, my hand still on the door handle.

She looks up quickly, wiping the tears away even as more keep coming. "Shit, sorry!" She leaps to her feet and smooths her clothing down.

When it looks like she's going to try and run, I close the door behind me, afraid to spook her.

"It's okay, really. You're not the first person to cry in this office." I try to lighten the mood, but she barely acknowledges my words.

"It's not okay. I should go."

"Hold on." I take her hand in mine as she moves to brush past me and open the door. "What's wrong?"

She glances down at our hands, and I let go, wary of overstepping.

"Just family stuff. I shouldn't have let it get to me at work. I just need a minute, and then I'll be fine."

Bugger that. Tears like these aren't easily overcome, and the last thing she should be doing is thinking about work when she's clearly incredibly upset.

"You don't have to tell me what's wrong, but I think you should go home. If something is upsetting you this much, then the office is the last place you should be."

She considers my words for a few moments, her eyes searching my face. "Why are you being so nice to me?" she finally asks.

I pause, not having expected this line of questioning. "Do you want me to be an arse? I mean, I could try to be one, I guess, but I'm not really built that way."

She deflates a little, seeming smaller somehow. "No, you're not, are you?" She's quiet for a few moments, and just as I begin to think that she's not going to speak again, she starts talking. "I just spoke to my father for the first time in twelve years."

Of all the things she could have said, that wasn't even on the table. "Shit, I'm sorry. That's a lot to deal with on a Monday morning."

She huffs a humourless laugh. "Right? I stupidly thought meeting him before work would give me an excuse not to hang around, but instead, I now feel like a completely garbage human being and am crying in my boss's office."

"You're not a garbage human being. I'm sure you had your reasons for not speaking to him all those years."

"Yeah." She shrugs. "But now that he's dying, I'm the bad guy."

I hide my surprise at this bit of news. I consider her words, cocking my head to the side while I watch her wipe another tear away. "I don't think dying erases the shit we do beforehand, Tara. Cut yourself a little slack." I really want to give her a hug, but I doubt she would welcome that.

She lets out a breath, nodding. "Maybe I should go home. I don't think I'm going to get much work done, anyway."

"Good idea. Whoever told you that must be pretty smart," I say with a smile, and am rewarded with a small laugh and a shake of her head.

"Thanks, Aiden. I'll speak to you tomorrow." She opens the door and, after squaring her shoulders and wiping away one last tear, heads back out to her desk.

I watch as she gathers her things, and she salutes me with her cup of hot chocolate before leaving.

Finally sitting down at my desk, I know it's going to be a while before I can concentrate myself. Every encounter with this woman leaves me wanting to know more. I know all too well how it feels to have a terminally ill parent. I just hope it's easier for her than it was for me.

A few hours later, Damien flags me down to see if I want to grab lunch out of the office together, which I'm more than happy to accept. It feels good to have finally made a friend, and the office has felt strange without Tara's presence all morning.

"So, where's your partner in crime?" Damien asks when we're heading down in the lift.

I can only assume he's talking about Tara. "She had a bit of a rough morning, so I sent her home."

Damien leans back against the wall and crosses his arms, considering me. "You're nothing like your old man, you know that?"

"I'll take that as a compliment."

"You should. Your Dad can be a bit of a -" he cuts himself off, so I finish for him.

"A bastard? Yeah, I know."

He laughs, looking a little surprised at my open assessment of my father's less than stellar qualities. "You're good people, Aiden."

"Thanks, I think..."

We head towards Post Office Square, and Damien shows me the food court hidden down below that I hadn't seen before. Each grabbing some sushi, we head back to the sunny grassed area and take a seat on a bench to eat.

"It always feels so much better to get out of the office for a bit." Damien takes a bite of his salmon and avocado roll.

"Yeah. I'm still discovering new places to sit and people watch. Certainly more interesting than that sad canteen."

He nods in agreement while he chews. "So what was up with Tara? It's not like her to take a day off."

I shrug. "She just had some personal stuff come up. I'm sure she'll be back in tomorrow like normal." Having her open up to me felt like such a step forward for us, so the last thing I'm going to do is betray her confidence.

Even if it means being evasive with my new friend

"She's an enigma, that one, that's for sure. She's so guarded with her personal life. It's kind of refreshing compared to some of the others who bring all their drama to work. I have a lot of respect for her."

I ponder his words for a few moments. When she'd opened up to me earlier, I had felt privileged that she'd finally felt comfortable enough to be honest with me. Now, knowing that she has kept colleagues she's worked with for years at arm's length... It feels a little heartwarming.

"Yeah... Me too," I reply quietly.

It's the last we mention the subject, but I carry the knowledge with me for the rest of the day and find myself looking forward to seeing her tomorrow.

After dinner, I bring my laptop to bed, ready for a video chat with Sarah.

"Hey, stranger. How's things?" The screen opens up to show the top of her blonde head and the wall above.

"Good. Can't see you properly, though. Still working on this technology thing?" I ask with a grin.

Although she's a teacher and works with computers all day long, technology and her have never been friends.

"Shit, sorry, I wasn't looking at my picture, was too busy admiring that handsome face." Her smile finally comes into view while she adjusts the screen.

From her surroundings, I can tell she's sitting on her sofa, and a stab of homesickness hits me in the chest. Many a night was spent on that sofa over the years.

"I miss you," I blurt out, not feeling even a little self conscious about the admission.

Sarah has been the only person I've ever been able to be completely candid with. She was the only friend to stick by me when everything happened with Mum and I had to step away from my studies. Watching her get to go on and live the life I'd hoped to have for myself was bittersweet. She helped get me through those dark days. When we'd both struggled with the loneliness of the single life, we'd sought comfort from one another, although it was more physical than emotional. Neither of us has ever developed romantic feelings throughout our friendship, but it was nice to at least have someone to turn to instead of always resorting to one-night stands with strangers.

"I miss you, too. Feels so strange not having you sitting on this sofa with me every night. Simon is a poor substitute." She smiles at someone off camera, and I hear Simon yell "hey!" in the background.

"Hi Simon!" I call, and he appears beside her, wrestling the laptop off her.

"Hi, mate. Or should I say, G'day Mate?" he replies in his thick Scottish accent.

They'd met a few months before I'd left, and so far, he seems to be a good match for my crazy best friend.

"I am yet to hear a single person use that phrase, so we'll just stick with 'hi'." I grin as Sarah's hand appears, and she steals the laptop back.

"Bugger off, this is my Aiden time. You can have him after I finish."

We settle in for a long chat, and I fill her in on the happenings over the last few weeks.

"So, what you're telling me is that you've found yourself a bril assistant that gets you all hot and bothered? I want to meet this woman that gets the usually unflappable Aiden all flustered." She grins evilly.

I roll my eyes. "She does not get me hot and bothered."

"Lies. I know you too well, remember? You are definitely into this woman. And I approve. Seems like she's got just the right amount of spark."

"I'm changing the subject. How's the break going?"

Sarah clucks her tongue, but allows me off the hook. "It's been good. We went up to Glasgow so I could meet Simon's parents and then into the highlands. You would have loved it."

We chat a little longer about her adventures while on the summer break from her job as a drama teacher at a posh school in central London. When we end the call, I feel a little lighter at having been able to have a conversation that isn't just surface level.

Now to just find myself friends like that in the same city I live in.

13

LAST BATH I'LL GIVE YOU

TARA

On Friday afternoon, I arrive home to find Bri sitting on the couch with a book open in her lap. Her long blonde hair is swept over her shoulder and she has cute little reading glasses perched on her nose.

"Hey! What are you doing here?" I ask, putting my bag down inside the door of my bedroom after kicking off my shoes.

"Like you even need to ask that. I wasn't going to leave you to deal with all this stuff by yourself. How are you going? Have you seen your Dad again?" She gets to her feet, her movements as graceful as ever.

I'd sent a message in the group chat with her and Kylie after my breakdown on Monday, and they'd both been checking on me daily since.

I shake my head. "No. I'm still processing everything. He wants me to meet his daughters."

Bri's face drops slightly, before giving me a hug and holding me tight until I sink into it.

It's been so long since I've allowed anyone to see my vulnerable

81

side that I'd forgotten what it's like to have my best friend here for me like this. Which makes it difficult for me to keep my composure.

I've felt like I was walking a tightrope all week. Ever since Aiden found me crying in his office on Monday, I've been fighting a constant internal battle with my emotions, which is not like me at all.

"Thank you," I mumble, and Bri squeezes me again before stepping back.

"You never have to thank me for being here for you, T," she says with a pointed look.

I let out a breath, nodding. "Still, you didn't have to leave your new husband to come and see me."

"Ha, Jake and I see each other so much, I'm sick of the man." She grins.

I laugh. "The day that you're sick of Jake Boyd, hell will have frozen over. He is the perfect man, after all."

She pokes out her tongue, unable to argue with me as we both know I'm one hundred percent right.

When we were growing up, it was obvious to Kylie and me just how right Jake and Bri were for each other. It just took them a good few years to work it out for themselves. But the three of us girls knew he was the kind of guy that other men should aspire to be like, even back in high school. I mean, the other guys in our friendship circle are pretty awesome as well, but there is just something about Jake. All caring and respectful, wrapped up in an incredibly good looking package.

My best friend definitely got one of the good ones.

"Where's Maddie?" I ask, looking around for her little dog that usually goes everywhere with her.

"I left her at home with Jake. You and I are going to get that kitten this weekend, and I figured it would probably be best not to make it deal with a dog just yet."

I feel the emotion rising in my chest again. I hadn't told Bri about the cat yet, not sure how to broach the subject with her, seeing as it's her apartment and all. But Kylie must have filled her in, and of course, not only is she fine with it, she's making it happen.

I might not have a partner, but I have two of the best friends anyone could ask for. If only they both didn't live so far away.

"Oh my gosh, he's adorable!" Bri scratches the fluffy little black kitten behind his ear while he purrs against my neck.

Julie, the foster carer, had happily let us come and see the litter of kittens she and her husband have hand raised since they were only a few days old.

"Isn't he? This little guy is the last of his brothers and sisters to leave us. I just find it so sad when the black ones are the last to go. They deserve love just as much as the others. Just be warned, he can be a little naughty once he feels comfortable." Julie wags her finger at the little ball of fur, who pushes his head further against my neck and purrs even louder.

I've never owned a cat, but how naughty can they be? I'm already in love with him, and I've only known him for ten minutes. While I'd been researching kittens, I'd come across countless profiles of little black balls of fur, looking absolutely adorable, but I think he might be the sweetest of them all, with big blue eyes that stand out against his jet black fur.

"Why do you have trouble finding homes for the black ones?" Bri asks, looking surprised.

"There's just so many superstitions about them, even now, which is so crazy. Who could possibly think this little guy would bring them bad luck?" Julie sighs, shaking her head.

"Well, I am not even slightly superstitious. I'll take him," I say with a grin.

Why not rescue a little soul who feels unloved? It might be nice to have a kindred spirit around.

I hold him out in front of me, admiring his fluffiness. He's all black except for a few tiny specs of grey and white scattered throughout his body. And although they've described him as a domestic short hair, the random long hairs make me think he might end up being even fluffier than he looks now.

"As if anyone could come and just see him without taking him home," Bri says while I pay Julie.

She sends us off with a bag full of cat food and a few toys. Bundling him into the carrier that I'd bought on my cat spending spree, she reaches in to give him one last ear rub.

"Do you have a name for him yet?" she asks, straightening up.

"I haven't been feeling particularly creative in that department. What do you think?" I ask Bri, who cocks her head to the side.

"What about a name from a show or movie or something?" I think about it for a moment, jumping when she claps her hands together loudly with a look of excitement. "Remember that movie we loved when we were in kindy? Aristocats. We were obsessed with that. What about one of the names from that?"

She's right, I absolutely loved the Aristocats when I was a kid and had forced her to watch it at every playdate we had.

"You're right. I really like the name Toulouse for him."

Bri scrunches her nose. "Isn't Toulouse the ginger one? The other one is the black one."

"Yeah, but I don't like the name Beliose. And as much as I'm against gendered names, he just doesn't look like a Marie."

Bri laughs. "True. Toulouse it is."

Bri drives us home, with Toulouse howling in his carrier the whole way. After five minutes, all we can do is laugh at how sad the little guy sounds. We stop laughing, however, when a horrific smell permeates through the car.

"Oh god, he's pooped," I say, gagging.

"My... That is potent." Bri presses the buttons on all the windows in the car, and both our eyes begin to water from the assault on our sense of smell.

This sets us both off laughing again. We arrive back at the apartment, and Bri parks her car next to mine in the residents' underground car park, leaving the windows open enough to air the smell out.

We get him in the elevator and realise too late that he's now covered in poop.

"Crap... we're going to have to give him a bath." I say, and we stare at each other.

"How... how do you bathe a cat?" Bri asks, sounding about as confident as I feel.

The elevator doors open on the ground floor, and I open my mouth to warn whoever it is that they might want to wait til it's empty, not wanting to subject anyone else to the smell. But the words die in my throat when I take in the appearance of the tall, slightly disheveled but incredibly hot man standing before me.

"Aiden?! What are you doing here?" I ask, blinking.

My words come out harsher than I meant them to, but seeing him in my building throws me off kilter.

He's still dressed in the same clothes he wore to work, and I notice his backpack slung over his shoulder. He must have just finished work. I hadn't realised how late he was staying. Or maybe he knows someone in the building and the backpack is full of clothes for a sleepover. I ignore the twisting feeling in my stomach at that thought.

"Um, hi to you too. And also, what the hell is that smell?" Aiden halts in the doorway, raising his hand to cover his mouth and nose.

"Her cat pooped," Bri offers up, looking between us both with wide eyes, and Aiden's gaze drops to the carrier in my hand.

"I didn't know you had a cat?"

"We just picked him up. But he pooped in the carrier on the drive back, and now he's covered in it," I reply, breathing through my mouth to avoid the smell.

"As fun as this is, we should probably get upstairs before more people need to use the lift and end up dying from the smell," Bri says.

Aiden gets in, looking at Toulouse who is screaming his little head off inside the carrier. "Cute."

We get to the top floor, and I realise Aiden didn't hit a button. "What are you doing here?" I ask again.

"I forgot to hit the button," he replies, holding his arm in front of the door to keep it from closing on us. "I live in this building."

Bri looks between the two of us, a smile slowly forming. "What a coincidence. So does she." She nods her head towards me while I stare at him in stunned confusion.

"Seriously?" he asks, looking at me.

I nod.

"You live in the penthouse?" he asks.

"Funny story. Wanna come help us clean a cat and we can tell you all about it?" Bri asks, ignoring my glare.

Aiden shrugs. "Sure. Why not?"

And that's how, ten minutes later, we're all standing in the bathroom, covered in tiny scratches with a wet black kitten who, thankfully, no longer smells like poop. Toulouse had clawed his way up my arm until Bri had dug out some rubber gloves I didn't even know we'd had, and I'd managed to avoid any more bloodshed.

"Poor little guy looks traumatised," Aiden says, scratching Toulouse's wet head while he shivers in my arms, bundled up in a towel.

"Yeah. Sorry, little man. I promise, that's the last bath I'll give you." I set the kitten down on the ground, letting him slowly start exploring his new home.

Bri opens the bathroom door, and the three of us follow while Toulouse tentatively steps out, keeping low to the ground while he takes in the large space.

"So, the penthouse, huh?" Aiden says, his gaze flicking to mine before looking over at Bri.

Bri launches into an explanation about how Jake won the place in one of those raffles several years ago and now I live here keeping an eye on the place for them while they live out in Stanthorpe most of the time.

"Wow. That's cool. I don't think I've ever known anyone who won a house or flat before," Aiden says, once she's finished talking.

I continue to watch Toulouse getting acquainted with the apartment while ignoring the mixed feelings I have about Aiden being in my home. We'd sort of come to a truce this week, after he'd found me crying in his office. I figure, he wasn't an asshole about it, so the least I could do was ease up on him. But it feels weird having him here. I'm not completely blind to the fact that the attraction I'd initially felt towards him was still there, but I've never socialised with anyone from work, other than Chris when he was still there. And having fuzzy feelings towards my boss just feels like trouble waiting to happen.

The fact that Aiden seems impervious to Bri's looks and is instead watching me is also disconcerting. I've never had a man pay this much attention to me when either Bri or Kylie (or both together) are around, and I don't know what to do with myself.

"Well, I should get back to my place. I guess we'll be seeing even more of each other now, Tara."

I nod silently while Bri lets him out, closing the door behind him and turning to face me. "Ah, you failed to mention that your boss is hot and clearly into you."

"He's not into me," I reply with a scoff.

She raises an eyebrow. "Yeah, he is."

"He was just being polite, that's all."

Bri shakes her head. "Oh T, when are you ever going to see yourself the way the rest of us see you? He was so into you. He helped us give your cat that was covered in poop a bath, and only a guy who knows you're a total catch would risk serious injury like that. The guy is smitten. He's a smitten kitten." She grins, pleased with her little rhyme.

"You're such a dork," I reply with a laugh, rolling my eyes.

"Yeah, I am. And you love it."

"I do." I hug her, before realising we've lost sight of Toulouse. "Crap. This is going to be fun."

We spend the rest of the evening playing with the kitten with no more talk of boys. But it's hard to forget that Aiden now lives in the same building, and I find myself wondering how often we're going to be running into each other.

And half looking forward to it.

14

ALL THOSE YEARS, WASTED

AIDEN

AFTER ANOTHER FRIDAY and Saturday night spent alone, I'm almost looking forward to having dinner with my father and his family.

Emphasis on the almost.

Although we've been working together for a month now, our relationship is still pretty basic. He only really knows how to talk to me about work. Anything personal seems to be too hard for him. Although judging by how I've seen him interact with others at the office, that seems to just be how he is.

I try not to think about how sad it is that my interactions with him are no different from my colleagues. At twenty-nine, I feel like I should just accept by now that I don't really have a father.

I decide to catch the ferry to his house in Bulimba. Now that I know my way around the city a little more, I'm determined to stop spending so much money on Ubers and take advantage of the public transport right on my doorstep. Although I do miss the reliability of the Tube in London.

A short walk up Oxford Street brings me to my father's street, and now that I'm on foot, I'm taken aback by the massive houses that I'd failed to notice last time. I knew he was well off, but I realise now that he's obviously sitting on some prime real estate, and that same resentfulness I'd felt last time I was here rises to the surface. I don't know that I'll ever be able to get past the fact that he gave my mother practically nothing to raise me while living such a luxurious lifestyle back here.

"It's good to see you again, Aiden." Like last time, Lisa is the one to answer the door.

She greets me with a smile, looking a little tired as she waves me through. I guess having toddlers in your late thirties is exhausting. After my interactions with my half-siblings last time, I'm not sure how I'd go in her position. Those two are full on.

"You too," I reply, following her through to the kitchen.

I'm surprised to find my father standing at the stove. I don't know why, but I just hadn't pictured him as someone who does any of the cooking. At least he does some of the domestic stuff around the house, I guess.

I'd learnt last time that Lisa is an interior designer, but she's been off work since the twins were born. From what I can tell, she's ready to go back to work, but Dad doesn't want the twins in nursery. I'd like to have kids one day - more than I realised, actually - but I don't know how I'd feel about not getting to go back to work because of a lifestyle choice that my spouse had an issue with.

"Ah, you made it. I was beginning to think you'd forgotten," Dad says, looking at his watch.

I'm only ten minutes late. "Sorry, I missed the earlier ferry."

"Oh, you caught the City Cat? Why didn't you drive?"

I look at him for a moment. "Um... I don't have a car."

"Don't you? Why not? Brisbane is a car city, after all."

Lisa and I exchange a brief look before I reply. "I've only been here for a month. It wasn't really a priority. And I didn't drive that much back home."

The fact that I still call London home speaks volumes about how I'm settling in here.

"Well, we should get you one. How have you been getting to client meetings?" Of course, that's his actual concern.

"Ubers or taxis," I reply with a shrug.

"That won't do at all. I'll arrange for you to get a company car this week." He turns back to the stove, done with the conversation now that he's made a decision, and I stare at his back.

I don't really get what the big deal is. Wouldn't the clients prefer to see me show up in a cab rather than some fancy company car?

"Um... do all the brokers have company cars?" I ask.

"No. Just the partners. But you're a Sanderson."

Great... more special treatment. Tara's going to love this.

I consider declining the car, but I know it's no use, as he will just do it, anyway. He's completely oblivious to any of the politics in that office. What's wrong with a healthy dose of nepotism, right?

As we sit down for dinner, I notice the absence of the twins finally.

"Where are the kids?"

"They're with my parents for the night. Your father needed a bit of a break," Lisa replies.

I don't know why, but something about that rubs me the wrong way. It's probably my own daddy issues, but it feels like he's just going back to his usual habits, foisting his parental responsibilities off onto others.

"They can be a little rambunctious, and we were out for an event last night, so they offered to have them an extra night," she continues, her gaze meeting mine.

I guess my thoughts were written all over my face, if she's coming to his defence like that.

I nod, serving myself some salad before reaching for the pasta dish Dad cooked up. Too late though, I realise it's covered in cheese. Not wanting to make a big deal, I serve myself the smallest portion possible.

Unfortunately, Lisa notices. "Are you not hungry?"

"Um... well it's just... I'm allergic to dairy."

Lisa turns to stare at Dad. "David. Why the heck did you use cheese when your son is allergic to dairy?"

Well, at least she has no problem on calling him out on a shitty parenting move.

"I forgot. Sorry. Although, to be honest, I always thought it was just your mother allowing you to be a picky eater." Dad doesn't look particularly concerned.

At the cavalier mention of Mum, I feel anger rising in my chest. "No. After having to call an ambulance for her baby because of an anaphylactic reaction, pretty sure she worked out it wasn't because I was a picky eater."

"Calm down. I was there. They told us you'd probably grow out of it."

Mum told me about that. He'd spent most of the time in the hospital emergency department on the phone to his assistant, getting her to sort out work stuff he had to reschedule and barely paid any attention to what the doctors said about their two week old baby.

"Well, I didn't. Still allergic."

Lisa watches the entire exchange with wide eyes, her gaze shifting between us both.

"Well, have some more salad. I can probably rustle something else up as well." He pushes the salad bowl towards me again.

"It's fine. Don't worry about it."

We lapse into silence while we eat. Lisa keeps casting looks towards her husband, almost like she's seeing him in a different light. Mustn't be nice, realising your husband is actually a pretty shitty father. Well, to his first born, anyway. I hope he's at least better with the twins.

After a few minutes, it appears as though she can't handle the silence any more. "So, Aiden. How are you settling in?"

"Good. I moved into an apartment in Kangaroo Point last week."

She nods. "And work?"

I shrug. "It's a bit of a learning curve, but I'm doing okay."

"Should have gotten you onboard sooner," Dad grumbles, and I raise an eyebrow.

"Well, I kind of had my hands full before," I reply.

He tsks, concentrating on his food and failing to see the disgusted look on my face. "All those years, wasted."

"I wouldn't call caring for my sick mother wasted years."

Yeah, Lisa is definitely seeing a new side of my father tonight. She looks horrified.

But Dad either doesn't notice, or doesn't care. "She could have had a carer, or lived in a facility. Instead, you lost those years that you could have been building your career back here."

"In what world do you think she had the money for a carer, even with the NHS? And I sure as fuck wasn't letting her live in extra-care housing." I push away from the table, getting to my feet.

Lisa looks up at me. "Don't go, Aiden."

"Sit down, Aiden," Dad says, sounding weary.

Like I'm the problem.

"I think I'm going to head home. I'll see you at work, I guess." There is no way I can continue to sit here, listening to him act like Mum was the problem.

Lisa follows me to the door. "I'm sorry, Aiden. I have no idea what's come over him."

I shake my head. "Don't worry about it. That's just who he is. I don't know why I thought it would be any different."

Walking back down the street, I shove my hands in the pockets of my jacket, kicking myself for even considering trying to build a relationship with the only parent I have left.

I should have just stayed in London.

15

HER NAME IS TARA, YOU PRICK

TARA

I DON'T KNOW why I thought going on a date on a Sunday night was a good idea, but here I am.

I'd had a few matches since I set up my profile again, but most of them seemed pretty creepy. One of them asked for photos of my feet, while another sent me a dick-pic before I'd even replied to his first message, which started with "wanna fuck?"

Charming.

When Daniel messaged after I'd spent the weekend with Bri, however, asking if I wanted to meet for a drink tonight, I felt braver than normal and actually accepted the invitation. I figured it would be a good distraction from thinking about my dad. Or daydreaming about ways to get Aiden to come back up to the apartment, which is the other thing plaguing my mind at the moment.

Daniel didn't look like a serial killer in his profile photo, had yet to send me a photo of his package or ask for photos of anything weird, so I decided to give him a chance. Pretty sad that the bar was so low, but that's modern dating for you.

So I put on a nice dress, applied more make up then I'd normally wear and curled my hair. Then I caught a cab to Howard Smith Wharves to meet him at the brewery. Not my usual scene, but it was his suggestion, as he apparently lives in New Farm, so this was kind of halfway for both of us.

Taking a seat on the river side at one of the high tables, I glance around to see if he's here yet, but it looks like I'm the first to arrive. The area is surprisingly quiet for a weekend, and I'm the only one sitting out here, but I guess most people have gone home to get ready for the working week. Like I kind of wish I was.

Once he arrives, the nerves I've been feeling disappear, replaced by disappointment. His profile photo was obviously a few years old, and I'm pretty sure he lied about his age, as there is no way he is only thirty. His hairline has receded a few inches since his photo was taken, and if he isn't at least forty, I will willingly eat dirt.

He's also wearing far too much cologne.

He orders for us both without asking what I'd like, and now I've got a beer in front of me along with a bowl of onion rings. I don't drink beer and I'm allergic to onions.

Why did I bother with this?

"So, Tina, what do you do?" he asks, chewing with his mouth open.

"It's Tara. And I work in insurance," I reply, already trying to work out how I can get out of here without causing a scene.

"Right, Tara. I'm a corporate lawyer."

I didn't ask. I can already tell he has an over-inflated ego. And when he launches into a long and boring explanation of what a corporate lawyer does, and how important he is, I nod along absently, wishing I'd thought to get Bri to call me with a fake emergency.

Rookie move, Tara.

Unsurprisingly, he doesn't notice that he is the only one eating and drinking, ordering another round of beers.

For some stupid reason, I stay at the table while he goes to the bar. All these years of being polite to assholes has trained me to put up with this shit, apparently. If this had happened to Kylie, she would have upended the beer on top of his head and marched right out of here. I really miss her when she's not around.

Daniel returns to the table while I'm still trying to work up the nerve to leave, and before I realise what's happening, he's standing next to my stool, staring down at me. He slides a hand behind my neck and moves to kiss me. His lips brush mine, and I recoil instinctively, the overwhelming smell of his cologne making me want to throw up.

"What are you doing?" I demand, pushing him away.

I guess I can get past the need to be polite after all.

"Come on, Tina. The connection between us is undeniable. No need to play hard to get." He leers down at me, his gaze bypassing my face and going straight to my cleavage.

"What connection? All you've done is talk about yourself for the past half an hour and ordered food and drink without asking me what I like." I get to my feet, grabbing my hand bag.

He grabs my arm. "Don't be like that. We were having a great time. I thought this was going somewhere. Come back to my place." He pulls me in closer and I struggle to wrench my arm from his grip.

As he tries to kiss me again, a hand clamps down on his shoulder and pulls him away.

"I'm pretty sure she doesn't want you to do that." I freeze when I recognise Aiden's voice.

"Who the fuck are you?" Daniel demands, while I step out of his reach, skirting around the table.

"Someone who is telling you to bugger off," Aiden replies.

His eyes flare while he stares at Daniel, his jaw clenched, and despite the situation, I don't think I've ever found him more attractive than right now.

"Tina and I were having a nice night. How about you fuck

off?" Daniel says, stepping closer to Aiden, who doesn't back down.

Aiden has a few inches on Daniel and is in far better shape. If I was to put money on who would win a fight, it would all go on Aiden.

"Her name is Tara, you prick. Tara," Aiden says, his voice deathly low as he turns to look at me. "Were you having a nice night?"

I shake my head. "I most certainly was not."

He turns to glower back at Daniel. "There's your answer. So get lost, perv. And the next time a woman tells you she's not interested, listen to the words coming out of her mouth."

Daniel glares at us both before throwing his hands up. "Whatever. You can have the fat bitch all to yourself."

He storms off, and Aiden looks like he's about to launch himself after him, but I place a hand on his arm. "Don't. He's not worth getting in trouble for. He spent half an hour telling me how much of an amazing lawyer he is, so he'd definitely call the cops."

Aiden lets out a breath, finally looking at me properly. "Are you okay?"

I nod, pretending that being called a 'fat bitch' didn't hurt. "I'm fine. Where did you come from, anyway?"

"I was out for a walk."

I raise an eyebrow. "Really? Here?"

He shrugs. "I needed to clear my head after a particularly shitty dinner, so I got off at Sidney Street and was planning to walk back over the bridge." He nods towards the elevators that go up the cliff face on the other side of the buildings.

"Okay... But why'd you come this way? This is out of your way."

He shrugs. "I was going to get a beer first. Never been here, so thought I'd check it out. Glad I did now. Are you sure you're okay?"

I let out a breath. "I won't lie and say that didn't suck, but I'm okay. I was pretty close to slapping him, though."

"Good. He needs a good slap. Why were you even on a date with him?" Something about his tone gets my defences up.

"Because he didn't seem like a creep when he messaged me on the app," I reply, raising my chin and glaring at him.

He raises an eyebrow. "You met someone from a dating app in a dark, secluded area?"

"Hey, drop the attitude," I reply, my voice raised as anger bubbles to the surface. At him or at myself, I'm not sure. "I agreed to meet him at a bar. It's not like I organised a tryst in a dark alley. I would have been fine. I didn't need saving."

Aiden looks like he's about to argue with me, but just shakes his head after a moment. "Sorry. I shouldn't have made it sound like you were in the wrong. I just had a shit night, and I am obviously more fired up than I thought."

I glare at him a little longer, not entirely sure I'm ready to forgive him so easily, but something in his eyes has me softening. "It's fine. Do you want to talk about it?" I ask, surprising both of us.

He shakes his head. "No, but thanks."

We both stand there awkwardly for a moment.

"I should let you get that drink," I say finally, sliding my handbag onto my shoulder.

"Don't really feel like it now. I'll walk you home."

I hesitate, not sure how we'll go spending the twenty minute walk back together. But what harm is it going to do? We live in the same building, and it's not like I can pretend I have somewhere else to be, seeing as my date just stormed off.

Nodding, I follow when he leads the way to the elevator. We join a small group gathered as the doors open, and I hold my breath most of the way to the top, the smell of urine overpowering everything else.

"My god, what is it with lifts and the smell of excrement?" Aiden says, once we're alone again.

I splutter a laugh. "Maybe it's you," I say with a grin.

"Ha, you were there both times as well. Maybe it was you." He grins back, a twinkle in his eye.

I gasp dramatically, pretending to be outraged, and his grin widens. We slip into easy conversation for the rest of the walk home, both of us avoiding talking about our crappy nights before seeing each other. It's surprisingly pleasant, and I'm reminded of our easy conversation the first night we met. Before everything else that happened.

Once we reach the lobby of our building, I've forgotten about my annoyance with him, reminded instead of the first night we'd met. He holds the elevator open and lets me go in first. He hits the button for the seventh floor and watches while I hit the penthouse one.

We fall silent, and once the elevator reaches his floor, he nods at me before stepping out. "Good night, Tara."

He stands outside the door, his hand holding it open while he looks like he's about to say something else.

"Good night, Aiden," I reply with a nod.

He nods back slowly, before removing his hand.

When the doors close, I feel a sudden emptiness that I can't quite describe. But I'm grateful for the little ball of fur waiting for me upstairs, realising how nice it is to have someone to come home to for a change.

Even if he does have four legs and likes to bite my toes.

16

DO YOU NEED SOMEONE
TO HOLD YOUR HAND?

AIDEN

MONDAY MORNING ARRIVES bright and sunny, and I drag myself into work. After last nights exchange with my father, the last thing I want to do is talk to him, but I can't really avoid him when he walks into my office five minutes after I arrive.

"I've asked Celeste to arrange your car," he says, not even bothering to say hello when he takes a seat on the other side of my desk.

I swallow the mouthful of coffee I was taking when he wandered in. "Great," I reply, unable to inject any enthusiasm into my voice.

He is, of course, oblivious. "And I'm arranging for you to attend the conference in Singapore on my behalf."

I pause in the process of raising my coffee to my mouth again. "What do you mean, on your behalf? I thought I was going as well as you?"

He shakes his head. "No. I can't be away from the family that long and I think it would be more beneficial for you to attend than me. I've been to so many of those over the years."

I regard him for a moment, a cold feeling of dread settling in the pit of my stomach. I'm nowhere near ready to attend a conference solo, let alone as the replacement for someone who has been in the industry for forty years.

I'm so focused on my own concerns that I miss what he says next. Not that he really requires a response from me. As far as he's concerned, this is a done deal.

"I can't go alone," I say, interrupting him while he's saying something about accommodation.

"What do you mean? Do you need someone to hold your hand?" he asks, frowning.

Yes.

"No. But I've only been in the industry for a month. If you're set on me going, I don't want to embarrass the company. So I'd like to take someone with me who has more knowledge."

He considers my words for a moment, which surprises me, as he very rarely takes into account what I have to say on any subject.

"Well, we do get two tickets for each office. Who do you suggest?"

I hesitate, glancing out through the glass towards Tara's desk, glimpsing her red bun over the top of the computer monitor. Would he even consider sending an assistant broker? I feel like this would be the perfect opportunity for her, but maybe I should suggest Damien? Oh, who am I kidding - there's no way I'll be suggesting anyone other than my slightly prickly, very attractive assistant.

"What about Tara?" I ask finally.

He doesn't reply straight away, studying my face closely while he thinks.

"Why Tara? She's good at her job, I'll give her that. But she's never shown any interest in furthering her career."

I'm too stunned to respond immediately. He truly is oblivious to the goings on in this office. In the month I've worked here, it's clear that Tara's talents are wasted in her role. Even the most experienced brokers in the office go to her for advice when they come up against road blocks.

"I think you'd be surprised. She is far overqualified for her job. If anything, I should be her assistant."

Dad looks horrified at the notion. "I think that's going a bit far. But if you think it would benefit you, I'll have Danielle make the arrangements," he says, referring to his personal assistant who has worked for him for as long as I can remember and basically runs this place.

That woman must have the patience of a saint.

I nod, determination setting in. "I think it would benefit Tara to come along."

He scowls a little, obviously not loving the fact that I'm advocating so strongly for the advancement of someone else's career, but I don't care. And hopefully, Tara will be distracted by the conference and won't notice the company car.

He leaves my office soon after, promising to have Danielle send through all the details once everything is booked. I turn back to my computer, staring at my over flowing inbox with a sinking feeling. Most of the client questions are still over my head, and I wonder if I'm ever going to get the hang of this. Or if I even want to. Insurance is so boring, and I just can't see myself doing this for the rest of my life.

It's not like I have any other prospects though, and it pays well. Probably better than it should, to be honest. I'm not stupid, I know that the pay I'm on far exceeds the experience I have. I can only imagine how it would feel to be in the position of someone like Damien or Tara and have the boss's son just step into a higher paid position, and have to explain everything to them. I'd probably be bitter about it, and can completely understand the resentment Tara has held towards me.

Will she consider this opportunity as a good thing, or be angry that I advocated for her?

Only one way to find out.

"Tara?" I call through the open door.

"Yeah?" She looks up, those big green eyes blinking at me slowly over the top of the computer monitor. The look on her face tells me she was in the middle of something important and isn't loving the interruption.

I swallow hard. She still intimidates the hell out of me at work, but the little glare does all sorts of things to my insides. My god, I really need to get laid, because I'm now fantasising ways to fuck the look off her face.

"Can you come in here for a sec?"

At least she manages to hold in her sigh this time while she gets to her feet and comes to sit in the chair in front of me. "What's up?"

"How was the rest of your evening?" I ask, figuring I'd start with some small talk.

She shrugs. "Fine."

Okay, so we're done with the small talk. I guess the events of the weekend still haven't won her over to my side. I'd thought that the walk home last night had thawed her out a little, but it looks like that was just wishful thinking.

I clear my throat. "So, we're going to Singapore."

She cocks her head to the side. "What?"

Honestly, I've had better conversations with a brick wall. "Dad has asked us to attend the conference in Singapore next month on his behalf."

She's quiet for far too long. "Really?" she asks, her tone incredulous.

"Yes."

"I get why he's sending you, being his son and all. But why me? I've never been to anything like that. I've had to beg to get to local ones that I need to attend to get my points each year, and that's a requirement of my job." She crosses her arms and lifts her chin.

Always so defensive. I really should not be picturing myself pinning her against the wall to kiss her senseless right now.

"I told him I believed you'd benefit from attending as well, and he agreed," I say, embellishing slightly.

She doesn't seem to believe me, going by the raised eyebrow, but nods slowly. "Okay."

I pause, waiting for her to continue speaking, but when that seems to be all she has to say, I let out a breath. "Okay."

"Is that all?" she asks.

"Ugh, yeah. Although... could you help me with replying to some of these emails?" I ask, really wishing I didn't have to ask.

I swear, she's about to sigh, but seems to remember the last conversation we'd had about that, as she pulls herself back. "Fine. Flag the ones you need help with and I'll rearrange my day."

She leaves without looking back, and I slump back into my chair, feeling like I've just gone three rounds in a boxing match.

What is it about this woman that drives me so crazy? Why am I letting her intimidate me when I'm technically her superior?

I decide it's best not to think on that too much and get to work flagging emails and praying she doesn't notice that I'm still struggling.

17
IT'S CLEARLY FATE

TARA

After Aiden dropped the bombshell about Singapore, I've been at war with my emotions. On the one hand, it's exciting to finally feel like my career is going somewhere. On the other hand, I'm pretty sure it was all Aiden's idea. I doubt David sees it as anything more than me attending to help his son seem like he has any idea of what he's doing.

While I've tried to keep myself from resenting Aiden, it's hard when I'm still basically doing the workload of a broker while being paid as an assistant. I've worked out that there is more to Aiden's story than just a case of nepotism, but that doesn't really make me feel any better.

But tonight I'm determined not to think about work. The time has come for my first salsa lesson on my own, and if possible, I'm even more nervous than I was before that lacklustre date on Sunday night. I've changed my outfit so many times, not really sure what to wear and hating my reflection. I'd signed up on a whim, determined to push myself out of my comfort zone (and off my couch), but now that the day has arrived, I'm filled with my usual self doubt.

When Kylie and I had gone to those few classes together, I'd been relatively okay. Clearly a beginner, but I had rhythm and was able to follow along with the basic steps. But that was with my best friend at my side, which made it easier to laugh off any mistakes, and not take myself so seriously. Now though... I'm ready to talk myself out of this.

But I decide to channel my inner Kylie and point at myself in the mirror. "No one is going to be looking at you. This is not serious. You are going to have fun and hopefully meet some new people. You are not allowed to spend the night on the couch."

Toulouse enters the bedroom, his little blue eyes meeting mine in the mirror while I give myself a much needed pep-talk. He meows, his tiny little kitten voice tugging at my maternal heartstrings, and I turn to scoop him up in my arms.

"You think I should stop being such chicken, don't you? There's only room for one fraidy-cat in this apartment, isn't there?"

He snuggles into my neck for a brief moment before wriggling, demanding to be let down. Unfortunately, he has already started to show signs that he's not a fan of cuddles. I find one of his little balls and toss it for him, and he scampers after it, running out of the room again. I smile when I hear him banging around in the lounge room before reappearing at the door with the ball in his mouth.

It appears I have a dog-cat who likes to play fetch.

He drops it and meows at me again, and I give in, throwing it for him on my way out of my bedroom. I've settled on jeans and a V-neck shirt, figuring I might as well go with comfort over style. I just won't look in the mirror at the dance studio if they have one.

. . .

I arrive twenty minutes early at the little hall in Bulimba and consider hiding in my car til the last possible minute, but force myself to go inside. I greet the pretty blonde woman at the door with a nervous smile, and she marks my name off on her iPad.

"Welcome, Tara. Go on in. We'll have the women on the right side of the hall, and the men on the left to start, so find yourself a spot where you'll be able to see the instructors in the middle."

I nod and follow her instructions, moving to the right side of the room and putting my handbag on one of the chairs lining the wall. Not knowing what else to do, I take a seat and look around at the few others that arrived before me. A few women mill around in the corner, chatting, and I wonder if they already knew each other, or are just better at socialising with strangers than I am.

While I'm considering if I should go and introduce myself, a petite woman sits down beside me. Looking like she's in her early fifties with a silver-grey pixie cut, she is dressed casually in leggings and a blue wrap-top, an air of sophistication about her that I wish I could pull off.

"Hi! I'm Sylvia." She smiles and puts her hand out for me to shake.

I take her hand, bemused. I wonder what it would be like to have the confidence to walk up to anyone and just introduce myself so easily.

"I'm Tara. It's nice to meet you. Are you one of the instructors?"

"Lord no! I've never done anything like this but figured it's never too late to give it a try." She grins, and her smile is infectious.

I find myself smiling back, listening as she tells me how she saw people dancing in the city and was handed a flyer about the class.

"I didn't realise there was somewhere for social dancing in the city. That sounds fun," I comment, and she nods with so much enthusiasm I briefly wonder if she's going to hurt her neck.

"Oh yes, it looks like so much fun, too. I saw some couples doing these really complicated moves and would love to be able to do the same one day. It also looked like a great way to meet people. I just moved here from Melbourne and don't really know anyone."

We chat for a little longer until the female instructor comes to stand in the middle of the room and claps her hands.

"Alright everyone. My name is Danika, and that tall piece of goodness over there is my husband, Rafael." The beautiful blonde woman points to a smiling, dark-haired man who is helping the woman at the front door with the line of people who had obviously waited until the last minute to arrive.

Rafael nods and leaves the woman to continue with the stragglers and joins his wife.

"Rafael and I have been dancing together for a number of years now, and have just retired from the professional circuit, but we love dancing so much that we decided to open up our own dance school. We have a passion for helping others find their love of dance, and can't wait to get to know you all over the next twelve weeks," Danika continues, turning slowly on the spot so that she's able to address everyone.

"The style of salsa that we are going to teach you is Cuban style. So it's a little different to what you might have seen if you've ever watched ballroom dancing, with a tap on the fourth and eighth beats. We're going to show you a routine now, and by the end of the twelve weeks, you will all hopefully be able to perform it with ease," Rafael says with a heavy accent, flashing his very white teeth.

The pair of them make an absolutely stunning couple. The kind that look like they could be the leads in a movie or something.

While we all watch, Danika pulls her phone from her pocket and starts the music, which pumps out through the small bluetooth speaker on the edge of the stage. It's a fast paced latin song, and I stare at their feet, mesmerised, while they start moving to the music. They move with ease, like the music is a part of them and dancing is as easy as breathing.

"Wow, that's amazing," Sylvia says, her voice full of awe as she stares at the couple.

"Yeah. No way I'll ever be able to look even half as good," I mutter, and she shakes her head.

"Don't be silly. You're here, aren't you? That's the hard part out of the way - finding the courage to step out of your comfort zone." She sounds far more confident than I think she should be, given she's not yet seen me attempt even the basic steps, but I smile nonetheless.

When the performance is over, the class erupts into applause while Danika and Rafael give a little bow. They begin to organise us into rows. The women position themselves behind Danika while she faces Rafael, and the men do the same behind him. I'm surprised to see that there appears to be a fairly even number on either side, which gives me some relief. The last class I'd attended, the women outnumbered the men by around two to one, which meant we'd often have to dance solo, or sometimes with other women. While it didn't bother me so much, it's nice to know I can focus on just the female's steps this time instead of having to learn the male's as well.

As they are about to start showing us the basic forward and back steps, a few more people enter the room, and my eyes widen when I recognise the last person. I'm starting to get really tired of seeing that handsome face everywhere I go. It's like the universe is playing a huge joke on me and my libido. Why does he have to be so damn good looking?

"You've got to be kidding me," I mutter, under my breath.

Sylvia glances over at me, momentarily distracted from watching Danika's feet. "What's wrong?"

"Nothing. I just recognised one of the guys who walked in," I reply, waiting for Aiden to see me.

He seems nervous while the woman at the front gives them all a quick overview of what's happening, and then points them towards where they should stand.

It's not until he's taken his place at the back that he looks around at the rest of us, and when his gaze finally meets mine, he blinks a few times. Like he's trying to work out if I'm a figment of his imagination.

I give a small wave before shifting my focus back to Danika, trying to ignore the way my heart rate has picked up when he smiles at me.

After about ten minutes, they ask us to pair up, and for a brief, terrifying moment, I freeze. I always hate this part in any activity. The fear that I'm not going to be picked and be left standing alone. Or worse, being the after thought and someone is forced to dance with me for lack of another option.

But Aiden makes a beeline straight for me, extending a hand for me to take. I pause for a moment, wary, but place my hand in his gingerly, and he slides his other hand to rest between my shoulder blades. Something about the way he does it gives me the impression that this isn't the first time he's danced like this.

Danika instructs everyone to form a circle with their partners. Aiden moves us easily into place beside Sylvia and her partner, an older man who seems to be a little enamoured with my new friend, looking down at her with a twinkle in his eye. I swallow a laugh when Sylvia giggles breathily at something he says.

"What are you doing here?" I mutter quietly, peering up at Aiden.

"Dancing," Aiden replies with a small smile.

"Ha ha." I roll my eyes. "I meant, how are you always every-where I am lately?"

"Fate, Tara. It's clearly fate." His hand squeezes mine.

I'm unable to respond, because Danika calls for all eyes to watch them while they start to break down the routine they showed us earlier. When they instruct us to try it, Aiden seamlessly leads me into the first turn, his movements fluid. My body responds immediately, and I turn gracefully on the spot, turning to face him again and blink at him in surprise.

"You can dance," I blurt out, stunned.

"I can," he says with a nod, smile still firmly in place.

He looks pretty happy with himself.

I have so many questions, but Rafael instructs the women to move on to their next partner. Aiden hesitates for a moment before letting me go, and for some reason, I feel disappointed while I step to my left and Sylvia's former partner takes hold of my hand.

The class continues on like this for the next forty minutes before Danika and Rafael end the lesson.

"We're going to play some music for the next half an hour, for anyone who wants to continue dancing," Danika says, before allowing Rafael to sweep her into his arms and spin her around the room.

My current partner definitely isn't anywhere near ready to try anything new, so I move towards my handbag, pausing when I see Aiden dancing with the woman from the front door. She'd joined the group to give extra instruction midway through the class, although watching how she's smiling at Aiden, I suspect she'd realised he wasn't a beginner and was excited to find an attractive man to dance with.

I swallow hard while my eyes follow their movements around the floor. A few other couples are also trying out some of their new moves, but it's obvious to all that Aiden is the most experienced of the class. He leads her easily into moves we haven't learned yet, and I don't want to think about the emotion that is rising up inside of me while I watch him dip her backwards.

There's no way I'm jealous of seeing someone else dancing with Aiden. I have no interest in him. I'm definitely not wishing it was me he was dancing with right now. He can dance with whoever he wants.

Sylvia appears at my side, elbowing me lightly in the ribs. "You seem to be watching him pretty closely," she says, the corners of her mouth lifting slightly.

"Nope." I turn back to my bag, pretending to be interested in my phone.

"Ha, you can't fool me. I saw you two, earlier. There's a spark there."

"Definitely not. All that's between us is a healthy dose of frustration," I reply, sliding my bag over my shoulder.

"Ah yes, frustration of the sexual kind. I understand," she teases, and I gape at her.

"No!" I splutter. "Just normal frustration."

She grins. "Whatever you need to tell yourself, darling."

I roll my eyes. I can tell she's just trying to get a rise out of me, so change the subject. "Did you want to catch up sometime outside of class? I can give you my number?"

Her smile changes to something softer, and she places her hand on my arm. "I would absolutely love that."

We exchange numbers and I leave without saying goodbye to Aiden, ignoring the niggling feeling in the pit of my stomach when he pauses briefly to watch me walk out.

I have got to find a way to get over these confusing feelings I have towards him. There's no way it can go anywhere, not while he's my boss and we work so closely together. That would just be a recipe for disaster.

18

SEE ANY DROP BEARS?

THE FOLLOWING EVENING, I arrive back at the apartment after work where Kylie is waiting for me by the door. Toulouse is hanging over her shoulder like he's known her all along.

"Not much of a guard-cat, are you, little man?" I scratch behind his ear, and he purrs.

"He is so freaking cute. He was playing fetch before. We'll be heading straight to the animal shelter as soon as we get off the plane when we get home," Kylie says, just as Seth comes in from the balcony.

He pauses at the door, raising an eyebrow.

"And who's going to take care of a kitten when we're both travelling for most of the year?" he asks.

Kylie turns to him with a smile. "Adele," she replies, batting her eyelashes.

I cough to cover a laugh. "Does your cousin know she's been nominated as the cat sitter?"

"Well, she basically lives at our place these days, anyway, so she can earn her keep," Kylie replies with a shrug.

From the look on Seth's face, I can tell he's resigned himself to the fact that he's about to become a cat dad.

"Anyway. I'm glad you're home. Go get ready, we're going out." Kylie points towards my room.

"Um... I really don't feel like going out."

"Tara. I am in town for one night, and then I'm gone for another six months. Get your ass in a dress, we're going out. Jake and Bri will be here in like half an hour." Kylie stares me down, and I sigh, giving in.

There really is no point in arguing with her. Just would have been nice to have advance warning that I was required to be social.

"So is it everyone, or just Jake and Bri?"

Please don't say everyone, please don't say everyone.

"It's everyone. Well, not Morgan. She had something on. But everyone else." Kylie at least has the sense to look a little sheepish.

Great, not only do I have to be social, but I have to be social with Will.

Seth gives me a sympathetic look when I walk past him, on the way to my bedroom. No doubt he wasn't given a say about being social either.

Kylie follows a moment later, going to my wardrobe to dig through my dresses.

"So, what are we doing?" I ask, taking the dress she hands me.

"We're going to South Bank for dinner, then we can go wherever the night takes us."

I guess that doesn't sound so bad. Hopefully, the night will bring us back to the apartment where I can get into my PJs and hang out on the couch.

Two hours later, we're sitting at one of the restaurants overlooking the river, the seven of us crowded into a booth with several plates of food in the middle of the table.

Kylie has been filling us in on their month long road trip

through outback Queensland and up into the tropics, and it's hard not to feel a little jealous. Since our holiday two years ago, I haven't really done much more travel, but she's well and truly caught the travel bug. Thankfully, Seth is more than happy to bank roll their adventures. At least she's got her job as a tour guide to keep her happy while he's playing hockey. I don't know if she would ever be able to go back to a regular job ever again.

"So, Seth. See any drop bears while you were out there?" Will asks with a smirk.

"Nope, but then, I guess they could tell I come from somewhere with real bears to worry about," Seth shoots back, a wry smile on his face.

This isn't the first time that someone has given the poor Canadian a hard time about the Australian wildlife, but he just takes it in his stride. He's pretty reserved, but it doesn't seem like much fazes him.

The guys start ribbing each other while Bri turns to me with a curious look. "So, what's this about Singapore?" She'd heard me mentioning it to Chris, who is attending on behalf of his office as well.

I shrug. "Apparently, I'm going to Singapore."

"That's huge, though, right? They don't send just anyone on those sorts of trips." Bri smiles, her eyes wide.

"Yeah, I guess. I don't know... It just doesn't seem like it means much. Aiden just pulled some strings with Daddy. For all I know, David will change his mind and I won't even get to go," I reply, aware of how bitter I sound.

"Well, good for Aiden. He knows you deserve it. I mean, I only met him for a few minutes last weekend, but he seemed really nice. And hot. And he is one hundred percent on the team Tara train." Bri wiggles her eyebrows.

Kylie snorts. "You've been waiting for years to do that to her, admit it."

"Do what?" I ask.

"That eyebrow wiggle. It's payback for all the times you did it to us when you knew we were being stupid about boys."

"I don't do that," I argue, and they both laugh.

I don't like this.

"Seriously though, what is it you don't like about him? He seemed really nice," Bri says.

"He's just... he's annoying! He keeps showing up everywhere I am. He acted all heroic last week when he interrupted my date, like I needed saving," I grumble.

"Which you did," Kylie replies.

I scowl at her before continuing. "And he was at my dance class last night. It's like he just knows everywhere that I'll be when I'm trying something new. I can't escape him."

"He was at your dance class? You didn't mention that." Bri completely ignores my complaining.

"Yep. Showed up late and was all 'look at me, I'm such a good dancer'." I sit back in my seat, crossing my arms.

Kylie grins. "Admit it. You were turned on when you saw he could dance."

"I will admit no such thing, because it's not true."

"Me thinks the lady doth protest too much." Bri's grin is almost evil.

"What happened to you? You used to be so sweet," I say, trying to glare at her, but failing because it's impossible to be mad at Bri.

She's too nice.

"Kylie happened," Bri replies.

Kylie laughs and gives a little bow. "Thank you."

"You both suck," I say, pouting.

They laugh again, before Kylie puts her arm around me and squeezes. "You know we're just teasing. But also... I think you should give him a chance. I mean, he did volunteer to wash your pussy."

My mouth drops open while Bri begins laughing so hard she almost falls out of her seat.

"I'm sorry. What was that?" Will's head snaps around and stares at his sister, his eyebrows shooting up.

Of course, this is the moment that the guys tune in to our conversation.

"Tara's boss helped them wash the cat last weekend," Jake answers, because both Bri and Kylie are still gasping for air, tears running down their faces.

"Trust you to make that sound dirty," Chris says, shaking his head at Kylie.

"There was nothing dirty about it," I interject, feeling my face heat up.

"There wasn't. But that was funny," Bri says, holding a hand to her stomach. "I don't think I've laughed like that in ages. I've missed you, Kylie."

"I haven't," I grumble.

"Don't lie. I'm awesome, and you know it." Kylie pokes me in the ribs and I bat her hand away.

"Nope, I haven't missed you at all." I poke my tongue out. "How do you put up with her, Seth?"

Seth just watches the pair of us from across the table, an amused smile on his face while he shakes his head. "Wouldn't have her any other way."

Kylie melts beside me, a soppy smile spreading across her face while she looks at her boyfriend.

Yeah, those two are pretty perfect together.

After dinner, we decide to walk into the city, the others not quite ready to head home yet.

As we cross the bridge from South Bank to the top of the Queen Street Mall, we hear music playing, and move towards it.

"Oh, this must be the dancing that Sylvia mentioned yesterday," I say, watching the crowd of dancers moving quickly to the latin music being played by a DJ.

"Who's Sylvia?" Kylie asks, her eyes trained on a couple who sweep past, their bodies moving in sync, as though they were born to dance together.

"A lady I met at dance class. She was saying she'd seen people dancing in the city and that's where she found out about the classes. This must be what she was talking about."

"This looks like so much fun! Let's get a table there." Kylie points towards the bar overlooking the makeshift dance floor.

We look at the guys, who shrug and follow behind us while we take over the only empty table left.

"So you're learning to do this?" Will asks, glancing at me before returning his gaze to the crowd.

I know it took a lot for him to start a conversation with me, aware of my feelings these days, so I decide to be charitable and not be a complete bitch by ignoring him. "Yeah. I've only had one lesson, though."

"Not true. We did those classes together a few years ago. You were pretty good, too," Kylie says.

The smile on her face when she looks between me and her brother lets me know she's happy we seem to be getting along. I don't have the heart to tell her that things will never be the same between Will and I.

"Wait, isn't that Aiden?" Bri asks, pointing to a couple in the middle of the crowd.

I sigh. "Of course it is. Because at this point, where can I go that Aiden isn't going to show up?" I look away, not wanting to watch while Aiden pulls his partner in close and then dips her backwards.

I refuse to acknowledge the stab of jealousy that appears when I recognise the woman from the door at our class last night.

"He's really good," Kylie comments, staring at my boss.

"Yep. He knows it, too."

"Seriously, T... If he can move like that... Imagine what he's like in bed," Kylie says.

Seth chokes out a laugh from where he's standing behind her, his arm slung around her waist. Kylie just shrugs, grinning.

"I don't want to imagine what he's like in bed, Kylie. He's my boss."

Chris looks over to where we are all staring. "Is that David's son?"

"Yeah. The one that knows nothing about insurance but got John's job anyway," I reply. Not that I'm bitter, or anything. "Maybe we should just go."

"No! Let's dance, come on." Kylie tugs my hand, trying to get me to follow her.

"You don't know how to dance like this," I protest, not ready to humiliate myself yet.

"So? There's plenty of people out there that clearly do not know what they're doing. Come on, T. Live a little."

I give in, allowing her to drag me behind her, but not before I grab hold of Bri's hand and force her to join us.

Within minutes, the three of us are laughing while trying to keep up with the beat. It's not until the next song that I notice Kylie has been moving us slowly towards where Aiden is dancing, and I glare at her.

"What?" she asks, batting her eyelashes at me.

"You are pure evil, you know that?"

"Moi?" She places a hand to her chest and widens her eyes.

"Oui," I reply, and she smirks.

"I have no idea what you're insinuating. I'm just dancing." She shimmies her shoulders, actually managing to keep time with the music as she does it.

As I'm trying to think of a reply, Aiden glances towards me, doing a double take when he recognises me. I give him a small wave, attempting to appear casual.

"And look at that. He's coming over here." Bri grins at me, while I pretend not to notice when he says something to his partner and turns our way.

"Hey. Wasn't expecting to see you here. Hi, Bri," he says once he's at my side, nodding towards my best friend.

"Hey, Aiden. You were pretty good over there." Bri nods back towards where his former dance partner is still watching him, her eyes narrowing slightly when she looks at me.

"Thank you." He looks at Kylie. "Hi, I'm Aiden." He extends a hand towards her, and she shakes it with a smile.

"Kylie. We actually met briefly, at the bar where you guys met."

Aiden cocks his head slightly. "Oh right, the bridesmaid with the giant boyfriend."

Kylie throws her head back and laughs. "Yep. He's over there." She points towards where the guys are chatting and glancing our way.

Keeping an eye on us without being overbearing.

"Would you like to dance, Tara?" Aiden's voice waivers while he looks at me.

I hesitate for a moment, not sure what to do.

"She'd love to," Kylie answers for me, pushing me towards him.

I stumble and place my hand against Aiden's chest to steady myself, before turning to glare back at her over my shoulder.

"Oh, look at that, Jake and Seth are calling us," she says with a grin, grabbing Bri's hand and pulling her back towards the guys.

None of whom are calling either of them.

Bitch.

"So, dance?" Aiden asks, raising an eyebrow.

I nod, because there's no point in trying to get away now. It would just be rude to say no, now that my best friends have abandoned me.

He takes my right hand and pulls me in closer, placing his other hand on my lower back. Wordlessly, he steps forward, and I mirror him, remembering the basic salsa step we'd learnt yesterday.

I'm surprised at how well I'm keeping up, but I guess when

you're dancing with a partner who knows what they're doing, it's easy to just let them lead you.

"So, that's all your friends?" he asks, looking towards where everyone else is gathered around the table.

"Most of them," I reply, Aiden's eyes meeting mine. "The other three guys are Kylie's brother, Will, Bri's husband, Jake, and our friend, Chris," I point them all out. "Chris used to work for Sanderson's," I add, and Aiden looks back over, his eyes resting on Chris while he laughs at something that Kylie just said.

"Oh yeah. Damien mentioned that a guy who used to work there got you the job."

I stiffen. "He didn't *get* me the job. I interviewed for it after he told me there was a job going," I say, moving to pull away.

His grip on me tightens. "Relax, Tara. I didn't mean it that way."

Although my defensive side wants me to walk away, there's something stopping me. Perhaps sensing my crumbling resolve, he leads me into a spin before dipping me backwards with practiced ease. My left leg lifts slightly of its own accord, almost as though my body automatically knows what to do.

I draw a sharp breath when his face hovers above mine, our lips only centimetres apart. I hold his gaze for a moment, before he moves us upright again. I'm basically a rag doll in this man's arms, and the non-feminist side of me is revelling in it, shutting down my usual defences.

By the end of the song, we're both breathless, and there is way more eye contact than I'm able to process.

"Ready for another dance?" We're interrupted by his former dance partner, who appears out of nowhere, placing a hand on his arm.

She barely looks at me, while Aiden hesitates, glancing at her before looking back at me.

I step back. "He's all yours. I'll see you later, Aiden."

I don't give him a chance to say anything else, turning on my heel and all but fleeing back to my friends.

"That was hot," Kylie says the second I'm in earshot.

"Shut up. We're leaving."

Although I'm met with six surprised looks, no one argues with me while I snatch up my jacket and handbag, marching off.

For the rest of the evening, I refuse to give any more ammunition to the mess of emotions cycling through my head. Because no good can come from admitting to myself that there is more to things with Aiden than I want to acknowledge.

<h1 style="text-align:center">19</h1>

SEXY AS HELL

AIDEN

CHANTEL STEPS in front of me and slides her hand into mine.

Disappointment surges through me as I tear my gaze away from Tara's retreating back, looking down at the blonde woman in front of me. There's no denying the glimmer of annoyance in her expression.

"Wasn't that one of the women from dance class?" she asks, placing her other hand on my shoulder.

"Yeah. We work together," I respond, guiding her into the next dance while keeping space between our bodies.

"Oh, I guess that explains why you were dancing with her then." Something about her tone sends a prickle down my spine, but I shrug, so she continues. "It's so nice to find a guy who knows how to dance. Other than Rafael, but he's always dancing with Danika, obviously."

I'd learned on Thursday evening that Chantel is Danika's younger sister and helping as a backup instructor.

"I don't know. Looking around, I can see plenty of guys who can dance," I remark, and she smiles.

"I meant from class. I expected to be dealing with novices, so it's nice to have someone to dance with at the end that I don't have to lead."

I get the feeling she's going to be expecting my undivided attention whenever there's dancing involved, and I'm not sure how I feel about that. She's attractive, but I'd joined the class to make new friends, and the last thing I want is to be seen as the teacher's pet. And, after that brief dance with Tara, a part of me can't wait to dance with her again. If I'm honest, that three minutes was the most intense dance I've ever had, and my body is still fighting off the attraction it stirred up.

Noticing Tara and her friends have disappeared, I try to push aside the sinking feeling in my gut, attempting instead to focus on dancing with Chantel.

We continue dancing for a few more songs, and when the DJ announces that he's only playing one more song, she pouts. "Damn. Wanna grab a drink after?"

I hesitate briefly before nodding. The last thing I want to do is lead her on, but I figure one drink can't hurt. And it beats going home to my empty apartment.

Once the song finishes, I follow her to the table she and a few of her friends had taken over with their belongings. She introduces me to them, taking a seat, and I let out a small sigh of relief when I realise it's not going to be just the two of us.

"So, Aiden, you're pretty good. What are you doing in a beginner's class?" Sunny, a petite woman with pink streaks in her black hair, turns her intense gaze towards me.

"I was handed a flyer when I came to check this place out after a friend recommended it to me. I figured the class would be a good way to meet people without being some weird guy lurking around," I reply, hoping I sound charming rather than creepy.

"You're new in town?" Chantel asks, cocking her head to the side.

I nod, ignoring the urge to remind her I told her that the other night. She doesn't strike me as someone who is too interested in others unless it serves her own agenda.

"Yeah, moved from London just over a month ago. I'm from Sydney originally, though."

"I thought I detected a British accent. You should definitely make sure you keep that. It's sexy as hell," Sunny says.

I feel my face heat up, and I cough a little to cover my embarrassment. "Uh, thanks?"

"It's nice to have some fresh meat around here."

Fresh meat?

I don't know how to respond to that comment, but it's clear from the way the conversation continues without me I'm not expected to take part any further. The two of them, along with their friend Diana, a leggy blonde, begin talking about people they know. More like gossiping, actually.

I quietly finish my drink before getting to my feet. "I'm going to head off."

Chantel pouts again. "So soon? Okay." She gathers her things. "I'll see you ladies later," she says to her friends, while I stare at her.

Did I miss something? Why is she acting like we came together?

Not knowing how to respond, I allow her to fall into step beside me.

"So, where's home?" she asks, placing a hand on my arm.

"Kangaroo Point," I reply.

"Oh, that's nice and close."

I honestly have no idea what is going through her mind, so I clear my throat. "Yeah. Can I walk you to your car, or something?"

She peers at me for a moment, the hint of annoyance I saw earlier returning.

But it disappears as she shakes her head. "No, that's okay. I stayed in after work, so I'm just going to catch an Uber home."

I decide not to point out that she hasn't requested a car. I'm pretty sure she thought she was coming home with me, but that is definitely not happening.

I say goodbye to her at the taxi rank and let out a relieved sigh once I'm alone again. Perhaps my empty apartment isn't so bad, after all.

Deciding to walk home, my thoughts wander while I head down to Howard Smith Wharves to catch the lift up again, deciding to take the longer way to clear my head.

I'd really hoped that after our walk home last week that Tara and I had reached a new understanding, but it almost seems like she's avoiding me even more now. It probably doesn't help that we keep running into each other, but those were all coincidences. If anything, it shows we have shared interests and could actually be friends.

Although, who am I kidding? If I'm honest with myself, I don't want to just be friends with Tara. The attraction that I'd felt for her from that very first night is still going strong. I'd never held much stock in the whole 'you only want what you can't have' mindset, but what other explanation is there for my feelings?

Clearly, I'm just a sucker for punishment.

20

AT LEAST ONCE, BEFORE I DIE

On Sunday morning, I head back to the hospital. This time, I go to my father's room, not wanting to put him through the exhausting exercise of going back down to the cafe.

Knocking on the open door, I'm surprised to see him sitting in the reclining chair by the window, rather than his bed.

"Hey, Dad," I say, plastering on a fake smile while I take in his appearance.

He looks like he's lost more weight since I was here two weeks ago, but his smile is wide when he looks over.

"Hi, baby girl. I'm glad you came back." His voice is shaky.

I swallow the lump in my throat, determined to put on a brave face.

"I brought you a danish from the bakery you used to like," I say, placing the brown paper bag on the table near his chair.

"Thank you. I still love that place," he replies, leaning forward to pick it up. He brings the open bag to his nose and inhales deeply. "Yum, that smells amazing."

I take a seat in the visitor's chair, holding my bag in my lap.

After an awkward few moments of silence, Dad speaks again. "So, how have you been?"

"Good. I started taking dance classes."

We chat a little about my week, and I tell him about the trip to Singapore. But it's all surface level. After twelve years, this man is a stranger to me. It makes me feel guilty, but I can't just let go of all the hurt he caused our family.

"Have you given any more thought into meeting your sisters?" he asks finally once we've exhausted the small talk.

I hesitate. It's been on my mind, but I haven't been able to bring myself to agree to meet them yet.

"I still need more time," I reply after a moment.

He sighs. "I'd just like to see all my children together, at least once, before I die."

Jesus, talk about a guilt trip.

"Well, while I appreciate that you aren't well, you can't just expect me to get over twelve years of hurt in the space of two weeks," I reply, fighting to keep control of my emotions.

"What about your sister? What does Annelisa say?"

I swallow hard. "Not much."

I don't want to repeat what Annelisa said when we discussed it via text. She's made it clear that she doesn't have any interest in reopening the lines of communication with Dad, and was even less receptive to the idea of meeting Jordan and Piper. Well, she didn't call them by name, instead referring to them as the children of the 'she-devil'.

I can hold a grudge, but Annelisa could win awards with her ability to hold on to stuff. She wasn't like that when we were kids, but once Dad abandoned us, it did something to her, breaking a part of her that she's never been able to mend within herself.

Dad looks sad, but nods, and I let out a breath, relieved he doesn't seem like he's going to push it any further.

That is, until I hear the sound of children's voices in the hallway. His eyes flick towards the door, and I know, without a doubt, that I'm about to come face to face with the sisters that, until two weeks ago, I'd been happy to pretend didn't exist.

"You've got to be kidding me," I mutter, getting to my feet and wrenching the strap of my bag over my shoulder.

"Tara, wait." He looks like he's going to try to stand up, and I wave my hand.

"No. You had no right to spring this on me. I'll... I'm leaving. Enjoy your danish." I turn towards the door just as Jo walks in, halting at the door and staring at me.

Looks like I wasn't the only one who didn't get the memo.

Two young girls follow behind her, each with the same deep red hair as Annelisa and I, and I feel something inside of me stretch tight.

If I don't get out of here now, there's every chance I'm going to fall apart again.

Without saying a word, I brush past them, trying not to notice the look of confusion on the younger girl's face, while her older sister seems to have worked out who I am and stares at me with wide eyes.

I move quickly down the hall, blinking rapidly while trying to keep my composure.

"Tara, wait." I consider running when I hear Jo call after me, but I stop walking, turning slowly to face the woman who my father threw his family away for.

I haven't seen her since I was fourteen. I rarely went to Dad's work, so never had a lot to do with his assistant, who was only in her mid-twenties at the time. She's still pretty, with long brown wavy hair and a youthful glow to her skin. But her eyes give away her exhaustion.

I wrap my arms around myself and eye her warily.

"I'm sorry. I didn't know you'd be here. He shouldn't have done that," Jo says, pushing her hair back behind her ear.

"No, he shouldn't have," I reply, not prepared to give her an inch of sympathy.

She's quiet for a moment. "You could stay? I can take the girls down to the cafe for a bit."

I shake my head. "No, it's fine. The girls should spend time with him. They still need a father." I turn to walk away, but she places a hand on my arm.

"So do you, Tara."

I face her again, anger rising inside me. "No. At fifteen, I needed a father. And he knocked you up and abandoned us. I'm all grown up now, but those girls don't deserve to feel the same way I did, so it's best I keep my distance. Because it's going to be a long time before I can forgive him for that."

I don't give her a chance to respond, unable to handle anymore. This time when I leave, she doesn't stop me.

By the time I get home, all traces of the make up I'd applied are long gone. I'd cried the entire way home, and now I feel so emotionally exhausted, all I want to do is curl up on the couch and cuddle my cat.

So, of course, Aiden steps into the elevator when I am on my way up to the apartment.

He pauses at the door, the smile on his face shifting as he runs his gaze over my face. "Are you okay?"

"Nope," I reply.

He hesitates before stepping inside to allow the doors to close behind him. "I take it you don't want to talk about it?"

I shake my head, feeling the small hold I have on my composure cracking.

He's quiet for a few seconds, hitting the button for his floor. He looks over at me again, flexing his hand at his side.

"Can I... can I give you a hug? You kind of look like you need it."

I don't answer at first, still trying to keep myself together. But when I nod, he steps forward and wraps his arms around me. The tenderness of his touch is all it takes for the dam to burst, and I begin crying again, burying my face in his chest. His arms tighten around me, and he rubs a soothing hand up and down my back while I sob quietly.

I don't even notice when he shuffles me out of the elevator and guides me towards his apartment. When he digs around in his pocket for his key, I go to step back, but he shakes his head.

"Come in. You don't have to talk about it, but at least let me make you a cup of tea."

"How very English of you," I reply, hiccuping slightly while I rub my face.

"Sh, don't tell David," he replies with a smile, and I laugh, despite how shit I'm feeling.

I allow him to lead me inside, taking me to his couch before heading into the kitchen. I look around the space, noting how empty the apartment is. I know he just moved in, but there is nothing to give it a homely feel. Besides the two seater couch, there's a small TV on a stand in the lounge area. There doesn't seem to be a table, just a single stool in front of the bench. The only thing that gives any warmth to the space is a single photo frame that sits on a shelf above the TV.

For the first time since I met him, it strikes me how lonely it must be for him. New city and starting out on your own must be incredibly difficult. Guilt takes over the grief that I've been feeling, thinking of how I've been pretty awful to him at work while he's been trying to find his feet.

"Sorry, I don't keep milk around, so I hope you're okay with black?" he asks, a lopsided smile on his face.

"Black's fine," I reply, getting to my feet.

I move closer to the photo. It's Aiden when he was younger, maybe in his late teens or early twenties. An older woman has her arm around him and they are standing in front of Tower Bridge in London. They are both laughing, and he looks happier than I've ever seen him look now.

"Is this your Mum?" I ask, although it's obvious.

She has his same smiling blue eyes and reddish-brown hair. A dusting of freckles across her nose gives her a youthful appearance, but it's the way she's looking at her son in the picture that makes my throat tighten. It's obvious just how much she loves him.

Aiden appears at my side, handing me a mug.

"Yeah, that's Mum." He picks up the photo and traces his finger over her face.

I feel a tightening in my chest. There's something about the way he's looking at the photo that tells me it's painful for him to talk about her.

"How old were you in that photo?" I ask, taking a sip of the tea before realising it's boiling hot and almost scalding my lips.

"Eighteen. I'd just started university."

"I didn't realise you'd gone to uni?"

He shrugs, putting the photo back on the shelf. "I didn't finish."

I cock my head to the side. "Why didn't you finish? If you don't mind me asking, that is?"

"It's fine. I only lasted one semester. Then Mum had a stroke."

Without thinking, I place a hand on his arm. "Oh Aiden, I'm so sorry. Is she okay now?"

He shakes his head, a sad smile on his face. "No. I became her carer, but she never really got better. Couldn't speak and had very little control over her limbs. She passed away six months ago."

An overwhelming feeling of sadness hits me, and I can feel my eyes welling up again. "I'm so sorry, Aiden."

I blink, trying to stop the tears, but it just makes my eyes sting more.

He hands me a tissue from beside the TV. "It's okay. She is finally no longer in pain. It was a really hard ten years, watching her go from this woman so full of life to a shell of herself, angry because she couldn't control what was happening to her. While I was sad when she passed, there was also a sense of relief that she wasn't suffering anymore."

I shake my head. "It's not just that I'm sorry for. I'm sorry about how I've acted since we've met. You've been going through all this, and I've been a complete bitch."

He laughs a little. "It's okay. You didn't know, and honestly, you've not been that bad."

My answering laugh is hollow, even to my own ears. "I've been horrible, and we both know it."

"How about we just agree to put it all behind us, and start over?" he asks, leaning his shoulder against the wall while watching me take another sip of the tea.

"I can do that."

"Good. Is the tea helping?"

"Is it meant to do something other than taste like tea?" I ask.

"It's meant to fix everything. That is the English way, after all." He grins, and my stomach does a weird little flip.

He really does have a gorgeous smile..

"Ah, right. Well, I guess it made me think about something else, but I think that was more you than the tea."

"I'll take it. Job done."

I place my hand over his and squeeze gently. "Thank you, Aiden."

He looks down at my hand before meeting my gaze. "You're welcome, Tara."

Every time he says my name, it sounds more and more seductive.

I'm just going to ignore the butterflies that seem to have taken flight in my stomach and drink my tea now.

21

THINK I BROKE SOMETHING

TARA

AFTER MY SUPER EMOTIONAL SUNDAY, which ended in a video chat with Annelisa that had me crying yet again, the last thing I felt like doing on Monday was getting up and going to work. I'd had a rather sleepless night. After telling my sister about my visit with our dad, she'd raged for half an hour, which just added to my stress. Seems like lately, all my conversations with Annelisa lead to stress.

But I'd arranged to have lunch today with Sylvia, so I drag myself out of bed and spend the morning dealing with client enquiries and a few claims. Aiden had a meeting all morning with the brokers, so other than when he deposited my hot chocolate on my desk, I haven't seen him. Which is probably a good thing, because I still feel guilty as hell about how I've been acting. I did a fair bit of soul searching yesterday and realised how bitter and crabby I've been lately. Not just with Aiden, but with everyone. Ever since Annelisa left, I've been bottling up so many feelings, and now, with everything with Dad and work stress, I've become someone I don't like too much.

. . .

Once lunch time rolls around, I'm over everything, and grateful to have a reason to leave the office. Meeting Sylvia outside the restaurant she'd suggested, I admire her outfit while she smiles warmly at me.

"You look amazing," I comment, eying the flowing blue dress that she's paired with nude-coloured sandals and matching handbag.

"Why thank you, darling." She kisses my cheek. "Looking good is a requirement of my business, so it's always nice when people notice."

We follow the hostess to the table Sylvia had reserved. This place is fancier than where I usually frequent for lunch, with the cutlery set out on white table clothes, wine glasses and water glasses sparkling in the light filtering through the floor to ceiling windows that overlook the river. Given I usually just end up in the David Jones Building food court if I haven't brought lunch in, this is a far cry from takeaway bags and containers.

"What is it you do for work, if looking good is a requirement?" I ask.

"I'm a personal stylist. People pay me to go through their wardrobes or take them shopping and put together outfits that suit their body shape and personal style."

I raise an eyebrow. "Wow. I didn't realise that was actually a job people had outside of celebrities."

"Oh, it's a huge industry. I've been doing it for twenty years now and absolutely love it. It's been a bit of a change, moving here and trying to build up a new client base, but there's been a lot of interest and business is starting to take off again." She smiles before opening the menu. "So, shall we make it a liquid lunch?"

I laugh. "As much as I like your thinking, I will have to stick with actual food. I've got quite a lot of work to get done this afternoon, and doing it half-cut wouldn't be great."

"Probably be more fun, though," she says with a wink.

I really like her. "Very true."

We put in our orders, and Sylvia regales me with stories of some of her latest clients.

"Maybe I should hire you," I say, intending for it to be a joke.

She cocks her head to the side. "I'd certainly be happy to help you, if that's what you wanted to do." I can't help but feel like she's suddenly inspecting me a lot closer.

Feeling self conscious all of a sudden, I shrug, pushing my hair back behind my ear. "I mean... I could probably use the help."

I've never been particularly into fashion. I've always struggled to find clothes I like in my size, so I've gravitated to baggier clothes that hide my body instead.

Sylvia smiles. "I never judge anyone by their clothes. But I definitely can see you in some of the cute outfits I've seen out lately. Let's book in a time to go shopping. We can do it just for fun, no charge and no pressure."

In my experience, shopping and fun have never gone together, but I'm willing to give it a go. Maybe she knows of shops that I've never ventured into.

We pass the rest of the hour chatting about her move up from Melbourne and how she's adjusting to life in Brisbane. Lunch was delicious, and I return to the office feeling so much lighter.

"Hey, you look happy," Damien says, passing by my desk as I'm sitting down.

"Yeah, I just had lunch with a new friend. Was nice to get out of the office for a change," I reply.

It's only after he wanders off that I think over his comment. Have I truly been so miserable that seeing me smiling is something that people need to comment on?

How sad is that?

"Tara, can I get your help with something?" Celeste appears at my side, fidgeting with her hands before shaking them out.

"What's wrong?" I ask, watching while she bites her lip and looks around before she answers.

"I think I stuffed something up," she whispers.

I smile. "I'm sure whatever it is, it can be fixed."

She shakes her head. "You're probably going to get really mad when you see what it is."

I follow her back to the reception desk. When she points at her computer, I read through the client email open on the screen. It seems she'd taken it upon herself to send a quote to them, but reading through the questions, I get the feeling she didn't get anyone to check it over first.

"It's okay. We can sort this out," I reply, sitting down and opening up the quote.

I hear Celeste let out a breath behind me, and I turn to see her sagging back against the bench that runs along behind the reception area. "Thank god. I thought you were going to get mad at me."

I smile and shake my head before returning to look at her computer. With a few clicks, I've sorted out the quote and responded to the client on behalf of Damien, who really should have been the one dealing with this instead of our receptionist, who doesn't have the right accreditations.

Once I'm back at my desk, I ponder over Celeste's behaviour and realise she was terrified of upsetting me.

Operation New Tara is definitely in force, starting right now.

22

WE WERE ALL
BEGINNERS ONCE

AIDEN

When I walk in the door at dancing, my subconscious narrows in on Tara immediately. She's trying to practice the routine we've been learning with one of the other men, Anthony, who is completely useless. Tara is laughing while Anthony tries to lead her into a spin, but he's stepping forward when he should step backwards, and it takes all my self control not to take over and show her how a proper partner should lead.

I do my best to swallow down the jealousy that is clawing its way up my throat by averting my gaze. While I search the room for a distraction, I find Sylvia watching me, a little smile playing across her lips while she raises an eyebrow and flicks her eyes towards Tara before looking back at me.

Feeling myself blush, I'm relieved when Chantel appears before me. But the relief is short-lived when she slides her hand up my arm and squeezing my bicep.

"Hey, I was wondering when you were going to get here. I want to get a good dance in before I have to take the losers through their paces," she murmurs in my ear.

"That's a bit harsh, don't you think? We were all beginners once," I reply, trying to remain polite when all I really want to do is shake her hand off me.

"True. I guess it's been so long I forget not everyone can just naturally move like us."

I don't know how to respond to that rather over the top assessment of our abilities. While she's a very competent dancer, it's not like she's the best I've ever seen. And I certainly wouldn't have described myself as having natural moves when I first started out. Pretty sure I almost broke Sarah's toes frequently before I finally got the hang of it all.

Against my better judgement, I allow Chantel to lead me out to the centre of the hall before leading her into the first few steps of the routine. It's not an overly complicated routine, so I add in a few steps to make it more interesting for both of us. Gradually, I become more aware of several sets of eyes on us and try not to let myself grow self conscious when I see Tara step away from Anthony to watch while I lead Chantel into the final dip.

"Excellent work!" Danika exclaims once the music ends, clapping her hands together while smiling at Chantel and me.

"Right? His talents are truly wasted in a beginner's class," Chantel replies.

I step out of her reach while Danika levels her with a warning look, and I'm glad I'm not the only one unimpressed with Chantel's attitude towards the people who are literally paying her wage.

Excusing myself from the tense atmosphere between the sisters, I head towards where Tara has now joined Sylvia.

"You make that look so easy," Sylvia says as soon as I'm in front of them.

I run a hand through my hair while I shrug, self conscious. "Believe me, when I first started, I had two left feet and was the cause of multiple foot injuries to my poor best friend."

"Well, that is definitely no longer the case. I can only hope I'll be half as good."

Tara has remained quiet throughout our conversation, watching me with an interested look on her face. I feel like we've come to a bit of a truce since that afternoon in my flat, but I'm still not used to her looking at me like this. Like there's more to me than just the boss's son she's forced to babysit.

Rafael calls out to get ready for warm up, and we move off to our respective sides, the women falling into line behind Danika while the men line up behind Rafael. We've done this enough times now to know the process, but there are still a few people struggling with the basic salsa steps that pull the teachers' focus throughout the first few songs.

Throughout the warm-up, my gaze keeps meeting Tara's. She smiles at me each time, but I wonder if she's finding it weird how often I keep looking her way. I can't seem to stop myself though. If anyone here is a natural, it's Tara. Her hips sway with each step, her movements similar to those displayed by Danika and Chantel. I force myself to concentrate on my own movements, lest I stumble and make a complete fool of myself by being distracted by the sexy woman dancing on the other side of the room.

When the warm-up is over, Anthony makes a beeline straight for Tara, and I'm surprised at the sudden urge to punch something. Jealousy has never been something I've really felt before, and I don't particularly like it. But when he puts his hand low on her back, I can feel a growl rumble low in my chest.

"Don't worry, Aiden. She would rather be dancing with you, as well." I turn to see Sylvia standing at my elbow.

"I don't know what you're talking about," I reply, blushing yet again.

She smirks at me. "I'm sure you don't."

Knowing there's no point in attempting to dig myself out of this little hole I've dug for myself, I put my hand out and pull her around to face me, putting my other hand between her shoulder blades.

I try not to look at Tara while we start to breakdown the routine further, learning the next few moves with relative ease. Once I lead Sylvia into the second spin, Rafael announces it's time for the women to move on to the next partner. Before stepping to her left, Sylvia flicks her gaze back towards Tara before giving me a stern look.

"If you don't make a move on that woman soon, young man, you are going to regret it for the rest of your life." She waggles her fingers in a little wave while I watch her twirl on to the man next to me, stunned.

Am I really that obvious that a virtual stranger has worked out my less than professional feelings towards my assistant? And if Sylvia has noticed... What must Tara be thinking?

Once class is over, I seek Tara out before Chantel can get a hold of me. The blonde woman narrows her eyes as she watches me walk across the room, and I wonder if she's finally getting the hint that I'm not interested in pursuing anything with her.

"Want to practice the routine for a bit?" I ask, feeling the nerves jangling away inside my stomach while I wait for her to reply.

"Sure," she replies, sliding her hand into mine.

I pull her in closer and we wait for the song to start again before beginning to move. She follows my lead with ease, and I have to marvel at how easily she follows my unspoken directions. For someone who is so used to being in charge in her professional life, it's surprising that she doesn't fight me to lead when we're dancing together.

I wonder in what other areas she'd be willing to let me be in charge?

Whoa, that was highly inappropriate. But that doesn't stop my mind from wandering... And hoping one day I'll find out.

23

IF YOU DON'T TRY NEW THINGS, YOU'RE NEVER GOING TO BREAK OUT OF THAT COMFORTABLE SHELL YOU'VE BUILT AROUND YOURSELF

TARA

I'VE NEVER BEEN the biggest fan of shopping, and I've been trying to think up excuses not to join Sylvia for days now. But I know, deep down, that I need to change things up in my life. Starting with my wardrobe.

So when Thursday night rolls around, I put my big girl pants on and get out of my car to meet Sylvia at the entrance.

"Okay. So what kind of budget are we working with?" Sylvia asks, leading the way into the large department store in the middle of the shopping centre.

"Well, I don't want to go too crazy, but... Well, I think I need to do a full wardrobe overhaul." I look down at my work attire before looking back at Sylvia.

She runs her eyes over my outfit, tapping her lip. "So, this is how you always dress for work?"

I shrug, crossing my arms in front of my body in an attempt to hide myself away. "Kinda... Yeah."

"There's nothing wrong with your clothes, Tara. But I get the sense you try to hide behind baggy clothes... Am I right?" Her tone is kind, and although we're talking about my appearance, she makes me feel comfortable.

She has such a warm and caring nature that I'm drawn to her like a moth to a flame. And I'm even willing to let her to treat me like a living doll for the next few hours.

"I never set out to do that... I've just always avoided fitted clothes because I know that I'm not the ideal body size for most of the clothes other women my age wear."

"I'm going to stop you right there." She puts her hands on her hips and gives me a stern look. "You are gorgeous, Tara. There's no ideal body size as far as I'm concerned, but even if there was, you are far from the opposite of that. Somewhere along the way, you've obviously decided that you needed to hide those beautiful curves. But I promise you, we are going to find you some stunning outfits that accentuate those curves and make you feel beautiful again."

I blink a couple of times, feeling a little emotional. Bri has often tried to tell me something similar. And Kylie has threatened to smack me frequently over the years when I've refused to wear the outfits she's tried to talk me into wearing. But hearing it from someone who was a stranger until a few weeks ago makes it feel like it's the first time.

Sylvia reaches over to squeeze my arm. "Come on. Let's ease you into this. I had a look online at a few pieces I thought might work. We can start in the corporate wear section and then move into the fun stuff."

I let out a breath. "Okay. Sounds good. Actually... I'm going to Singapore for work on the weekend... Can we... Can we find a few outfits for me to wear there, too?"

Her eyes light up. "Oh yes! This is going to be so much fun."

While I'm still undecided about the fun part of this excursion, I allow her to drag me towards the escalators and lead me towards the women's section on the second floor.

She starts loading my arms up with clothes in a blur, each one seemingly more brightly coloured than the last. Once there appears to be no more clothes left for her to grab, she turns and marches me towards the dressing room. It seems as though her soft, gentle ways are just for the initial pitch, as she has now turned into an army drill sergeant.

"I want you to try this one first," she says, handing me a gorgeous black dress with a plunging neckline. "We'll ease you into the colours."

I've seen Kylie wear similar dresses and could never in a million years imagine myself wearing anything like it.

I feel my eyes widen as I look at the short dress, beginning to rethink this whole thing. "I don't know, Sylvia... This isn't something I'd normally wear."

"Exactly. You don't have to buy it. But if you don't try new things, you're never going to break out of that comfortable shell you've built around yourself. And that includes trying on outfits you never thought you'd wear before."

Jesus... Talk about a reality check.

She leaves me with the dress, stepping back out of the dressing room and tugging the curtain closed behind her. I hang the dress on the hook and stare at it, letting out a long, noisy breath while I work up the courage to strip out of my 'comfortable shell' and attempt to squeeze myself into the dress. Because there is no way this is going to fit me. And it's too short. And my boobs are going to fall right out of this thing.

Eventually, I pull on my big girl panties and start undoing the buttons on my shirt. Once I'm down to my bra and undies, I stare at my reflection for a moment. At least my underwear has always been on point. That was one area Kylie has won when it comes to my clothes. She's always said that a woman should wear sexy underwear, even if no one else is going to see it. It gives us feminine power, or some such nonsense. And while I don't feel particularly powerful, it feels nice to wear pretty, lacy things.

I reach over and pull the dress off the hanger, giving it a cursory glare before sliding my arms in and wrapping it around my body. Once I tie the bow inside, I thread the sash through the hole on the other side. Refusing to look at my reflection until after I have it all in place, it's not until I've tied the two sashes together that I look up, expecting to see an elephant in a tutu in the mirror.

What I see instead is something I never expected. The dress fits me perfectly, creating an hourglass figure that I've never noticed before. I swallow hard while I run my eyes over my reflection slowly. My cleavage isn't entirely on display, but it's more than I've ever shown before. Instead of feeling self conscious though... Well, I guess I'm feeling some of that feminine power Kylie has been banging on about.

"Tara? Is everything okay in there?" Sylvia's voice drifts through the curtain, startling me out of my little reverie.

A smile slowly spreads across my lips and I spin on my heel, flinging the curtain open to grin at her.

She claps her hands together and bounces on the balls of her feet. "Oh, darling! This is perfect! If you don't buy this dress, it would be a crime. You realise that, right?"

I nod, unable to wipe the stupid grin off my face. "Give me more of those clothes."

"That's my girl." She hands me the next couple of dresses in similar styles. "Try the green one on, next. It will looks so good with that beautiful hair of yours."

I nod, closing the curtain once again and turning back to the mirror. I never thought I'd find clothes shopping so rewarding. But Sylvia seems to be my very own fairy godmother. And I'll happily play Cinderella if all the clothes in her hands make me look this good.

24
WE'LL GET YOU THROUGH IT

AIDEN

OVER THE PAST TWO WEEKS, I've noticed a marked change in how Tara is acting, almost as though that afternoon in my apartment flicked a switch within her. She's been smiling more, and hasn't once sighed when I've had to ask for help on something that I should definitely know how to do by now.

I still don't know what had caused her to cry that day, but I'm relieved that she seems to be doing better.

Or maybe she's just a fantastic actress and I'm completely off base.

She even agreed to let me drive her to the airport today, which is why I'm waiting in the hall outside her apartment with my suitcase beside me. It's been a few minutes since I knocked and she yelled out to give her a sec.

"Hey, sorry to make you wait. I was just getting everything ready for Bri when she arrives to look after Toulouse," Tara says as soon as she opens the door.

She looks a little flushed while she pulls her suitcase behind her, and a lock of her hair has escaped from the messy bun on top of her head. Despite her flustered appearance though, she looks stunning. While I've always found her attractive, there's something different about her today, and I forget to respond while I try to work out what it is.

"Why are you looking at me like that?" she asks, looking down at herself before meeting my gaze again.

"Nn... Nothing, sorry, was just lost in thought for a moment. You look nice," I reply, tripping over my words while I feel my cheeks grow warm.

What is it about this woman that makes me turn into a bumbling mess half the time?

She narrows her eyes for a moment, before turning to pull the door closed behind her and slipping her large handbag over her shoulder.

"Thanks. I let Sylvia take me shopping." She waves her hand down her body, and I follow its path, taking in her fitted jeans and wrap top.

And I realise that's what's different. Her clothes actually fit her, rather than the baggy clothes I've become accustomed to seeing her wear in the office. Although I've seen her outside of work a few times now, her casual dress seems to lean the same way, like she's trying to hide herself away from the world.

"Well, you look great," I say with a nod.

I try not to look at her for too long, wary of making her feel uncomfortable, but it's hard to tear my gaze away. I just want to drink it all in.

Her cheeks turn an even darker shade of pink, and she looks down again, before clearing her throat.

"Thanks. Again." She smiles, motioning towards the lift. "Should we go?"

I nod, moving aside so she can lead the way back down the hall.

We reach my car in the basement car park, and she eyes the white BMW SUV with a raised eyebrow. She hadn't seen the car yet, as it only arrived this week and we hadn't had any client appointments together.

"Fancy," she comments, and I hold my breath, waiting for the next comment.

But it doesn't come. She waits while I open the back of the car, placing her suitcase beside mine before I have a chance to take it from her.

Part of me wants to explain why I ended up with a company car. To defend myself against judgement. But I bite my tongue, determined not to draw more attention to it than necessary.

"So, have you been to Singapore before?" she asks after she slides into the passenger seat.

I turn on the engine and back the car out of my space, trying to appear more confident behind the wheel than I actually am. While I've had my licence for years, there hadn't been much cause for me to drive in London, and I'm a little rusty.

"Yeah, I had a stop over there when I came back, so I stayed a couple of extra days. It's nice. Hot, though."

"We flew through it when we went to Europe two years ago, but we just connected through and I didn't get to see anything." Out of the corner of my eye, I notice her gripping the handle on the car door.

Either my driving is really terrible, or she's a nervous passenger. I'm hoping it's the latter.

We make further small talk for the rest of the drive, but it's not until we're waiting in line to check our luggage that she seems to relax a little, and even start to show a little excitement.

"I see we're seated together. Think you can put up with me for the next ten hours?" I ask, grinning at her while I hold up our tickets and our suitcases disappear behind the counter on the conveyor belt.

She rolls her eyes. "Ugh, I should just leave now." She pokes her tongue out before giggling a little.

It's the lightest I've ever seen her, and I love it.

"Huh, I'll go flag you down a taxi then. Your bag's coming with me, though, sorry." I pretend to walk back towards the entrance, and she grabs my arm, tugging me back.

"Oh, shoosh you. Come on, let's go deal with security. I want to check out the business class lounge. I've never been in one before."

"I've only ever been to the ones in London and Singapore on my trip here," I say when we fall into step side by side, heading for the escalator leading down to security.

"Really? I would have thought you'd done it every time you travelled?" She cocks her head to the side.

"Why's that?" I ask, raising an eyebrow.

"Well... You're rich, right?" she asks, looking uncomfortable.

I laugh, probably harder than I should. "Uh, no. Far from it."

Her eyebrows knit together. "But... you're David's son."

"And until six months ago, I saw very little of him or his money. He kind of just left my mother and me with nothing." It's the closest I've come to telling anyone about my strained relationship with my father.

Tara looks horrified. "What?"

I shrug. "It is what it is. I think he's trying to make up for it all now, in his own round-about way."

She shakes her head. "I guess... You seem to be a little too okay with that, though," she says, coming to a stop at the end of the short line outside security, which is moving surprisingly quickly.

"Believe me, I'm not as okay with it as I seem. But I need a job, and after all the years of taking care of Mum, I have no qualifications. So I would have been stupid to turn down this opportunity. Besides, other than my friend Sarah, there's nothing left for me in London now. After Mum's stroke, a lot of my friendships disappeared, and once she passed... I guess this was just the only choice I had that didn't lead to me working in retail or hospitality and struggling to survive in one of the most expensive cities in the world." It's the first time I've admitted any of this out loud to anyone, as it had felt so pathetic that a man at my age is basically starting out.

Tara considers me for a moment, but we've reached the top of the line, and we have to split up, frantically dumping our laptops out of bags into the plastic tubs. I remove my belt, but the security agent waves me away when I go to remove my shoes, which is a relief. I always find this part of travel stressful - trying to move quickly while taking off the items that take the longest to put back on.

Once we make it through the gauntlet and have gathered our things, Tara is still looking at me with that sympathetic look on her face. It doesn't make me feel great, and I wish I'd kept my mouth shut. But what she says next surprises me.

"I understand how it feels to have a shitty relationship with your father. Mine cheated on my mother when I was fifteen. He got his assistant pregnant and abandoned us to start a family with her. I'm sorry you're in a position now that you have to work for the man who you have a similar relationship with."

I shrug. "Honestly, I've been trying to get past it. It's not easy, especially because quite often, it seems like he doesn't have a soul. A saying I heard once - You can't change the past, but you can choose how you frame it. I'm learning that forgiving him is more about helping me move forward than because he deserves it or because he's changed."

She stops walking for a moment, and I turn to look at her, stopping a few steps ahead.

"Is it that easy, though?" she asks, her expression thoughtful.

"It definitely isn't easy. I still have moments where I want to throttle him. Or throw a teenaged size tantrum. But it was something I needed to do for myself. I don't think he even realises anything has changed, to be honest."

She begins walking again, nodding while looking deep in thought, and we make our way through the crowd of people to get to the business class lounge for the airline we're using. While I speak to the woman at the front, Tara peeks through the door, her eyes wide. Once we get inside, she takes it all in silently, her mouth open in the cutest little 'oh', while her head swivels to look from one thing to another.

"You okay?" I ask, struggling not to show my amusement.

"Just drinking it all in. Don't know if I'll ever get to see inside one of these again," she says, her voice barely louder than a whisper.

"It's not a library, you know. We can have a conversation at a normal volume," I say with a grin.

She lightly smacks my arm. "Oh shoosh."

"If you think this one is special, wait til you see the one in Singapore."

Her eyes widen again. "I hadn't even thought about the return part. Okay, I'm looking forward to this now. If this is just the airport part, I wonder what our hotel is like?"

We find a table, placing our bags down before heading to the buffet to grab breakfast.

"Have you not looked it up?" I ask.

She gives me a sheepish look. "Um... I was too scared to, in case I didn't end up coming."

I raise an eyebrow. "Why did you think you might not end up coming?"

"Well... This all just seemed to be a little too good to be true. I kept waiting for David to say 'actually, scratch that, Tara's not going now'."

I shake my head. "I wouldn't have let that happen. We're a team, remember?"

She's quiet for a moment while she serves herself from the buffet, making sure her fruit doesn't touch her bacon and eggs. When she does look back up at me, her smile nearly knocks me off my feet. There's a warmth to it that I've only ever seen on her face when she's talking to or about her friends, and to have that smile turn on for me makes my heart feel like it's being squeezed.

"Thanks Aiden. I appreciate that. I really am sorry for being such a bitch in the beginning."

I shrug. "You had your reasons, and they were valid. But I'm glad we've been able to move past it all." I clear my throat. "I'd like to think that we're friends now," I add, feeling nervous in case I've overstepped.

She continues to smile. "Yes, Aiden. We're friends."

Well, thank goodness for that.

Over the next hour, I've noticed that Tara seems to grow increasingly anxious, her eyes constantly darting to the screen showing the departure times while she bites her lip. I don't think she's even read a word of the book she's holding. I didn't say anything while I've been trying to get on top of my emails so that we don't fall behind at work, because Tara's inbox is empty.

I wish I had her organisation skills.

By the time we're in line to board, Tara has gone almost mute, her face pale.

"Are you feeling okay?" I ask.

She shakes her head. "No... I kind of forgot how much I'm scared of flying."

"How do you forget that you're afraid of flying?"

"By convincing myself that I wasn't going to actually get on the plane, obviously. So I didn't think about this part. It's been two years since I flew anywhere, when we went to Europe. I had to take a Valium both ways."

I raise an eyebrow. "Did you bring any with you?"

She shakes her head. "No," she squeaks.

I reach down and take her hand, squeezing it gently. "It'll be okay. Maybe you'll be so distracted being in business class that you won't even notice," I say, hoping she believes that.

She glances down at our hands, our fingers laced together,

before looking up at me and letting out a long breath. "Thank you."

I squeeze again. "No worries. We'll get you through it and you'll see there's nothing to be scared of."

She smiles, appearing to be trying to put on a brave face. And my heart does a little skip when she squeezes my hand back.

And doesn't let go.

25
GOOD SURPRISE?

TARA

I can't believe I held Aiden's hand pretty much the entire flight.

I'm kicking myself for forgetting to get a script for Valium last week. I was so convinced that this opportunity was going to be torn out from beneath me that I hadn't thought about my ridiculous fear of flying.

I hate that he's seen such a vulnerable side of me. I've always prided myself on being the cool, calm and collected one. So having him see me jump at every slight noise that the plane made is just embarrassing. Although not as bad as when I'd practically climbed into his lap when we hit some turbulence.

He took it all in his stride, though, trying to distract me with movies and convincing me to have a couple of glasses of wine in the hope that it might help calm my nerves. Which they did, thank goodness. Although I'm feeling slightly tipsy on the cab ride to our hotel.

When we pull up outside, one of the staff opens the door of the cab for me, and I blink up at him for a moment, surprised. I don't think I've ever been anywhere that the staff opens the door for you. Another person has already begun unloading the back of the car, and Aiden is paying the driver, so all I have to do is stand there and wait, which feels very strange.

With our belongings safely loaded on to a trolley, we follow the staff inside. I hang back, staring around the opulent reception area while Aiden gets us checked in. Wandering over to the bar area, I look up and realise that there's no ceiling above it, creating a void. I can see all the way up to the roof of the hotel. The elevators are all glass, looking like something out of a sci-fi movie as they go up and down the wall. The bar area is amazing, with about twenty circular booths at different tiers, with wire cones above them, giving each one their own individual roof in the void. I've been to fancy-ish hotels before, but I've never seen anything like this before. It's the same hotel where the conference is being held, and I shudder to think how much this is all costing. But the insurance industry isn't known for being cheap at events like this.

Aiden appears at my side and hands me my room keycard. "We're on the 36th floor. Our rooms weren't ready yet, and they were so apologetic that they upgraded us both to something called a Panoramic Deluxe Room. I have no idea what that is, but it sounds like it'll be pretty fancy."

"I think fancy is the buzz-word for this entire trip," I reply, waving my hand up and down to draw his attention to the bar area and space-ship elevators.

He grins. "Worth the flight, then?"

"Ah, yeah. I mean, I love the apartment and am incredibly lucky to live there, but this place makes it look like a hovel."

He throws his head back and laughs. "I think that's a stretch. Your place is amazing. But yeah, this is next level. Come on, let's go see what our rooms are like."

He leads the way to the elevators on the right and soon, we're whooshing up towards the stars. Well, the 36th floor, which might as well be the stars.

It turns out our rooms are side-by-side. Aiden holds his keycard to his door, nodding before I step inside mine and let the door close behind me. The view that I'm met with takes my breath away. I barely even notice the room itself when I step around my suitcase that the very efficient bell-hop has already delivered, making a beeline straight for the floor to ceiling window that runs across the entire wall. Night has just started to fall, and the lights of the Singapore Marina and city skyline twinkle before me.

A thrill runs through me, unable to believe that I'm really here. We hadn't discussed plans for the rest of the evening, but looking out at the city before me, all I want to do is go and explore.

A knock at the door pulls me from my reverie, and I reluctantly tear myself away from the view to open the door to the hall, surprised when I find no one there. Another knock sounds, and I turn back into the room, spying a door to my right. I open it to find Aiden standing there with a massive smile on his face.

"Wanna go exploring?" he asks.

"You read my mind," I reply. "Have you seen the view?"

"Oh yeah, that's why I'm excited. There's an amazing street food area near here that I went to last time, and then there's somewhere I think we should check out, but it's a surprise."

I study him for a moment, noting the twinkle in his eye. "Okay. I wanna get out of these clothes and take a quick shower first."

I must imagine the heat behind his gaze, because there is no way Aiden is looking at me like the suggestion of me getting naked has gotten him hot and bothered.

Whatever that look was, it disappears quickly and he nods. "Good idea. Meet you in the hall in half an hour?"

"Perfect."

On my own again, I finally take a look around the room and am taken aback at the sheer size of it. The massive bed, which looks bigger than the king size one I sleep in at home, sits near the window, facing a large TV on the wall opposite. The bathroom has a rain water shower, and a spa bath tub sits against the window that overlooks the bedroom. Good thing I'm not sharing with anyone else, as there would be zero privacy, but it does mean I can look at the view from the bath.

I shower quickly before digging out one of the dresses that Sylvia picked out for me. This one is shorter than I normally would go for, fitted to the waist before flaring out at the hips, and it's much tighter than I ever would have chosen for myself, but after trying on that first dress, I'd become bolder with my choices. I stand in front of the mirror and admire the way the emerald green looks with my deep red hair hanging down my back.

I put on a small amount of BB cream and mascara, aware that it's about a thousand degrees outside and anything more would just melt straight off, anyway. Realising I've forgotten to pack a small handbag, I slide a hair tie on to my wrist in case I get over the feeling of my hair sticking to the back of my neck and slip my small wallet and phone into the surprisingly deep pockets on the dress, before heading out to meet Aiden in the hall.

As I open the door, I discover Aiden already waiting for me, and I feel a sudden loss of breath. I pause, taking in his fitted black T-shirt and dark jeans that cling in all the right places. His wavy hair hangs perfectly tousled around his ears, and he still hasn't shaved. The light stubble gives him a strikingly handsome look that apparently makes my insides go weak, reminding me of the beard he'd been sporting when we'd first met. Startling blue eyes meet mine, and he swallows hard, straightening up from where he is leaning against the wall and scrolling on his phone.

"You look... Yeah... You look amazing," he says, blushing a little.

It's good to know that he's just as affected by my appearance as I am by his.

"Thank you," I reply, a smile playing across my lips. Ignoring the way my heart rate seems to have picked up, I wave my hand towards the elevator. "Shall we go?"

He clears his throat and nods. "Ah, yeah. After you," he says, indicating for me to walk ahead of him.

I take the lead and wonder at our reactions just now... And feel my excitement growing in anticipation of what the night may have in store for us.

The open air market that Aiden takes me to amazes me with all the choices. I let him order for both of us and have the most amazing chili crab, along with a whole coconut to drink.

After we finish eating, he flags us down a cab and asks the driver to take us to Union Square, whisking me off to the surprise portion of the evening.

"What's Union Square?" I ask, unable to handle the suspense any longer.

"I told you, it's a surprise." He grins at me while I scowl.

"If you haven't worked it out, I am not a fan of surprises."

He laughs. "Oh, I've definitely worked that out, Tara. But you'll like this surprise, so just accept that you can't control everything."

I can't help the pout that crosses my face, and that just makes him laugh harder, before reaching over and squeezing my hand.

Sometime in the last fifteen hours, we've reached a point where hand holding feels normal, but I try not to focus on that. We're just friends, and he's my boss. So what if his touch makes me feel all warm and tingly, and the sight of him makes my mouth go dry. That's completely normal, right?

The cab pulls up outside a building that gives no clue as to what the surprise is. But when Aiden leads me inside and I can hear the latin music pumping, the apprehension I was feeling gives way to excitement, and I grip his hand tightly.

"We're going dancing?" I ask, my wide smile almost hurting my face.

"Yep. Good surprise?" he asks while paying for our entry.

"Great surprise."

We head inside and the place is jam packed with people. This is on a whole other level compared to the open air dancing back home, and I don't know where to look as couples whirl past me.

"What do you want to do first? Dance, or grab a drink and watch for a bit?" he asks, placing his hands on my shoulders while he stands behind me and speaks into my ear over the noise.

The sensation of his breath on my neck sends a shiver down my spine, and it takes all my concentration to focus on his words and not on how my body seems to be reacting to his touch.

"Let's grab a drink first. I'm going to need a little liquid courage to dance amongst all these pros." He takes my hand and kisses the back of it. I'm so stunned by the motion that I don't immediately realise he's speaking to me. "Sorry, what?"

"I said, no one is going to be paying attention to us. And you have nothing to be concerned about, anyway. You're a natural at this." He begins to lead me through the crowd. Once we make it to the bar, he waves down a bartender and orders a Singapore Sling before looking at me. "What do you want?"

You.

Where the hell did that thought come from?

"Um, what's in a Singapore Sling?" I ask, shaking off the sudden desire that I don't know how to process.

"It's gin based. Do you like gin?"

I shake my head. "I'll just get a French Martini, please."

The bartender nods and heads off to make both our cocktails.

"No Pina Colada's this time?" Aiden asks, leaning in close again so I can hear him.

All it does is ramp up the desire, the smell of his aftershave filling my senses.

What the hell do they put in the water in this country? Why am I suddenly so turned on by everything he does?

I shake my head, forcing myself to focus. "Uh, no. Not sure I'll be able stomach one of those ever again."

He grins, opening his mouth to reply, but pausing when the guy next to me accidentally bumps me into my side. Aiden raises an eyebrow and fixes our clumsy neighbour with a stern look before turning and pulling me close, pressing his chest against my back. He shuffles us around so that we are facing the dance floor, but he keeps me in place, his arms circling my waist.

Holy hell. The charismatic Aiden that I met that first night is definitely back with a vengeance and my body is completely on board with it. My head, however, is a swirl of confusion.

I'm not used to male attention like this and am so far out of my depth.

Should I do something to show him I'm interested? No, he's my boss!

While my body and my head have a stand off with each other, our drinks arrive. Aiden hands me mine before grabbing his and taking my hand again. We find an empty table and take a seat, both watching the dance floor. The absence of his touch gives me a chance to try to get my emotions under control. Because once we're dancing, it's going to take all of my self control not to do something stupid.

Like kiss him. Cause he's looking pretty damn kissable now.

"What's that look for?" he asks, his voice raised while leaning back in his chair and nursing his drink.

"Oh, nothing. Was just thinking." And of course, now I'm blushing.

I take a mouthful of my cocktail and turn to face the dance floor. I'm supposed to be watching the dancing couples, after all.

We watch in companionable silence, the music too loud to be able to have a meaningful conversation anyway. The chemistry between the couples is electric, and some of them look like they are seconds from tearing each other's clothes off. Trying to push aside the fact that I'm turned on by all the sexual tension in the air, I finish my cocktail far too quickly, and I look over to see Aiden draining the last of his.

"Alright, enough watching. Let's dance." He gets to his feet and takes my hand again.

Leading me out into the crowd of dancers, he finds a spot that's relatively free and turns to face me, pulling me in close.

"In a crowd this size, we're going to have to dance a bit closer," he says, his lips at my ear.

Grateful he can't see my face while I do my best not to turn into a puddle right here, I nod. He waits a few seconds, his body swaying from side to side, and I know he's getting a sense of the beat, before leading me into the steps.

I don't know how he does it, but I stop paying attention to my feet, and he guides us effortlessly into a fast-paced salsa, spinning me out and pulling me back in with ease. It's addictive, this feeling of dancing with someone who not only knows what they're doing but is able to take the lead and basically take control of my body. When my hair swings around and hits him about a thousand times, he pauses, pulling the hair tie from my wrist. Turning me so that I have my back to him, he pulls my hair back gently into a messy bun, and the feel of his fingers gently touching my scalp gives me goosebumps. It's such a tender action, so at odds with where we are.

Hair secured, he pulls me back into his arms and I lose count of how many songs we dance for.

The night eventually grows late, and I reluctantly point out that we have to get up early for the first day of the conference tomorrow.

He nods. "Last dance then?"

I smile, and the song changes to a slower paced one.

"Oh, this is Bachata. It's a bit different to salsa. It's still four steps though. Want to give it a try?"

I glance at the couples around us, noticing that the moves of this style of dance appear to have entered a whole new level of sexy. Swallowing hard, I nod slowly.

He pulls me in, wedging his thigh between both of mine. I

gasp when our bodies press flush against each other, our noses almost touching.

"Is this okay?" he asks.

Unable to find my voice, I simply nod, and he begins swaying us from side to side in time with the beat. The electricity between us reaches an entirely different level when he begins to lead me through spins and dips.

Without thinking, when he spins me in towards him, I rest my hand on his cheek, our gazes locking. His eyes flare and something almost primal seems to come over him. Spinning me so that my back is flush against his chest, he runs his nose down my neck while continuing to guide my body through the steps, pushing my hips away before pulling them back quickly in a wave like motion. Our bodies roll together and I'm pretty sure my heart is about to beat out of my chest.

As the song nears the crescendo, he spins me back around, hiking my thigh up to his hip and leaning back, my body following his so that I'm pressed entirely against him with only one foot on the ground.

Holy shit. Am I on fire? I feel like I'm on fire.

As the song ends, we stop moving, our bodies so close we may as well be one body at this point. Both of us are breathing hard, our lips only millimetres apart. All it would take is for one of us to move a fraction and we'd be kissing.

His gaze drops to my lips, and I can feel the war within his body, tension rolling through the muscles in his back beneath my hands.

With what looks like incredible restraint, he steps back a little and forces a smile.

"Come on, we should head back to the hotel."

He steps completely out of my arms, not taking my hand for the first time all evening, and it's like I've been left out in the cold. The loss of his touch leaves me feeling empty and wondering what the hell just happened.

Knowing he did the right thing by stopping, I follow him silently, and he keeps a healthy distance between our bodies while we wait for a cab. I pull out my phone for something to do, hoping to distract myself from what almost just happened.

The ride home is just as quiet. When we reach our floor at the hotel, he looks at me properly for the first time since we left the club when we come to a stop outside my door.

"Goodnight, Tara." There's something off about his expression, and I have to stop myself from reaching out to touch him.

There's no denying the desire on both our sides, but it has to just be the confusion from all the close dancing for the last few hours.

I tap my keycard to the door and push down the handle, still holding his gaze. "Goodnight, Aiden."

Once the door closes behind me, I lean back against it, placing a hand over my chest and feeling my heart racing beneath it.

And it's a long time before I hear the door next to mine open and close.

26

DAMN NEAR BROKE HIM

AIDEN

AFTER THE WORST sleep of my life, I've woken up this morning feeling like crap. It had been hours before I was able to get myself together enough to even attempt to sleep after all the sexual tension between Tara and I last night. And it had taken all my self control not to knock on the door between our rooms and kiss her like I've been dreaming about for weeks.

When I'd found the dance club online, sex had been the last thing on my mind, but now it's consuming my thoughts. Which is both frustrating and highly unprofessional.

After a cold shower that does little to help me, I get dressed for a day of sitting through what I imagine is going to be tedious sessions about the insurance world.

A knock at the door pulls me from my grumpy thoughts, and I open it to find Tara standing in the hallway, dressed in another new outfit that accentuates her curves. I really need to find a way to thank Sylvia for helping her find her new style, because she looks stunning once again.

"Ready for breakfast?" she asks, pulling the strap of her big hand bag up over her shoulder after it slides down.

"Yeah, one sec."

She holds the door open while I race around and grab my laptop and wallet, throwing them into my messenger bag before joining her in the hall.

I'm pleased to see that the weird tension between us last night seems to have dissipated, and she tells me about how great her sleep was before getting up early and having a cup of tea while staring out at the view. I'm glad at least one of us had a decent sleep. Although it bugs me a little that it seems like I'm the only one affected by the events of last night.

I felt her melt into my arms when I ran my nose along her neck while dancing. I saw how her breathing stopped when my gaze dropped to her lips when we finished that last dance. And the memory of her leaning in close and touching my face is burned into my mind.

So no, it wasn't solely one sided. But something is holding her back, and I don't know how to get past whatever it is.

Because I want her, and I've been pushing that thought aside for months now, to no avail.

I honestly don't think I've ever felt an attraction this strong for anyone before. Other than Sarah, I've only been with a handful of women over the years. And with Sarah, that was just scratching an itch for both of us while we dealt with the shitty hands we were dealt at the time. But I want more with Tara than just scratching an itch. And judging by the way we moved together last night, I wouldn't be surprised if the sex was the best I'd ever had.

And now I'm thinking about sex again. Get your shit together, Aiden.

"Are you okay? You've barely said a word." Tara's words pull me out of my head, and I find her watching me with a concerned look.

"Yeah. Sorry. I didn't sleep great. New bed and all." I stifle a yawn, and she nods.

"I'm normally like that. But the bed in my room was so comfy. I'm sorry yours wasn't as good."

I resist the urge to say that the bed was amazing, it was my libido doing the fucking tango that was the problem. Probably not the most professional way to start the day.

We enter the restaurant we were instructed to go to for all our breakfasts. Other conference attendees are already here, getting food from the buffet that is laden with every food known to man, and gathering around tables in groups.

"Aiden?" I turn to find my uncle standing next to me, a broad smile on his face.

"Hi Barry, how are you?" I shake his hand. "Have you met Tara? We work together." I wave towards Tara, who smiles back.

"We've met a few times when you came to the Brisbane office. It's good to see you again. I didn't realise anyone from Sydney was coming." She shakes Barry's hand.

"Would you like to join our table? Travis and I are just over there, along with Mitch and Paula from the Melbourne office." He points to where my other uncle, Travis, sits with a man and a woman who look to be closer to my age.

"Actually, I've just seen a friend. I'll see you at the first info session, okay Aiden?" Tara gives me a little wave before making a beeline to a guy around our age who gives her a hug.

I recognise him as her friend, Chris, that she'd pointed out when we danced together in Brisbane a few weeks ago. The one who used to work at our office. The one that she seems to be very close to, because he kisses her cheek.

"Come on, let's get you some food. It'll be good to catch up, it's been far too long since we've seen you." Barry motions for me to follow, and I reluctantly tear my eyes away from Tara and her 'friend'.

Perhaps that's why she's held me at arms length for so long -

because she's got feelings for her friend? Wouldn't be hard to believe. Why else would someone like Tara still be single?

I attempt to make small talk with my uncles and our colleagues through breakfast, but my gaze keeps drifting over to where Tara is sitting with Chris. It's just the two of them and she keeps laughing at whatever he's saying.

I've never been a particularly jealous person before, and I don't like this feeling at all.

Forcing myself to look away, I rejoin the conversation when Travis mentions how sorry he was to hear about Mum.

"I always had a soft spot for Anita. I'm sorry I wasn't able to make it over for the funeral."

I nod. "She always spoke highly of both of you," I say, looking between my father's brothers.

I haven't seen either of them since I was a kid, and aside from a yearly birthday and Christmas card, I've not had a lot to do with them.

"David tried to make it over to the funeral, but apparently the twins had croup and Lisa needed all hands on deck. It was so sad how things ended between your parents. He was gutted when she took you to London."

This is news to me. Mum had always lead me to believe that Dad hadn't put up a fight when she got eighty percent custody and decided to take me back to England.

"I didn't realise it had been such a big deal for him," I say, and Travis gapes at me for a moment.

"Are you kidding? His only child was suddenly taken half a world away and he had no way to follow. It damn near broke him. He couldn't live in the UK. Every time his gifts were sent back, it was like a piece of him shattered. It's why he eventually moved to Brisbane. Everywhere in Sydney was a reminder of the life he no longer had."

I look from one uncle to the other. Paula and Mitch glance at each other before making a lame excuse about needing to do some work before the first session and make a hasty exit.

"I honestly had no idea... Mum said he barely tried to keep in touch. I think I spoke to him maybe three times a year. And I don't remember any gifts." I shake my head, unable to reconcile their version of my father with the one I knew.

They exchange a look, and Barry's face softens. "There was a lot of anger between them in the end, Aiden. I'm sure your mother had her reasons for saying that. But David struggled for years. He made a lot of mistakes when it came to you and Anita. It's why he's more hands on with the twins. He doesn't want to miss out on a second of their lives."

I have no idea how to respond to that, but Travis looks at his watch and taps the table. "We should get a move on. The first session starts in twenty minutes."

I follow after them absently and find my name on the seating chart, trying to wrap my head around everything they just said.

Tara slides into the seat next to me a few moments later, pulling her laptop from her massive handbag.

"There's a few emails we need to respond to at the first break," she says quietly, and I nod, not really listening. She cocks her head to the side. "Are you sure you're okay? You seem really out of it this morning. You're not getting sick, are you?"

Her concern is nice, but it has me wondering again what is going on with her and Chris.

"I'm okay. Just don't do well without a decent sleep." My head is a swirling mess, between my weird feelings towards Tara and the bombshell my uncles just dropped, I'm not sure if I'm going to be able to take in a word that the speaker says.

Once everyone has taken their seats, the event coordinator introduces herself and explains how the rest of the day is going to go, before introducing the first speaker. Apparently he's some international insurance specialist, and he starts his speech off by giving a brief history lesson about the first insurance claim. It's actually more interesting than I was expecting. But once he starts to get into the more present information about changing policies and rattling off statistics, my brain shuts down.

Tara is madly taking notes beside me, her fingers flying over the keys of her laptop while she watches him with rapt attention. I envy her dedication. It's clear that she has a true passion for this industry, while for me, every moment is as boring as watching paint dry.

I wonder idly what it's like to find a job you're passionate about. I try to remember if there's anything I've enjoyed that I could see myself creating a career out of. Other than teaching, which was my dream as a kid, I can't think of anything. I feel like I'm too old now to go back to my degree, but the idea of staying in insurance feels like I'm looking down the barrel of a gun loaded with forty years of hell.

Surely there's got to be more to life than this?

27

TELL ME TO LEAVE

TARA

AFTER THE DAYS SESSIONS, I meet Chris in the bar for a drink before dinner.

"So, how did you like your first day of the conference?" he asks, pouring his beer into the rather expensive looking glass the waiter had left him.

We're settled into one of the booths, and I find it difficult to concentrate on our conversation while my eyes are drawn to the void above us, looking at the elevators and twinkling lights.

Pulling my attention back to my friend, I smile. "It was good. I found it more interesting than I thought I would."

"Yeah, they get some pretty good speakers at the international conferences. Not that we don't have decent experts back home or anything," he's quick to add, looking around to make sure no one overheard him.

In this industry, it pays not to get anyone offside, when you have no idea if you're going to need their help at a later date.

"This is your second one, isn't it?"

He moved up in the industry when he left our office, and has been making a bit of a name for himself, which is amazing to see.

"Yeah. Morgan was able to come along on the last one, when we went to Hong Kong, but she had some stuff she had to do this time, so it's just me."

Knowing how hard it is for them to spend nights apart, I assume it's something really important if she wasn't able to join.

"Yeah, now that you mention it, I haven't seen much of Morgan in a while, other than the wedding. Is work really busy at the moment?"

Chris shrugs. "Yeah, a little," he says, and I eye him closely, wondering why he's being so evasive.

Hoping nothing serious is going on with my friends, I allow the subject change when he asks me what I got up to last night.

"Aiden and I checked out the food market nearby, and then he took me to a dance club he found."

Chris whistles. "Wow, that sounds like fun. Better than my solo dinner and early night to bed."

"Yeah, it was, actually," I reply, smiling as I remember how fun it had been... until it got weird.

"So you're friends with him now?"

I shrug. "Yeah. I realised it was mostly me just being grumpy that was the problem. Things with Lis and then Dad have been getting to me more than I realised and I'd turned into a right old bitch."

Chris tilts his head to the side while he studies me. "How is Annelisa?"

"Well, she says she's fine, but she's rarely honest with me these days, so I don't know if I believe that."

He's quiet for a moment. "Did she mention Morgan reached out to her?"

I stare at him, stunned. "No. How did Morgan manage that?"

"Her author's social media profile. Guess her publisher forced her to have more of an online presence. They've chatted a bit.

Nothing too in depth, but Morgan was so happy when she heard from her."

I nod, remembering how hurt Morgan had been when Annelisa, her best friend since kindergarten, had just disappeared without a word. Of everyone, Morgan had the most reason to be hurt, after Will, of course, but she'd just been worried and hadn't shown any anger. Chris, however, has been pissed enough for the both of them, angry at Annelisa for abandoning not only his wife but his best friend. I'm actually surprised that Annelisa had replied to her, as she'd been so determined to only keep contact with Mum and me.

"Well, I'm glad she responded. I've been worried about her, over there by herself and refusing to communicate about whatever her problem was," I say, and Chris nods.

"Yeah... Will has said a few things over the years, but I guess... It's stuff she needs to sort through herself."

This is the first I've heard that Will has told anyone about what might have caused Annelisa to run off. I fight the urge to ask Chris about it, not wanting to get any further wrapped up in the drama around my sister and her ex. But in my role as little sister, it's fighting against years of needing to know everything there is to know about the woman I used to idolise.

"How is Will doing?" I ask instead, surprising myself.

Chris raises an eyebrow. "I thought talk of Will was off limits?"

I shrug. "I'm not a complete bitch. I might be mad at him about how he handled stuff with me, but I don't hate him. He didn't deserve what Lis put him through."

Chris' expression darkens. "No, he definitely didn't. It sucks watching him try to move on but being unable to put her behind him."

I know Will has become a regular guest at their house, and I'm relieved that he at least has people who love him to help him through it all. Even if it couldn't be me.

This conversation has taken a much darker turn than I

thought it would, and it seems to dawn on Chris at the same time as it occurs to me. He clears his throat and checks his watch.

"Anyway, I should probably call Morgan before I get ready for dinner. I'll see you in a bit?"

I nod, finishing my glass of wine. "Yep. Say hi to Morgan for me."

He nods and heads off towards the elevators. I wait a few minutes before doing the same, wanting to have a little time to myself while I process the conversation we'd just had.

I'm quieter at dinner than I intend. Aiden has given up on trying to draw me into the conversation he's having with his uncles when I'm unable to muster up more than a few words in response to his questions.

Once the meal has been cleared away, the band that had been setting up while we were eating starts playing, drawing a small crowd onto the dance floor.

"Dance with me?" Aiden asks, standing and reaching out a hand.

I take it, allowing him to lead me out onto the dance floor. The music has changed to a slower song, and he slides his hand to the small of my back, pulling me a little closer.

"You okay?" he asks, and I suspect that this is the real reason we're dancing, getting me away from the rest of our colleagues.

"Yeah. Just had a weird conversation with Chris earlier and it's messed with my head a bit."

His expression hardens a little at the mention of Chris, which I think is strange but don't comment on. He doesn't reply, simply nodding before leading me into a slow spin.

I swear, this guy can dance to anything.

. . .

After an hour, I've had enough of socialising, and excuse myself to head up to bed.

"I'll head up too. I need an early night after my crap sleep last night," Aiden says, nodding towards his uncles and the two people from the Melbourne office.

They seem like they are settling in for a late night, glasses already cluttering their side of the table. They wave goodbye, and Aiden follows me towards the elevators. He's been a bit weird with me ever since our first dance, and if I hadn't been so preoccupied with my thoughts, I'd be wondering if I'd done something wrong.

He walks quietly beside me as we head down the long hall towards our rooms. When I pull out my room key, he moves closer, and I look up to find him watching me with an expression I can't quite read.

"What's going on with you and Chris?" he asks.

I raise an eyebrow. "Um... what?"

"Are you into him? Is that why things were weird between us last night?"

I gape at him, trying to wrap my head around his words. "Um... No. He's just a really good friend. A very married friend," I add.

Aiden has the sense to look a little ashamed. "Oh."

"Yeah. So nothing is going on there. But what would it matter if something was going on?"

He groans, letting his head drop back and staring up at the ceiling. "All day, I've been trying to work out what happened between us last night."

I lean my shoulder against my door. "What do you think happened between us last night?"

He brings his gaze back to mine. "I'm pretty sure we were seconds from kissing."

My heart rate picks up while we continue to scan each other's faces. He takes a step closer to me, and my breath hitches when he pushes my hair back behind my ear.

"Aiden?" I ask, my voice barely louder than a whisper while he gazes at my lips.

"Tell me to leave," he whispers back.

I shake my head, unable to speak.

"Tell me it's all in my head."

Another head shake.

His lips hover over mine. "Tell me not to kiss you."

"Kiss me," I whisper.

He surges forward, claiming my lips with his own while holding my face, cupping my right cheek while guiding me back against the door. My arms move of their own accord, hands sliding up his back and pulling him close while I rise onto my toes to get closer.

It's a kiss unlike any I've had before, full of pent up frustration and weeks of dancing around each other. I can feel his hunger when his tongue swipes across my lower lip, seeking access, and I part my lips, stroking his tongue with mine.

A soft moan echoes down the hall, and I realise it's come from me, my body singing out for more.

"We should stop," he whispers against my lips, before moving to kiss my neck, and I melt further into his arms.

"Or... you could come in?"

He pulls back, looking me in the eye. "Are you sure that's what you want?"

In all my life, I've never considered sleeping with someone that I've not been on even a single date with, but my hormones are screaming at me. Years of involuntary celibacy ready to be broken.

So I don't hesitate for even a second when I bring my lips to his ear and whisper. "I want you."

I feel a shudder run through him, right before he grips my chin and devours me.

28
FOUR YEARS

TARA

No one has ever kissed me with this much intensity in my life.

Aiden presses me back against the door, sliding his hand down my arm to take the keycard from my hand while he continues to kiss me, his other hand cupping the back of my head, as though he's afraid I'll disappear if he lets go.

The automatic lock on the door beeps, and we stumble into the room. Once the door closes behind us, I let my handbag drop to the floor, and allow him to guide me further into the room. Bypassing the bed, he pulls me down to straddle him on the small couch, my dress riding up my thighs while I press against his semi.

The feel of him against my clit makes me gasp. He tangles his fingers in the hair at the back of my neck while he pulls my face to his and kisses me so hard my lips feel bruised. He uses his other hand to grip my hip, and rocks me back and forth. I grind down until we're both moaning.

"God, Tara, you feel so good," he whispers against my neck before nipping gently.

In the few months I was with my ex, we'd never once had an encounter like this. Like we would die if we stopped touching each other. No one has ever made me feel so desired, so needed, and it's a rush.

"I want to watch you come," he says, leaning against the back of the couch and gripping both my hips to urge me to move faster.

So caught up in the moment between us, I forget to be embarrassed by the thought of him watching me come. Placing my hands on his shoulders, I continue to grind down with a moan.

We lock eyes as my breath quickens. My eyelashes flutter while pleasure rises within me, unfurling itself in a way I'd long forgotten I could feel from another person's touch.

"Eyes on me, princess. I want you to remember who's making you feel so good." His words are like a trigger, and I cry out when the orgasm rips through me.

He doesn't allow me to catch my breath though, surging forward to claim my lips again, even while I'm still moaning and shuddering against him.

"That was beautiful," he says, lifting me with ease so that I'm on my feet once again while I'm still trying to regain my composure.

Turning me on the spot, he unzips my dress, sliding it down my arms and letting it fall to the floor. And I've never been more grateful to Kylie in my life than I am right now, standing before this gorgeous man in the sexy underwear that, until now, no one else but me has ever seen.

I keep waiting for the nerves to hit me, but there's something about the way that Aiden has taken control of the situation that makes me feel warm and safe. Stepping up behind me, he presses himself against my back, sliding my hair over my right shoulder while he kisses down my neck as I lean back against him.

"I've been thinking about how much I wanted to touch you like this for weeks," he whispers in my ear while his arms circle my waist. Another shudder runs through me when he traces a circle around my belly button. "I've imagined all the ways I can make you moan. Every pissed off sigh you've sent my way had my thoughts running wild about how I could make you scream instead." His hand moves lower down my abdomen, and I watch while he runs he runs a finger along the top of my underwear. "You're so fucking sexy it hurts. Will you let me touch you, Tara?"

His voice is cautious, like he's worried that I'll suddenly recoil from him.

I nod, my breath hitching a little.

"I need to hear you say the words out loud. I don't want there to be any regrets after tonight." He traces his nose slowly down my neck, before pressing a feather-light kiss to my shoulder.

I pull in a deep breath, the need for him to continue what he started overwhelming everything else. "Aiden. Please," I plead. "Please keep touching me."

I can feel a slight tremor run through him when his hand slides under the lace of my underwear, his finger moving to circle my clit. I jolt against him, and he chuckles a little while his lips press against the spot where my neck and shoulder meet. Applying a little more pressure, he continues to work my clit. But seconds later, I give a little cry of frustration when he takes his hand away. Grinning, he kisses my neck while he uses both hands to undo my bra, sliding both straps down my arms and letting it fall to the floor.

"As sexy as you look in this, I think you look even better in nothing at all," he whispers in my ear before moving his hands to my hips and sliding my underwear down my legs.

With a shuddering breath, I step out of them, and he returns to standing behind me.

Even though I'm now completely naked whilst he hasn't taken off a single item of clothing, I barely notice while he urges my legs further apart with his knee. Returning his hand to its former position, he uses the heel of his palm to apply pressure to my clit once more, while he slides a finger inside me. My head falls back against his chest while he gently thrusts his finger in and out, his other hand moving up to cover my right breast where his fingers tweak my nipple. All the while, he runs kisses up and down my neck, whispering praises with each of my moans.

My breath is coming out in short pants, my eyes half closed.

"Are you going to come for me again, Tara?" he whispers in my ear.

I nod, biting my lip. My legs tremble when he presses up against my back and applies even more pressure against my clit. Using a second finger, he thrusts harder and my legs move even further apart while he rocks my hips with his pelvis.

"I want to hear you cry my name this time when you make that beautiful sound. Because you need to remember that it's me bringing you close to the edge with my fingers. That it's me grinding your clit. That it's me who'll be deep inside you soon."

With each word from his lips, the orgasm that has been building reaches an almost painful level of pleasure. As it reaches its peak, I follow his command and his name slips from my mouth while I cry out. He keeps moving his hand, causing the orgasm to keep going, holding me tight against him with his arm wrapped around my waist. I moan, unable to keep my eyes open any longer as the ecstasy running through me overwhelms every one of my senses. My ears are ringing from the intensity of the orgasm, and it's only once he steps back to remove his clothes that I'm able to catch my breath.

I turn to face him, kissing my way up his neck before finding his lips again. He kisses me back slowly, before stepping back to reach behind his head to pull his shirt off in one quick movement. I've seen guys do that in movies and wondered how they did it without getting all caught up in the material, but Aiden makes it look effortless. My mouth goes dry as my eyes travel over his chest, sliding further south as he undoes his jeans. He smirks a little when I force myself to return my gaze to his, suddenly feeling very inexperienced. I've only ever seen one other man naked, and he was nowhere near as attractive as Aiden.

I swallow hard when my gaze dips lower again and take in his fully naked body before me.

My ex was also nowhere near as well endowed.

My movements tentative, I step closer and slide my hand between us, wrapping it around his shaft as his erection presses against my abdomen and squeezing gently. His breath hitches when I begin to move my hand back and forth, and he clasps my face with both hands while he kisses me with so much tenderness it almost brings a tear to my eye.

"I need you," he murmurs against my lips, and I nod.

Stepping back, he grabs his wallet from the pocket of his discarded jeans and pulls out a condom.

I raise an eyebrow. "I see you were expecting to get lucky on this trip," I tease.

He gives me a sheepish smile. "It's always best to be prepared. This has been in my wallet for a while... It's been a long time since I've been with anyone," he admits, dipping his head.

I place my hand on his chest. "For me, too."

"Probably not as long as me." His confidence seems to be slipping a little, the longer he's not touching me.

"Four years for me, Aiden," I say softly.

His eyes widen. "I don't understand..."

I take a deep breath, expecting him to cut and run at any moment. "Not since my very brief - and only - relationship when I was twenty-three."

He reaches up and places his hand over mine, running his thumb over the back of my hand. "Well, while it should be a criminal offence that no one has been able to make you feel good since then, I'm honoured that you chose me."

A part of me wants to point out that it's not like there has been a long list of men lining up to sleep with me, but that feels too negative for this tender moment between us. Instead, I smile and press a kiss to his lips.

"And I'm honoured you chose me, too."

He begins walking me back towards the bed, returning my kiss with renewed energy. The back of my knees hit the mattress and he pushes me to sit down, grabbing my legs to turn me so I'm lying in the centre of the bed.

"You're the most beautiful woman I've ever seen," he says while he rolls the condom on, and in that moment, I'm pretty sure my heart has just stopped beating on it's own and is completely controlled by him and the look on his face.

29
MY TURN TO TALK NOW

AIDEN

PART of me is still waiting to wake up and find that this moment between Tara and I is just another case of my imagination running wild. Because there is just no way that this goddess of a woman is lying before me, her eyelashes lowered, while she looks up at me from the bed.

Something had come over me when we first started this, and I'd tapped into the confident side of myself that rarely shows its face. But now, knowing that she's not been with anyone in four years, all I want to do is make it as enjoyable as possible for her.

Moving up her body, I settle between her legs and press a soft kiss to her neck. She shifts slightly, rolling her head to the side while she raises her hand to run her fingers through my hair. The urgency between us has shifted to something softer, and her breath puffs gently against my cheek when I slide a hand between us and ease my finger back inside her, a little gasp coming from her that is music to my ears. I lean on my elbow and watch her face while I move my hand back and forth, learning which spots to press and how fast to go by how her eyes roll back in her head and what pulls those little moans from her lips.

"Aiden, please," she whimpers, her eyes almost completely closed while she arches off the bed.

"I got you," I reply, lowering my lips to hers to kiss her softly.

She kisses me back, and I guide myself inside her, easing in slowly. She's tight, even after two orgasms, and I move my hips in slow, shallow thrusts until I feel her relax a little more.

She wraps her legs around my waist and pulls me in close while I pick up the pace, but still hold my weight off her, scared to hurt her.

"You won't break me, Aiden," she says, bringing her hand up to cup my cheek.

I let out a deep breath and begin thrusting harder. She meets each one of my thrusts, raising her hips and digging in with her heels. I groan and lean down to kiss her hard, my control starting to slip.

She throws her head back against the pillow and arches into me while a third orgasm rips through her, and she pulls me along with her and over the edge.

Moaning her name into her ear, I thrust a few more times until I'm completely spent, and we cling to each other while our hearts race together, and the enormity of what has just passed between us comes crashing down onto us both.

After I've caught my breath, I shift slightly to look down at her. "Are you okay?"

She nods, biting her lip. "Yeah, I'm okay... Wasn't quite expecting the night to go like this when we came up here."

She sounds wary, and I feel a prickle of apprehension. We've just crossed a line, and there's no way we can go back now.

Moving off her, I grab my boxers on the way into the bathroom to discard the condom, giving her a moment to sort through the emotions that are running over her face.

Once I've cleaned myself up and pulled my boxers on, I splash water on my face and stare at myself in the mirror.

What is she thinking? Is she regretting this already? Shit, have I fucked everything up?

Letting out a breath, I steel myself for whatever reception awaits me on the other side of the door and head out.

Tara is sitting up now, having pulled up the sheet to cover herself, clutching it to her chest.

"Um... bathrooms free," I say, immediately kicking myself for how lame that sounds.

She gives me a tight smile. "Okay... would you mind turning around?"

I nod, turning and grabbing my clothes while she makes a run for the bathroom.

Unsure whether she wants me to leave or stay, I take a seat on the couch after I pull on my jeans and stare at my hands while I wait for her to come back out.

After what feels like the longest time, she emerges, wearing one of the hotel robes.

"So... Um... What now?" she asks, looking as confused as I feel.

"That's up to you... I can leave? I don't want you to feel uncomfortable..."

Please don't tell me to go.

She bites her lip again, running her eyes over my face. "Was it... Was I not good? You can be honest. I don't have any expectations of you, I know I pretty much threw myself at you, and you probably felt like you had to sleep with me because I'm so pathetic and have only been with one guy my whole life," she rambles.

I can see she's working herself into a full on meltdown.

Getting to my feet, I move to stand in front of her while she keeps talking, seemingly convinced that it was just a pity fuck. She finally stops talking when I push her hair back behind her ear and cup her cheek, shaking my head.

"Okay. It's my turn to talk now." I place a finger over her lips and she stares up at me with wide eyes. "Firstly. You were amazing. I don't care how many men you've been with before me. And you didn't throw yourself at me, I kissed you first, remember? I only said I would leave because I was worried that I'd fucked everything up between us and now you didn't want to look at me again. I'm feeling just as nervous about how you're feeling as you clearly are about me. So how about this? We get into that bed together," I say, pointing to the bed, "and I hold you until you fall asleep? We can talk about what we both want from this like adults, and whatever happens, we don't let this affect our working relationship?"

She lets out a breath, like she had been holding it through my entire monologue, and nods. "Yeah... We can... We can do that."

I'm not used to this side of her. She's always seemed so certain of herself, but right now, the vulnerability on her face is almost heartbreaking. But I feel honoured that she's letting me see it, without putting on a show for me.

"Do you want me to turn around so you can get into your pyjamas?" I ask, pointing towards the pile of clothes next to her pillow.

She lets out another breath. "Do you want to turn around?"

"This feels like a trick question... If I say no, are you going to call me a perve?"

That finally gets a laugh out of her. "No, Aiden. I just... I've never really been naked in front of a man properly before..."

I stroke my thumb over her cheek. "If you're comfortable with me seeing you naked again, then I won't turn around, but the ball is completely in your court. But just to be clear... I think you are the most beautiful woman I've ever seen, and I don't want you to hide from me."

Her eyes are wide, full of emotion while she swallows hard. She steps back and carefully pulls the sash of her robe, letting it fall open. Not wanting to make her feel even a little uncomfortable, I keep my eyes locked on hers, letting her take the lead.

She reaches up to slide her right arm out, followed by the left, and the robe pools at her feet. Now it's my turn to swallow hard while she steps around me and moves to the bed.

I strip off, knowing that if I stay clothed, that will make her even more self-conscious. I've never had a sexual encounter like this one, but this feels like the most important moment of my life. Standing here with this woman who is trusting me when she's at her most vulnerable... Another man might crack under the pressure, but all I want to do is hold her and make her feel safe. And wanted.

Joining her between the sheets, I hold my right arm out, inviting her to cuddle up to my side. She hesitates for a moment before resting her head on my shoulder while draping her arm over my waist. I pull her closer and press a kiss to her forehead, relieved when I feel her relax against me.

After a moment, she lifts her head and looks at me. "Thank you."

I stroke her cheek before cupping her face. "You don't need to thank me for anything. I want to be here."

Her eyes glisten for a moment, and I can tell she's doing everything she can to hold back her tears. She nods and rests her head back down. I run my hand up and down her back.

After a few minutes, my curiosity gets the better of me. "Can I ask you something?"

She hesitates before answering. "Okay."

"You mentioned you'd only been with one person before now but had never really been naked with anyone, and it was four years ago?"

"Yeah?"

I pause, trying to find the right words. "Was he not... Did he hurt you? Is that why you're cautious?"

She shakes her head. "No. We were only together for a few months, and while he never hurt me, he had his own issues. We were only together a few times. I think he thought I'd been holding off on having sex until marriage, and felt like it was too much pressure. But really, it was just the fact that no one else had ever wanted to sleep with me before him. But he wasn't in the right headspace for a relationship, so it didn't last. And there's been no one else since then because of the reasons I'd told you about that first night I met you. Men only wanted to talk to me to ask about Bri or Kylie."

I let out a long breath, giving myself time to respond. "I don't know that I agree with that. I won't pretend I know what it feels like to believe that no one wants me for who I am, but from my perspective, all I've wanted since I met you was to truly get to know you. For who you are, not for your friends. And I can't be the only man who can see how beautiful you are, both inside and out. Bri and Kylie seem nice, but I was drawn to you. Is it possible that, over the years, you've built up this belief in your mind that people feel that way?"

She's quiet for so long that I'm worried I've taken it too far.

Finally, she speaks, her voice contemplative. "Maybe you're right... I've never considered that maybe it was my mindset that was keeping people at arm's length."

"Well, I'm not claiming to be an expert on how the human mind works, but if you ever need someone to remind you how amazing you really are, I'm your man."

She laughs a little. "Thank you."

I brush my lips against her temple. "You're welcome, Love." The endearment slips out, and I cringe, sure this is going to be the moment that she wants me to leave.

"I like it when your British side comes out," she says, biting her lip as she smiles. Another minute or so passes before she speaks again. "Will you... Will you stay with me tonight?"

I pull her closer and kiss her temple again. "I'll stay as long as you want me to."

Eventually, I feel her relax against me completely, her breathing evening out when she finally falls asleep. The lack of sleep the night before, along with our recent activities, has me exhausted, and I allow myself to drift off with my arm wrapped around her.

30
ABOUT LAST NIGHT

TARA

THE FIRST THING I see when I wake up is the clock on the bedside table, informing me that I've massively over slept. The second thing I see is a shirtless Aiden lying on his stomach beside me.

The memory of what we did last night comes back to me, and I don't know whether to run and hide, or play it cool. Either way, we're going to miss breakfast if we don't get up now.

"Aiden," I half whisper, not wanting to startle him.

He doesn't move.

"Aiden." I try again, louder this time.

Still nothing. I envy his ability to sleep so deeply, and it certainly had its advantages the last time I woke up beside him, but now it's just annoying.

"Aiden!" This time I poke him, and this finally seems to stir him from his deep sleep.

"Wha," he mumbles, his eyes still closed while he cuddles into the pillow further.

It would be cute if I didn't need him to get his ass out of bed.

"Aiden Sanderson! Wake up right now!"

He finally opens his eyes and lifts his head. "Did you just full name me?"

"Yes I did. Has anyone ever told you how hard it is to wake you up?" I grumble.

He rolls over before sitting up, running a hand over his face. "It was my mother's number one complaint about me when I was growing up."

"I can see why."

He grins, and my stomach does a little flip flop. At least when he does wake up, he's fully functioning.

"So... about last night..." He starts, but I shake my head.

"As much as we should probably talk about it, we only have twenty minutes before they stop serving breakfast and we have to be in the first session, so it's going to have to wait. I need a shower."

He considers me for a moment before nodding and getting out of bed. I stay where I am, the sheet held firmly over my chest. I may have been brave enough to be naked in front of him in the lamp light last night, but in the harsh light of day, it's not happening. I know he notices, but he doesn't comment while he pulls his jeans on.

"I'll meet you out in the hall in ten minutes," he says, heading towards the door between our two rooms.

"You don't have to wait for me," I say.

He turns, hand on the door handle, and gives me a pointed look. "I'll meet you out in the hall in ten minutes." There's no arguing with that look, so I nod and he disappears through the door.

Finally alone, I'd love nothing more than to pull the covers over my head and overthink about every detail of last night, but my growling stomach informs me that's not an option. I head into the bathroom and have the quickest shower I've ever had, before throwing on another one of my new dresses and throwing my hair into a messy bun. With only two minutes left, I don't have time for full make up, so BB Cream and mascara it is.

Grabbing my handbag from where I'd dropped it on the floor last night, I don't have time to do anything more than shove my feet into my high heels before I'm running out the door.

Aiden is leaning against the wall opposite my door, typing something into his phone when I open the door. His head snaps up immediately, and he runs his gaze over me. Sliding his phone into his pocket, he moves to stand in front of me while I pull the door closed behind me, causing me to press my back against the door while my eyes meet his.

"Good morning, by the way," he says, a soft smile playing over his lips.

I feel breathless all of a sudden. I'd managed to push all thoughts of last night aside while I raced around getting ready, but now that he's standing right in front of me, all the emotions I was feeling when I fell asleep have come racing back.

"Good morning," I say, the words feeling like they are lodged in my throat.

He moves closer still. "Can I kiss you, or are you freaking out?"

Unable to find my voice, I simply nod.

"Is that yes to a kiss or yes, you're freaking out?" he asks, the smile widening.

"Kiss," I whisper, licking my lips.

He bends his head to bring his lips to mine in the sweetest, most gentle kiss I've ever had while his hands grip my hips, pulling me closer. Lifting on to my tiptoes, my arms circle his neck while I deepen the kiss, parting my lips when his tongue sweeps across them. I sigh as I melt further into his embrace, and he laughs a little, moving to kiss the tip of my nose before stepping back.

"As much as I would love to take this further, we really need to get downstairs," he says, and I'm pleased to see that he seems just as affected by our kiss as I am, his cheeks a little flushed.

I nod, and he slips his hand into mine, tugging me along gently towards the elevators. Once we're inside, he tucks me into his side and presses a kiss to my temple. I've never experienced tenderness such as this, and a wave of emotion threatens to overcome me. I swallow hard, determined not to let them get the better of me and just enjoy this moment without thinking about what it all means.

Yesterday, I'd been determined to take everything in through the day sessions, wanting to learn as much as I could. But that is pretty much impossible today, because Aiden is sitting right beside me with his thigh pressed against mine under the table. We'd managed to grab a plate of fruit and pastries each before making our way into the conference room and finding the only two chairs left together at one of the shared tables. Out of sight of our colleagues, our chairs seemed to have gravitated closer all on their own until I was all but sitting in his lap, his hand on my thigh while the guest speaker drones on about liability insurance.

By the time the morning session is over, my libido has well and truly woken up, and I'm seconds from dragging Aiden back upstairs. But we need to keep this professional. No matter how good it feels to be with him, we're here for work, and the last thing I need is for either of his uncles, or our Melbourne colleagues, to work out something has happened between us. While it probably won't have any impact on Aiden, it would definitely ruin any chance of me moving further up the ranks if they think I'm sleeping with the boss's son.

Even if that's exactly what I'm doing now.

Because as much as I plan on keeping things professional in front of others, I also know that I want to continue sleeping with him. And from the way his hand has been inching higher up my thigh for the last hour, I know he wants that, too.

Chris finds me as we're heading back into the restaurant for lunch, eyeing Aiden cautiously before asking if I want to sit with him.

"Sure. Grab us a table?" I ask, and Chris nods, heading off. I turn to Aiden, who's watching Chris's retreating back with an unreadable expression. "Do you want to join us?"

He brings his gaze back to mine and smiles a little. "It's okay. I should probably make an appearance with my uncles. I'll see you back in there?"

I nod, and he heads off towards the table that our colleagues have commandeered already. I watch him for a moment, wondering if he's still jealous of my friendship with Chris, before shaking it off. If this is going to end up being something more between us, I need to make sure it doesn't completely take over my life, and we don't need to be together all the time. In fact, maybe a little distance right now is what we both need.

After grabbing some food from the buffet, I find Chris sitting at a table for two and pull out the chair across from him.

"Is it just you here from your office?" I ask, realising I haven't really seen him talk to anyone other than myself while we've been here.

"One of the guys from Sydney is here somewhere, but no one else from the Brisbane office."

I raise an eyebrow. "That's pretty impressive, right?"

He shrugs. "I guess. I think none of the higher ups really felt like going so just handed it off to the new guy." He nods towards where the rest of the people from Sanderson's are sitting. "What's up with you and David's son then? You guys seem pretty cosy now." There's a little smirk threatening to break out on his face.

I narrow my eyes at him. "I have no idea what you are implying, Christopher."

He laughs. "Oh, the full name. Yeah, there's definitely something going on there." His expression softens into the caring older brother look he often gets towards myself, Bri and Kylie. "Seriously though, T. If you're happy, that's pretty cool."

This is why I get along so well with Chris. He doesn't pass judgement, just gives support where needed. All the guys in our friendship group are like this, even Will, who I begrudgingly admit is pretty awesome, even though I'm still hurt by how he pushed me away after Annelisa left him. Although I tried to take a step back from the group a year ago, our little found family wouldn't let me go far, and I'm grateful to them for that. It turns out, I need them all more than I realised.

"I think I might be happy... At least, in that regard. There's still so much other crap going on though," I say, looking down at the untouched food on my plate.

In the whirlwind of getting organised for this trip and my changing feelings towards Aiden, I'd been pushing aside thoughts of my father and the whole 'other family' situation. After twelve years, it's easier to just pretend he doesn't exist rather than deal with all the stuff going on. And that just makes me feel guilty now.

"Yeah. I wish I had some words of wisdom on that. Bri mentioned your dad sprung meeting the kids on you the last time you saw him." Chris sits back in his chair, studying my face.

"Yeah. That was really shit. But I shouldn't have expected anything different. He was never great at respecting boundaries. Add in the whole dying thing and his selfishness is really coming out." I take a sip of my drink just for something to do.

Chris knew our dad back when we were kids, so I'm grateful not to have to elaborate further. He was one of the people who was there for Annelisa and I when it all exploded.

"Well, you know we're all here for you. And from the looks of it, your guy over there will be, too." He nods towards Aiden, who keeps glancing my way while talking to the others at the table. "I know you think you have to deal with everything on your own, but that's never been the case. So just remember you have people you can lean on."

I smile gratefully. "Thank you."

"Don't mention it."

We leave the heavy stuff there, and spend the rest of the meal chatting about the conference and work stuff. By the time we need to head back in for the afternoon session, a lightness has settled over me that I haven't felt in a long time, and I squeeze Aiden's hand under the table when he sits down next to me.

He flashes me a sweet smile, and the little butterflies in my stomach take flight once again.

31

TAKE WHAT YOU NEED

AIDEN

AFTER YET ANOTHER boring conference session that felt like it would never end, I'm so grateful that the second day is over. Attempting to care about insurance while imagining all the things I could be doing with - or to - Tara has been driving me nuts since we sat down for the morning session. Knowing that we still have to sit through dinner with everyone is excruciating. At least this time, dinner is out at a different location, so we can maybe sneak off early without being noticed. The event organisers had arranged for dinner to take place at the hotel where the Singapore Sling was invented, and I figure maybe we can swing by the dance club again. We only have one more night here, as we're on the red-eye flight home tomorrow, and I'm determined to spend as much time with Tara as possible before we return to reality. The fear that she'll push me away once we're back on Australian soil is real, so I want to make sure she realises how good it could be between us, if she just gives it a chance.

. . .

When she opens the door between our rooms, I can't help but run my eyes over her. Swallowing hard, I take in the black dress that skims along every curve, stopping just above her knees. The new confidence she exudes since her little makeover with Sylvia is amazing, and I love that she seems to be embracing her figure, rather than hiding it away behind the baggy clothes. Her long red hair is out, and I'm pretty sure she's spent some time curling it, as it's falling in waves over her right shoulder.

"You look... Fuck..." Words have completely escaped me.

It takes all my willpower to stop myself from pressing her against the wall and having my way with her right now, but we need to get downstairs for the shuttles they've arranged for us all to get to the hotel.

"Are there other words in that sentence?" She smiles, looking a little nervous while she fidgets with the one of the straps on her dress.

I step closer and take her hand, pulling it away gently. "You look absolutely stunning. And if we didn't have to leave right now, I'd be stripping that dress off you immediately."

Her eyes widen a little, and she blushes, which is very cute. It also doesn't help my desire to just spend the rest of the evening alone with her in one of our rooms and no clothes on either of us.

"We should go," she says.

I nod. "Agreed. I have plans for us tonight, so let's get the dinner part out of the way." I take her hand and lead her out the door of my room.

"And what are these plans?" she asks while we wait for the lift.

"Well, I figure, we make an appearance at dinner, then head back to the club? And then, we'll see where the night takes us."

A smile grows steadily on her face and she nods. "That sounds good."

I squeeze her hand and grin. "Good. It's a date."

Her breath hitches a little, and she looks down at our hands before meeting my gaze again. "Yes. It is."

. . .

Whilst dinner has been good, I'm struggling to concentrate on anything that Travis and Barry have been saying for the last hour. When we arrived, Tara had excused herself to go to the bathroom and I'd gone to find our table. But when I'd sat down, both uncles had sat on either side of me, and I've been forced to endure endless shop talk while Tara has been smirking at me from across the table. Travis has been droning on for the last twenty minutes about the importance of remaining compliant, and when Barry jumped in to point out we need to review our internal dispute resolution process, I could have easily throttled him, because it meant the wait staff has been holding off on serving us our dessert while he's been gesturing wildly. By the time the final course is done, I'm desperate to be free of the rest of the conference goers.

"So, shall we go out for a drink?" Travis asks, getting to his feet as the staff clear our table.

I flick my gaze towards Tara before shaking my head. "I need an early night, unfortunately. But I'll see you at breakfast."

"Oh, that's a shame. What about you, Tara? Will you be joining us?"

Tara stares at me for a moment, doing her best impression of a deer caught in headlights, before shaking her head. "Oh, I'm pretty tired, too. I didn't sleep very well last night, so I'll sit this one out."

I cough to cover my laugh when she adds a very convincing fake yawn to really drive it home.

"You kids have no stamina. Back when I was your age, I was partying all night at these events." Barry looks put out, but I shrug.

"Sorry guys, what can I say? Our generation is just weak, I guess," I say with a smile, and Tara looks away while she attempts to keep a straight face.

"Fine. We'll see you in the morning, then."

"Yep, bye," I reply, ushering Tara ahead of me.

We make it outside before we start laughing, and manage to

flag down a taxi with relative ease, heading off towards the club once again.

It's just as busy tonight as it was on Sunday, and we don't bother with drinks when we arrive. I lead her straight out onto the dance floor as soon as we get inside, grateful that the current song is a fast salsa. It feels like we need to ease into this part of the night, and a repeat of Sunday's bachata may cause us both to spontaneously combust if we start that way.

I lead her into a spin, loving the smile that makes her entire face light up. I don't know if she has any idea how sexy she looks when she's dancing, but it's honestly one of the hottest things I've ever seen. I've danced with quite a few women over the years, most more experienced than Tara, but the way she surrenders to the music and allows me to lead her into each move without resistance makes the experience of dancing with her better than anyone else I've danced with in the past. It's like she's tapped into a new side of herself since starting lessons, and I'm glad she's found something that brings her joy.

It's even better that it's something we can enjoy together.

Pulling her in close after the next spin, I wrap one arm around her, keeping our bodies pressed together while we continue moving to the music, and I can't stop myself from running my nose up her neck, breathing in the scent of her perfume.

I feel her shudder a little, and press my lips just below her ear when she melts into my arms. Perhaps dancing in the club wasn't the right way to go. It would be better if we weren't surrounded by other people right now, cause all I want to do is undress her and kiss every inch of her body.

The song changes, and Tara clears her throat.

"Maybe we should get a drink?" She sounds breathless, and I'm relieved to see that she's just as flushed as I feel.

"Sure, come on." I lead her off the dance floor and order our drinks at the bar.

Once the bartender hands us our cocktails, we move to the side of the dance floor, watching the other couples while we sip our drinks. Not wanting to let her go, I step behind her and wrap an arm around her waist, pulling her close to my chest. She rests her head back against my shoulder, and we continue to stand like this until we finish our drinks. Placing our glasses down on a nearby table, I move to lead her back out onto the dance floor, but she tugs me close and kisses me.

"I know you really want to make this feel like a date, but my entire body feels like it's going to explode from how badly I want you right now," she says after bringing her lips close to my ear.

I look down at her while she steps back, watching me through lowered lashes. Knowing the amount of courage it would have taken her to admit that, all I can do is nod and take her hand, leading her back outside. Thankfully, there's a taxi rank nearby, and we slide in to the back seat of the one at the front of the line, sitting as close as possible without her actually sitting in my lap.

The drive to get to the hotel is almost painful, hands exploring discreetly so as not to draw attention from our driver. By the time we get there, I need to keep her in front of me to keep my raging hard on from the view of others.

I've never been more grateful to see an empty elevator when one arrives, and as soon as the doors close, I tug her around to face me. Pushing her back against the wall, I kiss her hungrily, and she returns it with enthusiasm. Hitching her leg up to my hip, I grind myself against her centre, and she moans against my lips while her grip on my shoulders tightens.

Once we reach our floor, we're both out of breath. Her hair is a mess, her lipstick smudged, and I'm ready to tear our clothes off right here in the hall.

She leads the way into her room, and as soon as the door is closed, the intense need to feel her body under mine is overwhelming. Pressing her against the closed door, I run my hand up her leg, pushing the skirt of her dress aside to grab her ass before hiking her leg up to my hip and resuming grinding against her, needing to hear those moans grow louder.

When I can tell she's on the edge of coming undone, I pull away, and she huffs out a frustrated sigh.

Grinning, I pull her towards the bed, turning her so that I can unzip her dress. Letting it fall to the floor, I look towards the mirror and appreciate her reflection in yet another gorgeous matching underwear set. This one is a deep red, moulding to her curves perfectly, and it sends my desire for her sky rocketing.

"You are the most beautiful woman I've ever seen," I whisper into her ear, watching her face in the mirror.

The mood has shifted slightly, and I know she's a little less certain now that we're in front of the mirror. Shifting her hair out of the way, I trail little kisses down her neck, circling my arms around her waist and pulling her back against me so that there isn't even a millimetre of space between us.

Making sure she can feel how badly I want her, I bring my lips back to her ear. "Let me make you feel good."

She swallows hard, and her eyes meet mine in the mirror while she nods.

She lets out a little sigh and leans her head back again, watching through half-closed eyes while my hand slides beneath the band of her underwear. She's already so wet, and I force myself to take my time, wanting her to be completely at ease while I continue learning what brings her the most pleasure.

Applying pressure to her clit, I press a kiss to her neck when she moans, her hips shifting while she seeks more friction. Stroking her a little faster, it isn't long before she's writhing against my hand, and she gasps when I slide a finger inside her and continue applying pressure with the heel of my hand.

Her eyes flutter closed, and I gently bite her ear lobe. "Look at me, Tara. I want you to watch while I make you come. I want you to see how fucking beautiful you are when you're coming undone."

A tremor runs through her body, and she opens her eyes, locking her gaze with mine when she cries out.

"Good girl," I murmur into her neck, continuing to move my hand while she shudders against me.

Once she's finished, I pull my hand away, turning her so that she's facing me. Her cheeks are flushed, and her breathing is uneven when I bend to kiss her. I reach around to undo her bra, before kneeling to pull her underwear down slowly, pressing a kiss to her abdomen. I feel her tense against me, and I look up to meet her gaze. With a shaking hand, she runs her fingers through my hair while watching me, and I can tell she's nervous about the position I'm in.

"Has no one ever knelt before you like this?" I ask.

She blushes, even darker this time, and shakes her head.

Mentally cursing the ex that seemed too inexperienced to be with anyone, let alone a woman as beautiful as Tara, I stand again, kissing her hard.

Guiding her backwards until the back of her knees hit the mattress, I urge her to sit. Making quick work of removing my own clothes, I pull a condom from my pocket and toss it onto the bed beside her. She eyes it before looking back at me.

"Out of curiosity, how did you happen to have condoms available last night and now?" she asks.

"Last night was the one I've had in my wallet for a while. This one is from the packet I bought before dinner tonight, hoping we might end up doing this again," I reply, not even slightly embarrassed. She needs to understand how badly I want her. Although that want is fast turning into a need. "Lie back," I say, cupping her face and forcing her to look me in the eye.

She goes to move back on the bed, but I hold her legs while I kneel in front of her, and her eyes widen when she realises what my intentions are.

"Do you trust me?" I ask. She hesitates before nodding. "Good. Lie back then, beautiful, and let me make you feel good."

She leans back slowly, resting on her elbows, and I bend to kiss her abdomen, keeping my eyes on hers. Her stomach clenches, and I run feather light kisses across it, until she relaxes a little more. When I finally make it to the apex of her thighs, she seems to be comfortable with this position, and when I suck her clit between my lips, she moans and bucks her lips a little. I find a rhythm that works, and she slides her hand through my hair while she grinds against me.

I suck harder before sliding a finger inside, appreciating her ability to silently communicate her needs. She cries out, flinging her head back, and I know I've found the right spot. Working harder, it's not long before her breathing becomes erratic, and the sound of her moans fills the room, growing louder while she clenches around my fingers and practically sobs when she comes.

She's struggling to catch her breath while holding her hand on her chest, and I withdraw my hand before move to her side. Leaning down to kiss her, I run a hand through her hair before grabbing the condom. Motioning for her to move to the centre of the bed, I sit against the head of the bed and pile up the pillows behind my back, before leaning back. She watches me curiously, and after I roll the condom on, I motion for her to come to me. She crawls up the bed, and once she's at my side, I grab her hips to pull her up and straddle my lap. Her eyes widen when I pull her down, easing inside her and guiding her hips to move back and forth once she's fully seated.

"You have the control here. Take what you need."

She rocks, slowly at first, but when she picks up the pace, I clench my jaw and concentrate on my breathing to keep from coming too soon.

She brings her face to mine, kissing me hard while she moves against me, before throwing her head back. I bring my mouth to her breast and suck, and she moans, cupping the back of my head and holding me there while she rolls her hips.

I can feel my orgasm building, moaning against her skin when

I feel her begin to tighten around me. Finally, I can't hold it back any more, and pleasure rocks through me, our cries mingling together. The entire experience is so amazing that I have to fight the overwhelming emotion threatening to overcome me.

We lie together after cleaning up, and I brush a kiss to her temple while she cuddles into my side.

"So... We should talk about what this is," I say, my voice sounding out of place in the comfortable silence.

I feel her tense up a little, and run my hand up and down her side.

"What do you want this to be?" she asks after a moment.

Continuing to move my hand in what I hope are comforting strokes, I clear my throat, suddenly nervous. "Well... I'd be interested in seeing where this could go... I mean... If you want?"

I'm pretty sure that I just undid all attempts to appear confident with that one sentence.

She lifts herself to rest on her elbow and look down at me, a small smile on her face.

"I'm interested in seeing where this could go, too."

I let out a long breath, relief flooding through me. Reaching up, I push the curtain of her hair back over her shoulder and cup her cheek, rubbing my thumb back and forth gently. "Thank god," I say, lifting my head to kiss her.

I feel her smile widen against my lips, and we soon become lost in each other's touch once more.

32
FAMILIES ALWAYS HAVE ISSUES

TARA

"So... How are we playing this at work?" I ask Aiden on Friday morning.

He had arrived at my apartment with a hot chocolate in hand for me, shyly admitting that he'd made it himself before coming up. The nervous smile on his face as he said it was enough to melt any woman's heart, and I'd gratefully accepted it while hiding the keep cup full of tea that I'd just poured myself.

I'm now sipping the rather delicious drink while holding his hand as we walk across the bridge into the city.

He shrugs. "Well, as far as I'm aware, there's no rules about colleagues dating, right?"

I shake my head. So many people have dated in this office, it's almost ridiculous. But in a company of this size, it's not particularly surprising.

"Do you want to just keep it between us for now?" he asks, stopping to the side of the bridge so that he can look at me while allowing others to pass by.

I contemplate our options for a moment. While yes, others

have dated, those people weren't the boss's son and his assistant. The vipers in the admin team would love nothing more than to make this seem like something sordid, when Aiden and I both know that his status as the boss's son has nothing to do with it.

"I think we should play it cool, at least to start with. I don't want anyone gossiping about us. I have nothing to hide, but I've always kept my personal life to myself and I'd prefer to keep it that way."

He nods. "I'm on board with that. I don't want our relationship to cause you any issues."

I smile. "Relationship, huh?"

He grins and tugs me in close, pressing a soft kiss to my lips before stepping back. "Yep, you're in a relationship now, Tara. Deal with it."

We continue walking, and I'm glad he doesn't see the goofy grin that has taken over my face.

Once we reach the building, he lingers downstairs while I head up first. Five minutes later, he saunters past my desk and heads into his office. Once he's seated at his desk, he looks up at me and gives me a cute little wink, and I muffle a laugh before getting started on dealing with the mess in both our inboxes.

Just over a week after our return from Singapore, Aiden is sitting on my couch, waiting for me to finish getting ready before our first official date. Although we've yet to actually go out anywhere, we've spent every night together since we got back. But I realised last night that we can't just spend all our time together naked in my bed, no matter how good it feels. So I'm taking him out to check out the Eat Street Markets in Hamilton. It's long been one of my favourite places to go on the ferry when I'm over the city and South Bank, and he hasn't been very far outside the CBD limits yet.

When I appear at my bedroom door, I find he's been entertaining himself by throwing Toulouse's favourite ball for him, laughing when the kitten keeps bringing it back to him.

"Are you aware that your cat thinks he's a dog?" he asks, turning to look at me when I round the couch to stand beside him.

"Yeah, he definitely seems like he's having an identity crisis." My stomach does a little flutter when his eyes widen, taking in my outfit, and I'm glad I put in the extra effort.

He stands and pulls me in for a long, slow kiss that causes me to melt against him.

"I changed my mind. Let's stay right here," he murmurs against my lips, before slowly kissing his way down my neck.

It takes every bit of my willpower to resist giving in, the feel of his hands making their way towards my butt making it very difficult.

"Nope. We are leaving this apartment tonight." I step out of his arms and pat his cheek.

He pretends to pout, but I can tell he's looking forward to our night out as much as I am. Slapping his butt as I pass, I reach down to pat Toulouse's head before grabbing my handbag and lead the way out the door.

It's almost scary how easily I've fallen into things with Aiden. Perhaps it was because we'd sort of become friends before we started sleeping together, but he manages to make me feel comfortable around him in a way that I never felt with Travis, the ex who I'd met through an old school friend. Or maybe it's just because Aiden has age and experience on his side, unlike the twenty-two year old who wanted to spend all his time partying with his boys. Either way, it's been the best week and a half of my life and I'm determined to hold on to this feeling for as long as possible.

Hand in hand, we walk down to the City Cat terminal at Mowbray Park and wait for the next ferry. I feel my phone buzz in my pocket and pull it out, smiling when I see a text from Bri.

I snort, knowing she had fun writing that. Given that she and Jake no doubt had sex on every surface possible in the apartment when they first got together, she definitely can't give me a hard time about enjoying being dick-matised by Aiden.

Aiden raises an eyebrow and I show him the message.

"What's Riverfire?" he asks.

"You haven't seen all the signs about the Brisbane Festival everywhere?"

He shrugs. "Maybe... I hadn't really been paying attention."

"Riverfire is this massive fireworks display that opens the festival for all of September. It always the last weekend of August. It's takes over the whole city, the Story Bridge closes down and fireworks are going off everywhere. We've got one of the best views of it from the penthouse."

"That sounds fun," he replies, nodding.

I cock my head to the side. "So, are we at the 'meet the friends' phase yet, or do you need to hide at your place next weekend when everyone takes over my place?" I try to sound casual, but I keep waiting for him to run away scared because everything is moving too quickly for him.

I mustn't be that great at hiding it though, because he pulls me in closer and nuzzles my neck. "I'd love to meet your friends properly, Tara. I can tell they are important to you."

I grin and give him a quick peck on the lips before texting Bri back.

Another thought occurs to me then, and I feel my smile drop slightly.

TARA

I'm assuming everyone includes Will?

I wait while the little text bubble shows up, sighing when Bri confirms that Jake wants to see Will, too.

"What's wrong?" Aiden asks after I type back "OK" and pocket my phone again.

I haven't filled him in on the drama between myself and Will yet, so once we're on the ferry, we settle into seats on the back deck and I give him a brief overview of the events of three years ago.

"Why do Bri and Jake think it's okay to invite him over when you're not comfortable with him being around anymore?" Aiden asks, looking like he's ready to throw down.

I smile softly, squeezing his hand. "While I'm hurt by how Will handled the fallout with Annelisa, he's still like family. I've been trying to work on getting over how it all went down, because my friends have always had my back. Even Will."

"Still... You know you can say you don't want him there, right? It is your home, after all." As much as I love that he's concerned, it's clear that he doesn't understand our group dynamic.

"If I really couldn't handle having him around, I would tell Bri. But it's not that big of a deal, really." His expression tells me that he doesn't agree, and I stroke his cheek. "I promise. You'll see when you meet everyone that they really are like family. And families always have issues, mine included."

He considers me closely for a moment. "What does your sister have to say about it?"

I shrug. "I've never told Lis how people reacted after she left. I don't talk about them at all with her."

His eyebrows raise higher. "Not even once in the three years since she left?"

I shake my head. "She was the one who chose to leave in such a spectacular fashion. She doesn't get to ask me about the others when she broke so many hearts with the way she left."

Aiden is quiet for a few moments, processing my words. When he finally speaks again, I can tell he's trying to choose his words carefully. "It seems like you've got a lot that she's just left you to deal with on your own." He squeezes my hand. "This, and the stuff with your dad." I'd opened up about the situation with my father two nights ago when Dad had sent me a message asking me again about meeting the girls.

I take a deep breath, about to admit something out loud that I've not said to anyone since Annelisa left. "How do you tell your sister that her own selfishness has upended your life over a video chat? If she hadn't left the way she did, then she'd be here with me and I wouldn't be dealing with all of this alone. But Annelisa didn't take anyone else's thoughts into account when she ran away from whatever happened three years ago. And I'm still trying to pick up the pieces."

Aiden wraps his arm around me and pulls me into his side. "And she's never said what happened to make her leave?"

I shake my head. "Only she and Will know what happened, and neither of them have told us what it was. I know he wouldn't have done anything to hurt her, that's just not who he is. In the months before she left, she was acting weird. We all noticed it. But no one expected her to just up and move to the other side of the world without so much as a goodbye. My heart broke. Not just for me, but for Will. They were each other's entire world. So whatever it was had to have been pretty serious for her to do what she did. She has never been great at dealing with her issues. When Dad left, it was like something inside her broke, and the carefree sister I grew up with disappeared overnight."

He kisses my temple, and I close my eyes, allowing myself to draw comfort from his presence. It's been so long since I've felt like I could be so open with someone, and it feels like a weight has been lifted slightly off my shoulders to get these words out that I've long been choking down.

"Well, I don't have any advice other than to say that you don't need to do all of this on your own. If your friends are family like you say they are, I don't think they'd want you to pretend you're okay all the time. And I certainly don't expect you to pretend you're not hurting when you're around me either. So anytime you need to let it out, I'm here."

What did I do to deserve this man?

The rest of the evening is perfect. We wander through all the food stands in the brightly lit open air food market, buying a wide array of foods to share and just people watch while we sit near the river to try a bit of everything. I love being able to show Aiden one of my favourite places, and he takes it all in with a wide smile.

But my favourite part is when he just stops in the middle of all the activity to kiss me whenever he feels like it. Since that first night together in Singapore, he's been openly affectionate in a way that I'd always hoped for in a relationship but never thought I'd find. After watching my friends happily settle down over the years, it had felt like it was never going to happen for me.

I just have to stop myself from getting too comfortable, because good things like this never last.

Not for someone like me.

33

NO ONE IS THAT
WELL ADJUSTED

TARA

ON FRIDAY EVENING, I have to tear myself away from Aiden to go and have dinner with my mother. While I'm prepared to introduce him to my friends on the weekend, meeting the parents seems a little too soon, and I also have stuff I need to talk to her about without an audience.

"So, I saw your father yesterday," Mum says after I've been in the house for half an hour.

Her little black and tan sausage dog, Mandy, sits next to me on the couch, sniffing my hand and prodding me to pat her.

"I didn't realise you were planning on seeing him," I reply, surprised.

"We were married for twenty years. As much as things ended terribly, I'm not interested in holding a grudge. I never was."

I stare down at Mandy while I play with her ears. "How do you just forgive him for what he did? He ripped our family apart and broke your heart." I can't even begin to understand how anyone wouldn't hold a grudge after something like that.

"I've always been of the belief that forgiveness is more for the benefit of the wronged party than the one who did the hurting. It was only going to hurt me more if I continued to hold it against your father. He didn't take my feelings into account when he did what he did, and I wasn't prepared to become someone I wasn't because I'd been hurt. And I certainly never wanted either of you girls to carry the anger you both did." Mum delivers this information so nonchalantly, while all I can do is stare at her.

"No one is that well adjusted, Mum. Surely you were angry with him, at the very least?"

"Oh, I was livid. You remember what it was like those first few months. If it hadn't been for the Anderson's, I don't know how we would have gotten through. But we did. And once I pulled myself from the pit of grief and humiliation, I knew that the only way I'd be able to move forward was to forgive him."

I wrack my brain, trying to remember when it was that Mum had seemed like she'd found some sort of peace. I know that Will and Kylie's Mum pretty much lived at our house for the first few weeks, making sure we were all fed and that Lis and I were still going to school. Will and Kylie had camped out at our place most nights as well. But there was obviously a time when things slowly returned to a new sort of normal.

It's strange, looking back at that time from the perspective of an adult. Lis and I had been fifteen and sixteen, and dealing with the usual teenage emotional rollercoaster when it felt like the world was falling apart. But now that Mum mentions it, I don't recall her ever encouraging us to stop talking to Dad. If anything, she tried to get us to continue seeing him. But Lis was adamant that he was dead to her, and I always followed her lead. I wonder how things would have been if I hadn't pushed him away? The anger I've held for him has been like a weight around my neck for twelve years, and I can never get those years back.

I must be quiet for longer than I realise, because Mum gets up and comes to my side, giving me a squeeze when she sits down next to me. "You and Annelisa were always going to have to deal with your feelings towards him at some point. I've watched you both over the last twelve years while you pushed yourselves to just pretend he didn't exist, and it has concerned me to no end. But if you don't find a way to get past the hurt soon, it is going to eat you alive when he's gone."

I chew my bottom lip, aware that she's right but still not sure I'm well adjusted enough to simply forgive him.

"He wants me to meet the girls."

Mum nods. "I know. He mentioned that when I saw him. I think it would be good for you and for them. Those little girls are not to blame for what happened, and as much as you don't want to hear it, they are your sisters. They are still at an age where they'll be able to forget that you weren't around when they were young. But once they hit the teen years, there's no telling how they'll feel. You don't want to become the villain in their stories, Tara. And they certainly aren't the villains in yours."

I swallow hard, her words hitting me harder than I ever thought possible. I've not once thought about how Jordan and Piper must feel, knowing that they have two older sisters who have refused to meet them. Annelisa and I are the adults in all of this, and Mum is right, if we keep ignoring their existence, they are going to hate us, and rightly so. They aren't to blame for the actions of their parents. Just like our father's faults do not define Annelisa and me.

"How do we just forgive him, though? I don't know how to suddenly just let go of what happened and pretend to be okay."

"You are both more like your father than you are ready to admit. He was always one to hold a grudge and hold people to unrealistic expectations. Perhaps it's worth speaking to someone, a professional, who can help you work through your emotions and help you find what works for you? But it's not about pretending to be okay, Tara. It's about forgiving him so that you can let go of the hurt and anger that has festered inside you and tainted how you view the world. I'd hoped that Annelisa was able to find happiness with Will and not let it affect her relationships. But when she ran away, I knew I'd failed her by not insisting she speak with someone. I don't want to see the same thing happen with you. You always looked to her for how to handle life, but you are your own person. Seeing how much you both changed after he left was heartbreaking, but you needed to navigate your feelings yourselves, and all I could do was be there when you needed me."

This is the most open conversation I've ever had with my mother, and I don't know how to process it all.

I do have to find a way to get through it all though, because I know she's right. If my father dies before I am able to get past what happened, I don't know that I'll ever be the version of myself that I need to be. For myself, and for the people in my life.

Something that Aiden said to me swims to the surface of my consciousness - You can't change the past, but you can choose how you frame it.

I can't let how Annelisa is dealing with it affect me anymore.

Guess it's time to stop pushing my emotions aside and deal with them, once and for all.

Once I get home, I send Annelisa a message to see if she's around for a quick chat. Moments later, my laptop starts ringing, and I take a deep breath before answering.

"Hey, is everything okay?" she asks, her concerned face filling the screen.

"Yeah... I just had a few things I wanted to talk to you about." I carry my laptop to my bed, leaning back against the pillows and resting it on my knees.

"Okay..." Her expression turns wary.

"I just had dinner with Mum. And she said some things that I think are important that you know." She remains quiet, waiting for me to continue. "She thinks we should meet Piper and Jordan."

Annelisa shakes her head immediately. "No. No way."

"Let me finish, okay?"

"Fine." She leans back and crosses her arms over her chest.

I take another deep breath. "She said some things that made a lot of sense. The only ones who were really hurt by all of this was us. Dad got his new little family, but because we cut him out and didn't really deal with the hurt it all caused, I think it's affected both of us more than we realised."

"How so?" I can tell she's going to be defensive, which is her usual way of dealing with things when she doesn't agree.

"Well - and I say this with love - the way that you dealt with the end of your relationship with Will is a pretty good example of your unhealthy coping mechanisms." She opens her mouth, looking like she's about to breathe fire, but I hold up my hand. "No one has called you out on this Lis, but what you did was shit. You hurt so many people with how you just up and left, myself included. Do you have any idea how badly you broke his heart? And you left me here to deal with the fallout alone. He wouldn't talk to me for a year, avoiding every social event where I might be and making it all really fucking awkward. It wasn't until Kylie told him you were in London that he finally apologised for how he'd treated me, but by then, the damage was done. I've been holding on to so much hurt and anger for the last three years that it turned me into someone I couldn't stand anymore." Throughout my monologue, Annelisa's eyes have begun to fill with tears, but I can't seem to stop the flow of words now that they've started. "I've been so miserable for so long, and I'm tired of it. We should never have just cut Dad out without at least discussing how it all hurt us. We let that one really shitty experience define the rest of our lives, and I can't do that anymore. I can't risk damaging my own relationships the way you did, and if I let those two little girls feel like I hate them, I'm scared of the person I'm going to end up being."

I finally manage to stop talking, my throat feeling like it's closing up while I fight back my emotions. Annelisa remains silent, and I keep waiting for her to slam the laptop shut and never speak to me again.

We stare at each other for a few moments before she finally opens her mouth, wiping away a tear. "I'm sorry that my issues affected you so much."

I wait for her to continue, but that seems to be all she has to say.

"Is that it?" I ask, unable to believe that is all she took away from my word vomit.

"What else do you want me to say? I'm glad you've had some epiphany after speaking to Mum about how she just let Dad walk all over her after he blew up our lives, but I can't just get over twelve years of hurt in a single moment."

I shake my head. "She didn't let Dad walk all over her. She forgave him so that she could move on. Of the three of us, she was the one who should have been the most hurt, and yet, she's the most well adjusted. Maybe that's something worth thinking about while you hide away from everyone on the other side of the world."

She glares at me. "Is that all you wanted to talk to me about? I'm on a deadline."

I glare right back. "Well, I was going to talk to you about the guy that I'm seeing, but if you're going to be like that, I guess, that's all there is for us to talk about."

After a moment, when I think she might be about to change her mind, she nods. "I guess it is. I'll talk to you later."

The connection ends and I'm left staring at my laptop, feeling like crap but not even slightly surprised that, instead of talking about things, she chose once again to run away.

34
YOU SNOOZE, YOU

AIDEN

On Saturday evening, I feel like a kid on his first day at a new school. While Tara has assured me that her friends are great, my nerves have been jangling away all day, and by the time I arrive at her door with a bottle of wine clutched in my hand, I feel sick. Which is ridiculous because I'm a grown man, for fuck's sake.

"Hi, Aiden." Bri stands at the door with a smile, stepping aside to usher me in. "This is my husband, Jake." She nods towards the guy standing in the middle of the kitchen surrounded by enough food to feed a small army.

"How's it going?" Jake nods, moving to wipe his hands on a dishcloth before coming to shake my hand.

"Good. It's nice to meet you," I reply, shaking his hand firmly.

"Tara's just finishing in the shower, she'll be out in a minute," Bri says, taking the bottle when I hold it out towards her. "Thank you."

"So, Aiden. How are you settling in?" Jake asks while I take a seat on one of the high stools behind the kitchen counter.

"So far, it's been fine," I reply, nodding my thanks to Bri when

me a glass of the wine. "I mean, I'm still trying to wrap
around all the insurance jargon, but everything else has
y."

h, Tara mentioned you'd had some issues."

mirk. "I'll bet she did."

was only a little mean," Tara says, coming out of her
oom. She stops beside me and gives me a quick kiss before
ing my hair. "And it was all before I got to know you
perly."

I run my eyes over her, still having trouble believing that I get
o check her out as much as I want now. "I guess I'll let it slide
then."

"Good idea," she replies with a grin, leaning in to my side
when I put my arm around her waist.

She reaches across the bench to grab a carrot stick from a
platter that Jake is working on.

"Oi! I haven't finished putting that together yet! Hands off."
He slaps her hand away, but she manages to steal the carrot and
crunches it loudly, grinning.

"Sorry Jake, you snooze, you lose."

"Get out of my kitchen, Tara," he replies, and she raises an
eyebrow.

"Whose kitchen?"

Jake shrugs, unperturbed by the reminder that she lives here all
the time. "When I'm in this kitchen, it's all mine. Unless you want
to miss out on the food?"

She laughs. "Well, given how awesome your food is, I guess I
better accept that it's yours when you're here."

"Wise decision."

I relax a little, enjoying watching her interact with her
friends. I can see now what she meant about them being like
family. She and Jake continue to bicker good naturedly while Bri
looks on, shaking her head with an exasperated sigh for my
benefit.

"I'd hoped that having new company around would make them be on their best behaviour," she says, smiling at me.

"Wait until Morgan gets here, then it'll be ten times worse," Tara responds.

"Who's Morgan again?" I ask, trying to put together all the connections between them.

"My best friend," Jake replies, at the same time that Bri says, "My sister."

I look at Tara with a raised brow.

"Also known as Chris' wife," she contributes with a shrug.

"Right. And this is the Chris who used to work at the office, yeah?"

She nods. "Yep. The one you thought I was madly in love with."

I groan while Jake and Bri both snort with laughter. "We promised never to speak of that again."

She crunches on the carrot again. "I made no such promise. You must be imagining things." She grins and winks.

This is the side of her I've been falling in love with since we met. In this moment, she is exactly like the version of herself I met that first night.

While I'm momentarily awestruck, a little white dog comes trotting into the room from the balcony. Toulouse hisses at her from the top of the couch, but she ignores him and makes a beeline straight for me.

"Who's this?" I ask, leaning down to pat the dog's soft head while it stands on its back legs to paw at my calf.

"That's our dog, Maddie," Jake says, walking to pick up the intercom when it rings, alerting them to more guests arriving.

I lean down to lift Maddie up onto my lap. "She's adorable," I reply, scruffing her up while her whole body wriggles with excitement.

"Yeah, she knows it, too," Bri replies, watching with a smile while Maddie tries to lick my face.

Not keen on getting covered in doggy kisses just now, I pop her back down on the floor, and she heads around the bench to sit by Jake's feet. She stares up at him with wide eyes, and Jake drops a carrot on the floor for her. She grabs it and tears back outside.

"Not sure I've ever seen a dog eat a carrot before," I comment.

"She's obsessed with them. As soon as she sees me get the packet out of the fridge, I can't get her away from me." Jake shakes his head. "She's definitely an odd little one."

As Bri opens her mouth, no doubt to defend the dog, a knock sounds at the door. Tara moves from my side to open it, standing aside as Chris leads the way inside, followed by a blonde woman who bears a striking resemblance to Bri, and a tall brown-haired guy. I recognise him from the night I danced with Tara in the city and assume this must be the infamous Will.

"Hey guys," Jake says, nodding towards the newcomers before bending to get something out of the oven.

A delicious smell wafts out, making my mouth water.

"Hey," the blonde woman gives Tara a quick hug before moving into the kitchen to join Bri, giving her a squeeze.

This has to be Morgan. They could almost pass as twins.

Tara introduces me to all of them, and the guys shake my hand. Will eyes me with interest but seems hesitant to say more than "hi". I'm not sure if it's because I know their history, but I can see the awkwardness between him and Tara, although I'm determined not to pass my own judgement until I get to know him a bit more.

"Alright, dinner's ready. Everyone, grab a plate or something," Jake announces, nodding towards all the side dishes he's got spread out, while he holds up the oven tray.

"What are we having?" Morgan asks, sniffing the air.

"Lamb." Jake holds the tray out towards her to inspect, and she nods her approval.

We all grab something and I follow Tara outside to the balcony.

As the evening wears on, the conversation flows naturally. Tara's friends are welcoming - asking questions about London and how I'm settling in. My nerves from earlier have eased, and it's nice to feel like I'm a part of the group.

"Oh, we've only got a few minutes before the fireworks start," Bri says, jumping up to race inside.

"What's she doing?" I ask Tara.

"Putting the TV on so we can hear the soundtrack they've put together. That's the only down side to watching it from here, away from the crowds. We can't hear the music that they have timed everything with. But it's so worth it. Come on." She grabs my hand and drags me to the end of the terrace that overlooks the Story Bridge and city.

Across the river, I can see a huge crowd of people lining every available space along the fence line and am grateful I'm up here rather than being squashed amongst so many bodies.

Music starts playing from inside, and Bri makes it back to stand in front of Jake, who pulls her backwards so that her back is pressed against his chest, just as the first firework goes off.

Mirroring Jake and Bri, Tara and I stand in awed silence while the impressive display continues.

"Oh, look at the Bridge!" Tara calls, pointing ahead of us all.

We watch, open mouthed, as a curtain of flames fall from the bridge. I've never seen fireworks like this before, and the hairs on my arms raise while an old Aussie rock song starts playing.

Throughout the twenty minute display, the atmosphere is electric, and my arms tighten around Tara as I stare up at the explosions occuring above the river all around the city. While we can't see the fireworks happening on the South Bank side, we can hear them, and it amazes me how much is happening all at once.

"What do you think?" Tara says, looking up at me over her shoulder.

"It's awesome," I reply, truthfully.

I never thought I'd be so excited about fireworks at my age, but I can understand why they make such a big deal out of this event.

She looks up at me with an expression full of joy, and my attention is pulled from the rapid fire explosions that signal the end is near. Leaning down, I brush my lips to hers, and she reaches back to grip my neck, deepening the kiss.

"Alright, you two, settle down," Morgan says from beside us, laughing when we don't immediately respond.

"Shoosh, leave them alone," Bri says, and I assume the slap I hear is her smacking her sister's arm.

We pull apart and Tara gives me a sheepish little smile before we return our attention to the last of the display

Afterwards, Bri starts gathering plates, and Will, Tara and I move to help her.

"Shall we move this party to the spa?" Jake asks.

"Well, we have some news," Morgan says, and I glance over to see her exchanging looks with Chris.

The others have paused in helping clear the table. Bri has a smile slowly appearing on her face, and I have a feeling I know what's about to happen.

"Morgan's pregnant. So, no spa for her," Chris says a moment later, confirming my suspicions.

"Oh my gosh! That's so great!" Tara exclaims beside me, and she rushes around the table to give her friends a hug each.

From the smiles on their faces, it's obvious that Bri and Jake already knew. The stunned look on Will's face tells me this is definitely news to him, though. He stands frozen for a few moments, before shaking his head and going to join the others.

I hang back, politely nodding and smiling, while the group shares hugs. Tara glances over, cocking her head to the side before making her way to my side.

"Hey. Sorry, this is probably a bit uncomfortable for you." She places a hand on my bicep and squeezes.

I put my arm around her, tucking her into my side. "Nope,

I'm fine. It's nice that your friends are able to share their excitement with you."

The rest of the evening buzzes with conversation about babies and Morgan's well-being. I catch Tara looking at me a few times, perhaps waiting for me to freak out, but I just smile, hoping to ease her anxiety.

Around ten, Morgan yawns, and Chris declares it's time to go home. Will follows them both out the door after saying his own goodbyes, and it's the four of us left in the apartment.

"We might head to bed, too," Tara says, grabbing my hand.

Jake and Bri exchange grins before Jake shrugs. "No worries. We remember how it is."

Tara blushes and shoots him a glare, but doesn't let the innuendo stop her from dragging me into the bedroom. I give them a smile and a wave before closing the door.

"If you were going for subtle, I think you failed," I say, grinning and reaching to pull her close.

She steps out of my reach, biting her lip. "I have no idea what you're implying, mister. I'm just going to sleep."

"Oh, well, in that case, goodnight." I flop down on the bed and close my eyes.

Tara laughs and curls up beside me. "Okay, you got me. All I really wanted was to come in here and ravish you. You handled all the baby talk very well."

I shake my head. "It was honestly fine. We're at that age where people are settling down and starting families. I'm not freaking out."

She props herself up on her elbow and peers down at me. "You really are one of the good ones, you know that?"

I stroke my thumb over her cheek. "I find it quite sad that such a simple thing makes me one of the good ones."

"It's not only the fact that you don't turn into a freaked out mess at the mention of babies, and spending time with my friends.

Thank you for just being you." She turns to kiss the palm of my hand.

"You're welcome. You're pretty amazing, too," I reply, pushing her hair back behind her ear.

She peers at me, her expression thoughtful. "I don't feel so amazing at the moment. I spoke to Mum yesterday, and she basically told me off for not wanting to meet Jordan and Piper. Told me I don't want to be the villain in their story. And then I pretty much told Annelisa she was a terrible person."

I pause in the motion of rubbing her back and raise an eyebrow. "Okay, you're gonna need to walk me through all of that."

I listen while she goes over the details of her conversations with both her mother and her sister the previous evening, letting her talk it all out while I continue to run my hand up and down her back. Once she's finished speaking, I nod my head.

"Well, I think it's good that you did finally tell Annelisa how her actions have affected you. And I also kind of agree with your mum. The girls are at that young age where they will still forgive you for not wanting to meet them before now, but if you leave it much longer, the older one is going to hit those fun teenage years, and then you may never be able to go back."

Tara nods. "Yeah, I know... I just don't want to meet them on my own. I'd really hoped I might be able to convince Annelisa to see it that way, but I think that might be a lost cause."

"I'm sorry that your sister isn't able to find it in herself to be there. But you're not alone. You still have me. And I'm sure if you asked any of the friends that you had here tonight, they would be with you as well. You've got a good support network around you," I remind her with a smile.

"You'd really come with me?"

I nod. "I know a thing or two about meeting younger half siblings. Just tell me when you need me and I'll be there."

She smiles and places her hand on my chest. "Thank you."

I shake my head. "There's no need to thank me. It's what any good boyfriend would do."

She pauses, a small smile playing across her lips. "Boyfriend, huh?"

"Yeah. Pretty sure we're at that step now. If you don't mind me calling you my girlfriend?" Despite the smile on her face, my heart races a little while I wait for her to reply.

"I'd really like that, Aiden." She bends to kiss me, and I cup her face in my hands, savouring the gentleness of her lips on mine.

I could easily spend the rest of my life on this bed with her by my side.

35

DON'T WANT YOU TO SETTLE

AIDEN

THE NEXT DAY, I pull up in the driveway of Dad and Lisa's place. Opening the rear passenger door, I take out the tray of cupcakes that Lisa had asked me to collect on my way over. It's the twins' birthday party, and I was surprised when I received the invite in my inbox.

"Are you sure it's okay that I'm here with you?" Tara asks, smoothing down the skirt of her dress when I join her at the front of the car.

"Yes, I promise. I checked with Lisa, just to be sure," I reply, giving her a quick kiss before taking her hand in mine.

Making sure the cupcakes are safe in their little carrier, I lead her up the stairs and into the house. The sounds of children squealing with excitement greet us when we enter the kitchen, and I can see a number of small children running around in the back-yard. Someone has organised several inflatable houses and castles, each with large slides, and I spy a small fenced off area behind the pool that seems to have a number of farm animals in it.

"Wow. Inflatables *and* a petting zoo? This is the coolest party ever," Tara comments, her eyes wide while she takes it all in.

"Yeah... I can't even remember having a birthday party, let alone one with live animals," I say, trying to keep the bitterness out of my voice.

She catches it anyway, squeezing my hand without saying anything.

Dad walks in while I'm looking for a place to put down the cupcakes, stopping when his gaze drops to Tara's hand in mine. He raises an eyebrow but doesn't say anything. I wonder how long it will be before he asks me about it though.

"Hey, here's the cupcakes," I say, handing them to him.

"Thank you. Head on out if you want. There's beer and wine in the fridge on the patio, and the caterers have just started serving the food." He nods towards the open patio doors.

"Okay," I reply, leading Tara outside.

We find Lisa running after the twins looking absolutely exhausted, while the tiny terrors seem to have more than enough energy to spare.

"Hey. Need a hand?" I ask, reaching down to capture Mitchell as he tears past.

Lisa looks like she's about to cry. Exchanging a glance with Tara, she grabs Daisy before she can escape, and we each hold a screaming toddler while looking at their mother.

"Thank you. I'm trying to get them wrangled into their outfits but as soon as the animals arrived, they were off and I've not been able to catch them," Lisa says, a tiny sob escaping her lips.

"How about, we'll go and get them changed and you get a glass of wine?" I suggest.

Lisa hesitates for a moment, looking between Tara and me. "Are you sure?"

"Yes. We've got these two, just go take a few minutes to yourself."

She smiles gratefully, and then heads for the fridge while Tara and I carry the two squirming three-year-olds inside. We head for their room, and I'm relieved to see that Lisa has laid their outfits out on their beds.

"Now, Mitchy, buddy. How about we give the screaming a break and get into your party clothes?" I ask my little brother, who glares up at me from where he's thrown himself on the floor.

Tara deposits Daisy next to Mitchell, and the little cherub faced demon bops her brother on the head while giggling. This sets Mitchell off again, and they start rolling all over the floor, hitting and biting each other.

"Jesus!" Tara leaps in and pulls them apart.

Getting down on their level, I look them both in the eye. "Hey. We do not hit and bite," I say, pulling out my sternest voice.

Daisy's lower lip starts to wobble, and I sigh, scooping my little sister up and sitting on the edge of her bed with her on my lap. Mitchell toddles off to the toy kitchen in the corner of the room, giving up on his pursuit of freedom.

"Now, Daisy, why'd you hit your brother?" I ask, looking her in the eye.

"Wanted to," she replies.

Tara covers a laugh with a cough before grabbing Mitchell's clothes from the bed and going to sit at his side while he plays.

"Well, it's not nice. Now, you two have all these people here to celebrate your birthday with you. But they can't do that if you are both being mean to each other, can they?" I level Daisy with what I hope is my most convincing gaze.

Wide blue eyes stare into mine while she considers her options. She cocks her little head to the side and then looks at the dress on the bed beside me.

"Don't want that," she says, her little voice showing her grumpiness.

"Well, what do you want to wear?" I ask.

She hops off my lap and goes to the cupboard, tugging on the door. I move to stand behind her and open it up for her. She hones in on a long, blue dress, tugging on it while looking up at me.

"Elsa," she says, and I look at the dress again.

Of course she wants to dress up like an ice queen.

I help her into her costume, and she grins up at me, giving me a cute little curtsey before racing off again. I move to follow her, but Tara stops me.

"I've got her. You work that magic on your brother." She disappears out the door in pursuit of my blonde headed tiny sister, leaving me to negotiate with Mitchell.

It appears that the large part of their issue was that they didn't like the outfits their mother had picked for them, so I cave and let him dress in his own Elsa costume. I carry him back out to the party, and Dad sighs when he sees what he's wearing.

"Mummy picked out such cute outfits. Couldn't you both give up being Elsa for one day?" he asks, taking Mitchell from me.

"No," Mitchell says, kicking to be let down.

Dad sighs again and puts him down. Mitchell races off to join his sister in the bouncy castle. Tara is standing nearby, watching Daisy bounce around with her little friends.

"We can keep an eye on the kids, if you want?" I say.

Dad raises an eyebrow. "You're volunteering to look after the two demons?"

I splutter a laugh. "I didn't realise you had nicknamed your offspring the two demons?"

He shrugs. "If the shoe fits. They were sweet when they were babies, but as soon as they started walking, it was like their energy levels went through the roof. Poor Lisa is exhausted. They are like this from the moment they wake up until they go to bed."

"That sounds full on. Well, Tara and I can give you both a break if you want to try to mingle with all your guests?"

"Tara and I, huh? When did this happen?" he asks, nodding towards Tara.

"Singapore. We're keeping it private for now, though." I grab drinks from the fridge for myself and Tara.

"Good idea. The last thing we need is anyone claiming she's using you to work her way up the ladder," he replies, to my disbelief.

It sounded almost supportive of Tara.

I nod before heading down the stairs to join Tara beside the bouncy castle and hand her a can of soft drink.

"I volunteered our services as tiny human watchers," I tell her, and she nods.

"No problem. They're actually kind of cute."

"Dad just referred to them as the two demons." I smile and take a mouthful of drink.

At that moment, Daisy jumps on top of Mitchell while he's rolling around in the corner of the bouncy castle, and they both begin screaming blue murder.

Tara raises an eyebrow. "Oh, he's definitely right about that."

We spend the rest of the party keeping an eye on the twins and making sure they don't injure themselves or each other. There was one hairy moment when I thought they might hurt the calf in the petting zoo, but thankfully, we got them under control before there were any disasters.

On the drive home, Tara turns in the passenger seat to look at me. I decide this is a small victory, as she's usually clinging to the passenger door handle and trying not to scream.

"You're really good with kids, you know that?"

I glance over at her before returning my eyes to the road. "I guess. I'd actually wanted to be a teacher when I was younger. It's what I'd planned to do after university. But life had other plans for me."

She's quiet for a moment, studying me closely. "You said you didn't get to finish your degree, right?"

I shake my head. "No. Only got to do one semester before Mum had her stroke."

"Have you thought about finishing now? You were so good with the twins, I think you'd have the patience needed to be a teacher."

I mull over her words before shrugging. "I can't really afford to study. I need to be working, and I feel like I'm too old now, anyway."

She shakes her head. "Plenty of people start new careers in their thirties. And you hate insurance. Wouldn't you rather try to do something you enjoy?"

"Maybe."

She reaches over and places her hand on my thigh. "I won't push it anymore. I just want you to be happy."

I cover her hand with mine. "I am happy."

"I meant happy at work."

"Is there anyone who is really happy at work?" I ask, deflecting.

Tara isn't to be swayed. "I think there are plenty of people who like their jobs. Bri certainly does. I don't mind certain parts. Kylie and Seth love their jobs."

I laugh. "I don't think I can compare myself to a professional hockey player. He'd have to love his job to put up with all that attention."

"True. But people find jobs they enjoy. I just don't want you to settle. You're still young, with no responsibilities yet. Promise me you'll think about it?"

I pat her hand. "I promise I'll think about it."

"Good. Now both hands on the steering wheel." She resumes her normal passenger position and I laugh, returning my hand to the steering wheel while shaking my head.

There is truth to her words. Plenty of people start again when they don't find satisfaction in their first career attempt. Why can't I?

36
NOT HAVING A GREAT DAY

TARA

AFTER SEEING Aiden with his young siblings yesterday - and dealing with my ovaries screaming when I saw how good he was with them - I'm about to take him to meet with my own half-sisters.

We came straight to the hospital after work, and I'd barely been able to concentrate all day.

"I'm sorry I dragged you along," I say to Aiden once he's returned to his seat across the cafeteria table, after getting us both drinks.

"Don't be silly. I wouldn't have offered to come if it was a problem. I just want to be here to support you."

I bite my lip. "At least meeting Mum last night was fairly pain free."

I'd refused to let Dad be the first parent to meet Aiden, so had staged an impromptu Sunday roast dinner at home with Mum and Aiden last night. It had gone well, which shouldn't have surprised me, because Aiden gets along with pretty much everyone.

"It's going to be okay. I'm right here," he says, stopping my fingers from tapping on the arm of the uncomfortable metal chair .

"I know... I'm just freaking out a little." My leg starts to jiggle, my body determined to find a way to expel the nervous energy swirling inside me.

"Tara?" I look over my shoulder to see Jo standing a few steps away.

I get to my feet, nodding towards Aiden. "Hi Jo. This is my boyfriend, Aiden. Where's Dad?"

She grimaces. "He's not having a great day. He asked if you could come upstairs to the room. I'm sorry, I know you preferred to meet the girls down here."

Emotions swirl within me. I can handle the change of location, but the knowledge that my father isn't doing so well has set off something inside me that I've been refusing to acknowledge. That I'm running out of time with him. That Annelisa is going to miss him if she doesn't get her head out of her ass and get back here.

I swallow hard before nodding. Aiden gets to his feet beside me and takes my hand, leading me along to follow Jo back to the elevators.

The atmosphere in the elevator up to the ward is tense. While I know I need to make peace with my father, I'm not sure I'll ever be able to forgive the woman who tore him away from us and started a second family with him. Logically, I know it took two people to do what they did, but logic plays no part in a broken heart.

"Do the girls know I'm coming?" I ask, breaking the silence between us as we walk down the hall to my father's room.

"Yes. I'd say they are about as nervous as you are," Jo replies, frowning a little.

I can tell she wants to say more, a mother bear protecting her young, but we reach his room before she has a chance. The door is open, and I can hear two young voices chatting away excitedly.

From what I can tell, they are telling Dad about their day at school.

"And then Amber told Peter that she hates him and they aren't boyfriend and girlfriend anymore. So Peter told me he never liked Amber anyway and he always liked me more."

I shoot a glance towards Aiden, who appears to be trying to fight back a smile when we overhear the last of Piper's story.

"You shouldn't accept someone else's damaged goods," Jordan tells her sister, with more wisdom than I expected from an eleven-year-old.

"Your sister's right." The change in Dad's voice is so strong that it feels like I've been punched in the stomach.

He's hooked up to an oxygen tank again, and his breathing seems laboured. Face pale, he appears to be struggling just to keep his eyes open, but he's doing his best to seem like nothing is wrong.

But it's all wrong.

They haven't noticed us yet, so I step back slightly, nodding my head towards Jo for her to follow. I keep a tight grip on Aiden's hand as I turn to face her again, hopefully out of earshot of the room.

"How much longer has he got?" I ask, doing my best to keep my voice from wavering.

She takes a deep breath, and for the first time, I realise just how hard this all is for her. "They've said it could be in the next few weeks. Did he tell you the details?"

I shake my head. "No... our visits have been a bit... fraught."

I've been so caught up in my own emotions that I haven't even asked for more information about how my father has become so sick in the first place.

Aiden squeezes my hand gently, bringing me back to the conversation while Jo gives me a sad look.

"By the time he showed any symptoms, he was already stage five. He was on the transplant list, but it's gone too far for that. It's now caused heart problems. He won't be coming home from here." She chokes on those final few words, and I take a deep, ragged breath.

Aiden pulls me in to his side, wrapping his arm around me and pressing his lips to my temple while I blink rapidly.

Jo stays quiet while I pull myself together, the fatigue on her face seeming to age her beyond her years. I can tell just how much of a toll this is all taking on her, and can only imagine how it must feel having your husband so sick while raising two young girls.

"Do the girls know how bad it is?" I ask finally.

"Somewhat. Jordan has more of an understanding of it all, but Piper has always been quite sensitive, and we've tried to only tell her what she needs to know. She's a real daddy's girl, so this is going to hit her hard."

At the mention of Piper being a daddy's girl, my stomach flips, and I have to fight to keep my expression neutral. I was a daddy's girl once. Until I wasn't.

Jo must see the conflicting emotions on my face, because she reaches forward to squeeze my arm gently. "I'll give you a moment."

She heads back into Dad's room, and I turn to bury my face into Aiden's neck while he rubs his hand up and down my back.

After a few more moments, I take another deep breath, steeling myself to go back in there. Aiden kisses my forehead when I look up at him, giving me some of his strength.

This must all be bringing back memories for him, and I feel guilty for dragging him into my family drama so soon after dealing with the loss of his own mother.

Pushing aside the thoughts that will need to wait until later, I lead the way back towards the door. Hesitating for only a moment, I step inside, closely followed by Aiden, and plaster a smile on my face.

Dad's eyes meet mine, and he smiles, his head resting back against his pillow. "Hi Tara." His voice cracks a little, and two little red heads swing around to look at me.

"Hi Dad." I give a little wave, letting myself look at my younger sisters properly for the first time.

It's alarming how much they remind me of Annelisa and myself at their ages. I'd always thought we looked more like Mum, but seeing these two little clones has me questioning everything I ever believed about myself.

"Girls. This is your sister, Tara," Jo pipes up, squeezing Dad's hand while he struggles to hold back his emotions.

Jordan is the first to speak, putting her arm around Piper. "Hi."

I smile at them both, the first real smile I've used since I got to the hospital. "It's nice to meet you both."

"Who's that?" Piper asks, pointing at Aiden.

"This is my boyfriend, Aiden."

"I've got a boyfriend. His name is Peter," Piper replies with a big smile.

Jordan makes a disgusted noise. "He's not your boyfriend. You're not allowed to be boyfriend and girlfriend with someone who was just going out with your best friend. It's against the girl code."

"Am too. Amber was so mean to him all the time. I don't even like her anymore."

They start to squabble, and I glance at Dad. He seems unaffected by the arguing, but Jo steps in before it can escalate any further. Diverting the conversation from boyfriends and ex-best friends , she asks the girls to tell me what they like to do for fun.

Piper is a talented gymnast, and has to be stopped from showing me some of her tricks right there at the end of Dad's bed.

Jordan is more reserved, watching me closely, and I can tell she is still deciding whether she can trust me or not. They really are so similar to Annelisa and me, and I can understand now why Dad wanted us to all meet.

"How come we've never met you before," Jordan asks, interrupting Piper as she excitedly tells me about her next gymnastics competition in a few weeks.

I exchange a look with Dad, who nods slightly.

"Well... Dad and I haven't really spoken very much for a few years. But we're working on that now. I'm sorry I wasn't around before now."

Jordan narrows her eyes while she considers my answer. To my own ears, it was pretty weak, but I don't think she needs to know the details of her conception and the fallout from it.

"So why isn't our other sister here? Doesn't she care that Dad is dy-" Jordan slams her mouth shut, looking at her mother quickly before speaking again. "Doesn't she care that Dad is sick?"

Piper's eyes swing from Jordan to me, and I wonder if she picked up on her sister's slip-up.

"Annelisa lives in London now. It's a long way for her to come. But she does care."

Even if she won't admit it to herself, she cares so damn much it hurts.

Jordan looks like she wants to argue, but Jo rests a hand on her shoulder, shaking her head when Jordan looks up at her.

"Let's try to have a nice visit, hey?" Jo gives Jordan a pointed look, and she nods before looking back at me.

"So, Aiden. How did you and Tara meet?" Dad asks.

"Well, we met when Tara was hiding from the wedding she was part of." He grins at me, before turning back to Dad. "But now we work together."

I lean into his side a little more while he and my father talk. Piper has moved on to playing a game on her iPad, but Jordan is still studying me closely. I give her a little smile, which she eventually returns.

We spend another half an hour with them, but I notice Dad seems to be struggling even more. Exchanging a look with Jo, I pat Dad's hand, and he turns his head slightly to look at me.

"We're going to head off. But I'll come back on the weekend, okay? I can bring you something from the bakery again."

He smiles at me. "I'd really like that, Tara. Thank you for coming."

Nodding, we say our goodbyes to everyone and I let Aiden lead me towards the door. I pause before walking out, turning back to look at Dad and Jo. While the girls are preoccupied with their technology, Jo is resting her forehead on Dad's temple, and the sight of it makes my heart feel like it's cracking down the middle.

Despite my feelings about their relationship, I can see how much this is hurting them both, and seeing them like this reminds me just how precious life is.

I have got to find a way to get Annelisa here before it's too late.

37
WHAT WAS THAT FOR?

AIDEN

ON FRIDAY EVENING, Tara and I are due to go on our second official date, and this time it's my turn to organise it.

After she'd shown me the Eat Street Markets, I've been trying to work out what we could do that would be something different for her. After asking Damien for tips, I'd settled on a late afternoon drive up to Mount Coot-tha to watch the colours change over the city while the sun goes down. Then, dinner at a small Italian restaurant he'd recommended in Paddington, before heading back into the city and the open-air dancing once again.

We've not had a chance for much social dancing since Singapore, so have had to settle for the small amount of free dance time after our class each week. I'm really looking forward to just being able to dance with her, without having to change partners or focus on the one routine.

Knocking on Tara's door, I wait while I hear her rushing around on the other side of the door, a small smile on my lips while I imagine her running after Toulouse, trying to put him in her bathroom while she's out.

The little kitten has been getting into all sorts of mischief when left in the main part of the apartment. Last night, Tara had gone to bed before me, and I'd spent almost an hour frantically searching the place for the little rascal. I'd finally given up and gone to get Tara, worried I'd lost her cat. Only for her to open the top drawer of the dresser in one of the other bedrooms and there he was, curled up without a care in the world. So now, he has lost access to all bedrooms except Tara's, and when she's not home, he's in the bathroom. At least until he grows bigger and can no longer fit into tight spaces.

"Sorry," Tara says as she flings the door open. "I finally got him. I think he knew what was going on when he heard you knock on the door." She pushes her hair behind her ear, her cheeks flushed from the flurry of activity. "Should we go?"

I step closer and place a finger to her lips. "You look gorgeous," I tell her, and her lips curl up slightly behind my finger.

I lower my head and kiss her softly, feeling her relax against me as she sinks into it. Her arms come around my neck as she deepens the kiss, opening her mouth to me. I groan and grip her hips, pulling her flush against me.

"Well, that's certainly a good start to the evening," she whispers when we pull apart.

"Yeah. We should go now, before my resolve crumbles, and we end up spending another night in bed instead," I reply, taking her hand.

"I certainly wouldn't complain if that happened." Tara grins when I pretend to be shocked.

"Why, Miss Tara, are you asking me to spend the night ravishing you in bed?"

"That depends. What will you do if I say yes?" She laughs when I swoop down and nuzzle her neck. "Ack, that tickles!"

"Good. Your punishment for being a brat and putting dirty thoughts in my head." I smack her on the butt, making her laugh harder.

"Whatever. Those dirty thoughts were well and truly already there." She swats my hand away and steps around me to head towards the elevator, still laughing.

I love it when things between us are fun and easy like this. I don't get to see this side of her often enough with everything she's got going on, but I'd give anything to have more of these moments. She deserves to smile more.

We make it to the view point at Mount Coot-tha with only a few minutes to spare. Twilight is already starting to fall, and Tara rests her head on my shoulder while we watch the lights of the city turn on below us.

"It's so pretty. I don't think I've ever been up here at this time of day," she says, her voice filled with awe.

"Oh good, I found a new experience for you," I reply with a laugh.

She lifts her head and regards me closely. "I've had so many new experiences with you."

I put my arm around her and draw her close. "That's good to hear. Cause I want to keep finding new experiences with you every day."

She smiles up at me and lifts on to her tiptoes to kiss me softly.

"What was that for?" I ask when she pulls away.

"For being so perfect."

I raise an eyebrow. "I don't know that I've ever been described as perfect before."

"Well, get used to it, mister." A small smile plays across her lips, and I kiss her temple before we turn to look back at the lights again.

A feeling I've not felt before settles over me, burrowing into my chest and blooming so fast that it almost takes my breath away. I rub my chest absently while I mull over the meaning behind it.

Is this what love feels like?

It's terrifying and exhilarating all at once, and I could easily become addicted to this feeling. Just like I'm addicted to this woman.

After dinner, we drive back to the apartment building before walking into the city. Tara swings my hand in hers while we walk along, a relaxed smile on her face. After a fairly emotional weekend, it's good to know that she's still capable of smiling like this. I remember all too well how it feels to watch a parent slip away, and I know that she's in for a lot more pain over the next few months. So far, she's leaned on me for support, which I am more than happy to provide. But I wonder how long it will be before anger sets in. Anger at the unfairness of it all. At being forced to deal with the strained relationship with her father before she was ready.

She hasn't spoken to her sister since their disagreement, and I can tell that's been weighing on her as well. But all I can do is be here when she's ready and hope that when she falls, it won't be without me.

"Have you given any more thought to what you're going to do with yourself long term?" she asks, pulling me from my reverie as we walk up towards the casino.

"Why, are you over working with me already?" I grin at her when she rolls her eyes.

"No, but I also know how bored you are by insurance."

I sigh. "I told you, I can't afford not to work, so I'm kind of limited."

She pulls me to a stop, swinging me around to face her. "That's just an excuse. I think you've convinced yourself that you aren't good enough, for some reason. But you would be an amazing teacher, Aiden. You're so patient and kind. Any kids who had you in their corner would be so lucky."

I consider her for a moment, reaching up to cup her cheek. "You're the one who's perfect, you know that?"

She scoffs and shakes her head. "Hardly. I'm nowhere near it. I'm angry all the time, and can't even get my stupid sister to get over herself and come back for Dad."

I cut her off by kissing her hard. After a moments hesitation, she kisses me back, and I run my fingers through her hair.

Eventually, I pull back and hold her gaze. "You are perfect. You are enough. And I'm in love with you."

Her mouth opens slightly, her lips open in the cutest little "Oh" while she stares at me.

"It's okay. You don't have to say it back. But I just needed you to know that I'm all in. You're it for me."

She swallows, her eyes tracing the features of my face as though she's trying to memorise them. "I love you, too. I didn't think I was ever going to find someone that I would say that to, but I know in my heart that you're it for me, too."

I pull her in again, kissing her forehead before wrapping my arms around her and holding her close. She melts into my embrace, and for a brief moment in time, anything feels like it could be possible with this amazing woman by my side.

38
DON'T NEED TO DO THIS

AIDEN

WHILE I'VE BEEN TELLING Tara that I'm not interested in going back to finish my degree, the more I think about it, the further the idea has burrowed its way into my brain. So much so that I've started looking into distance education options so that I can still work while I'm studying, at least for the non-practical components.

"I think it's a great idea," Sarah says during our weekly Face-Time catch up.

We do it every Sunday, and this week is the first time she's meeting Tara. So far it seems to be going well. It helps that they are both in agreement about what I should do with my future.

"I think I'm just hesitating because the idea of going back to studying at my age scares the absolute crap out of me," I reply, rubbing my hand up and down Tara's back while she snuggles into my side, her legs curled under her.

Tara looks up at me. "But why? It's not like you're retirement age or anything. You still have plenty of years in the workforce ahead of you, and I can tell you're far more interested in teaching than insurance. That's my wheelhouse, not yours."

I laugh a little. "True. You definitely have more of a knack for it than I do."

"So, it's decided. Aiden will be going back to university to become the amazing teacher I know he'll be." Sarah claps her hands together, conversation settled as far as she's concerned. "Maybe you can move back here afterwards and we can finally work together."

Tara's grip on my waist tightens. "No, sorry, he's an Aussie again now." While her tone is joking, I can tell she would fight Sarah on it if she had to.

I brush a kiss against her temple. "Don't worry, I'm not going anywhere. Sorry, Sare, you're just going to have to move here."

My best friend taps her cheek thoughtfully. "Hm. It sounds interesting. I've never been to Australia. Maybe Simon and I can come for a holiday first before I drag him all the way down there with a one-way ticket." She grins at Simon, who just rolls his eyes.

As much as I'd love to have my best friend on the same continent once again, I can't imagine her making the move here. She's a creature of habit, and if she ever left London, it would be because something drastic had happened.

"How do you think your Dad is going to take it?" Sarah asks, her expression serious now.

I sigh. "I've got a meeting with him tomorrow. I might try and bring it up with him then."

"How sad is it that it takes a meeting at work for you to be able to have a conversation with your father," Sarah says, and Tara gives my waist another gentle squeeze.

Offering silent comfort, and understanding what it's like to have a fractured relationship with a father.

"I guess I don't really know much different. But anyway, enough about all that, how are things with you guys? How was the first week back at school?"

We continue to chat for another hour, only wrapping up the call once Tara starts yawning.

We've fallen into the habit of spending every night at her place. I do wonder if maybe we've moved a little fast, but the desire to spend every moment possible with her is hard to fight, and I know she feels it too.

"Bed time?" I ask, cuddling her close once we hang up with Sarah and Simon.

"Yeah. I think today's visit with Dad has drained me more than I realised."

We sit quietly for a moment while she musters the energy to get to her feet. I try not to think too hard about how worn out she'd looked when she'd returned from the hospital a few hours ago. She'd mentioned her Dad wasn't particularly chatty today, and I can tell that the reality of his declining health is setting in.

"Come on, let's get to bed." I get her moving, and while she goes into the bathroom to clean her teeth, I move around the flat, turning off lights and finding Toulouse, carrying him into her room after I scoop him out from behind the TV cabinet.

The little kitten burrows in my neck and purrs, which makes me a little emotional. Who would have thought that the love of an animal could make you feel special?

Tara comes out of the bathroom and a soft smile spreads across her face when she takes in the view of me sitting at the end of her bed with a small black ball of fluff pushing its head against my neck.

"Just when I thought I couldn't be more attracted to you," she says, coming to stand in front of me and runs a hand through my hair.

"Oh really? Tell me more about this attraction," I reply, resisting a little when she takes him from me.

She gives him her own little cuddle before safely depositing him in the bathroom with his bed and shuts the door before moving to stand in front of me again. I slide back slightly and pull her forward so that she's straddling my lap.

"Well, in case you haven't worked it out, I'm really, really hot for you," she whispers in my ear.

The feel of her breath against my neck makes me groan, and I turn my head to capture her lips with mine, sliding my hand up to clasp the back of her neck.

"Funny. Cause I'm really, really hot for you, too," I reply, before giving her lower lip a soft nip.

We continue kissing while our hands explore each others bodies at a leisurely pace. She pulls my shirt over my head, and all thoughts of going to bed seem to have fled her mind when she begins rolling her hips, grinding against my semi. I slide my hands up her sides before pulling her singlet over her head and sucking her right nipple into my mouth while tweaking the other between my fingers. She gasps and tips her head back, a moan escaping her lips. Moving both hands down to her hips, I guide her against me, moving her faster until she begins to whimper, a sign that she's close.

"That's it, Love. Let go," I whisper against her breast, and she cries out.

I slow her movements while she comes back down, and she presses her forehead against mine, our noses touching while we close our eyes and just breathe together. We sit like that for a moment, the peacefulness of the room settling around us.

"Take off your pants," she whispers eventually, and I open my eyes to find her looking at me with a twinkle in her eye.

My heart rate picks up when she gets to her feet, looking utterly delicious in nothing but her lace g-string and her hair hanging over both breasts. If I wasn't hard before, this would certainly have set me off.

I stand up, and she tugs my sweatpants down my legs, kneeling before me. I swallow hard when she looks up at me with wide eyes, before dropping her gaze to my erection.

"You don't need to do this," I say quietly.

She shakes her head. "I want to make you feel good," she replies before running her hand up and down my shaft.

I inhale sharply, and feel a muscle in my jaw tick when I grit my teeth, fighting against the urge to pull her up and bury myself inside her. She's become more adventurous each time we've been together, but this is the first time she's knelt before me like this, and I want to let her lead this time.

With a tentative swipe of her tongue, she moves forward and takes me into her mouth. I groan, holding perfectly still while she moves her head back and forth, trying to take more of me each time. She eventually finds her rhythm, and my eyes roll back in my head when she reaches up to cup me, massaging while she moves her head faster. Taking my hand, she moves it to the back of her head, urging me to guide her how I need her.

Cautious about making her gag, I apply only a small amount of pressure. Eventually, my body takes over, and I hold her head still while my hips thrust forward. She massages harder, looking up at me with an intense look in her slightly watery eyes.

"I'm so close, Love. You're gonna have to decide how you want to do this," I manage to get out between clenched teeth.

It's like I've presented her with a challenge, and she takes me further in her mouth, her eyes watering more when I hit the back of her throat. Taking that as my queue, a few thrusts later, I'm spilling down her throat.

Breathless, she pulls away and I collapse back down to sit on the edge of the bed again.

"Was that okay?" she asks, still on her knees before me.

I urge her back up and pull her onto my lap again. "That was amazing."

She smiles and I pull her face to mine to kiss her once again.

I don't know if I'll ever get used to this feeling, but I know I never want it to stop. She's pulling me right in to her orbit and I don't know what I'll do if she ever decides she's had enough.

. . .

Two hours after arriving at the office the next morning, I meet Dad at reception when I'm on my way to the printer.

"Got time for that meeting now?" he asks, nodding towards the conference room.

"Sure. Can we grab a coffee from downstairs first, though? I was just about to get one." He nods, and I grab my paperwork, handing it to Celeste when I can see that Dad isn't keen on waiting around. "Can you take this to Tara, please?"

Celeste glances between us both before nodding and heading back towards the main office area. I follow Dad to the lift and we head downstairs together, neither of us really feeling the need to fill the silence between us.

After ordering my almond milk latte, I wait for Dad to get his long black before following him back to the lift.

"So, what did you want to talk to me about?" I ask, taking a seat across from him at the long table.

"We got the numbers through for the last quarter and I wanted to congratulate you. You've exceeded John's numbers and actually set a company record."

I take a moment to process his words. "I'm sorry, but how is that possible?"

"Well, you've brought in almost double the amount of clients that John was bringing in, and you've made a few significant sales on top of that." Dad looks so proud, but something doesn't feel right about accepting this without Tara sitting next to me.

"If anyone deserves the congratulations, it's Tara. There is absolutely no way that I would have made the sales without her, and honestly, most of the clients only signed up because of her knowledge."

Dad shakes his head. "Why are you so determined to keep mentioning your assistant?"

"Because she's more than an assistant, and you seem determined not to notice the value she brings to the company," I retort.

"Is this because you are sleeping with her?"

I am genuinely trying to understand just how oblivious he is to how talented Tara is, and also incredibly pissed off that he'd bring that up in the office.

"It's got nothing to do with our relationship. Since the day I arrived, Tara has carried the majority of the load while I wrapped my head around everything, and she more than deserves to be rewarded for all her hard work."

Dad lets out a frustrated sigh, shaking his head. "Well, that's not how it works here. Advisers have their assistants, and that's that."

"Well, maybe it's time you considered making her an adviser then?" I say, throwing down the challenge.

"But then, how will you keep going without her? If she really is the one keeping you afloat, you need her."

This conversation is going around in circles, and I'm over it. "Well, maybe I won't be here for that to be a problem."

Dad freezes, his coffee half way to his mouth. "What's that supposed to mean?"

I shrug. "I'm just saying, I don't find insurance particularly riveting. I've been considering going back to finish my degree."

Dad laughs. "You can't be serious? There's no money in teaching."

I'm impressed that he even remembered that was what I'd wanted to do before everything happened.

"Not everything is about money. It's just something I'm thinking about. Shouldn't you, as my father, want me to do something I enjoy instead of ending up in a job that I hate?" He studies me for a moment, sitting back in his chair with his arms crossed. After a few more moments of silence, I shake my head and get to my feet. "Never mind. I can see this conversation is going nowhere. I'd better get back to work."

39
YOU SHOULDN'T SETTLE

Monday arrived far too soon. It followed a weekend that had both been one of the happiest of my life, yet one of the saddest after a visit with my father. While my personal life has become tough to navigate, work has also been incredibly busy. Now that Aiden and I are working as a team, we've been bringing in more work than any of the other advisers, which has been both a blessing and a curse.

"Have you got those quotes sorted for the house for Deidre?" I ask Aiden, walking into his office after lunch.

I've barely seen him all morning, since Celeste had dropped off the documents he'd gone to collect and said that David had kidnapped him.

"Yeah, I just finished it. You've finished their other quotes?" He rolls his chair back and stretches his arms above his head.

"All ready to go. I'll send them all over now. How did it go with David?" I lean against his desk, and he rolls forward slightly to run his hands up the outside of both of my thighs.

I glance over my shoulder to make sure no one is watching us from outside, but our colleagues all appear to be otherwise occupied.

"Playing it a little dangerous there, mister," I say, smiling a little when he plays with the hem of my skirt.

"I like this outfit. Another new one from your latest Sylvia shopping trip?" he asks, sliding his hand up a little further, grazing the skin of my inner thigh.

I fight back a gasp when he lightly traces a path up and down with his finger, watching my face with a dangerous look in his eye.

"Yes. I'm slowly replacing my entire wardrobe," I reply, my voice shaking a little.

He smirks, sliding his hand up a little higher. Finally reaching my self preservation limit, I bat his hand away, and he laughs, rolling back again to create some space between us.

"So what did David want?" I rest my hands on either side of my hips and slide back on the desk a little more. Aiden's expression changes slightly, and I cock my head to the side. "What's that look for?"

"He wanted to congratulate me on the sales coming in." He looks over my shoulder before bringing his gaze back to mine. "Apparently we broke some sort of quarterly record."

"Oh. Well, that's good news then. Why don't you seem happy?"

He lets out a sigh and runs a hand through his hair. "Because he was making a point of congratulating me. Like I was the only one doing the work. You should have been there with me."

"Ah... I see." Warring emotions rise up within me. Happiness that we work so well as a team clashes with frustration that no matter how hard I work, David seems determined to disregard the value I bring to not just this team, but the company as a whole.

My feelings must be showing on my face, because Aiden moves forward again, taking my left hand and squeezing it gently. "I reminded him that I didn't do this alone."

I smile, squeezing back. "I know you're championing for me.

But it seems like he's pretty determined to ignore the fact that I'm doing work above my pay grade."

He sighs. "I'm sorry. When my bonus comes through, I'm splitting it with you."

I shake my head. "I can't ask you to do that."

"You're not asking me to do anything. You earned it just as much as I did, if not more. It's your knowledge that is giving the clients confidence to go with us."

"It's not really about the money, though. I mean, yes, the bonus would be nice. But I think I'd like the recognition more. I work my ass off for this company. I carried John for years without so much as a thank you from David. I kept thinking, if I just continue proving my worth, one day he will have to acknowledge everything I do." I shrug, a lump forming in my throat. "But I'm starting to realise that it's never going to happen."

His eyes widen. "You're not thinking about leaving, are you?"

I smile, reaching forward to touch his cheek before remembering where we are. I let my hand drop back to my side. "I don't know. But something needs to change."

"I'll talk to him again. I'll make him understand." Aiden looks so frustrated, and I know, if I let him, he'd march into his father's office right now.

"It's okay. If he hasn't worked it out by now, he's never going to. I'm just glad that I was able to help you find your feet. At least for now, until you start studying."

He shakes his head. "I still haven't decided if I'm doing that yet."

"But I can tell you want to. We can make anything work, if that's what you want to do."

He raises an eyebrow while the corners of his mouth lift a little. "*We* can, huh?"

I smile again, and this time I do allow myself to touch his face for a moment. "Yep. We're a *we* now, sorry."

"I think I can handle that." His gaze drops to my lips, and I can see the war within him as he fights against the urge to kiss me.

"Hey Aiden, have you seen -" Damien's voice startles us both, and we jump. "Ah, Tara, there you are."

I shoot to my feet, realising how close we'd moved towards each other throughout the conversation. "Yep, here I am. Do you need help with something?"

Damien hesitates, looking from me to Aiden, and then back again. "Uh, yeah. Can I get you to look over a quote for me? Sarah's off today and she normally double checks my quotes before I send them to the clients," he says, and I nod.

"Yep, I can do that." I know I sound far too eager, and try to dial back the nervous enthusiasm. "Email me the client details and I'll check the system."

Damien waits a moment, and I can tell that he's noticed the weirdness. But he doesn't say anything further, just nods and heads back to his desk.

I look back at Aiden and let out a breath. "Perhaps we should continue this conversation later?"

He nods, glancing over my shoulder again. "Probably a good idea."

I make a beeline for my desk and avoid looking over at Damien in case he's watching me. The last thing we need is anyone talking about Aiden and I. It would just add an extra layer of stress to our lives that neither of us needs right now.

Maybe it really is time for me to start looking for a new job.

Several hours later, I look up to see that the office has emptied while I've been frantically trying to work through several detailed quotes. When the requests had come through, I'd put my earphones in and knuckled down, determined to get it done before I went home.

But now that I'm looking around, I've realised that not only has everyone gone home, the sun has set, making the florescent lights appear even harsher than usual.

"Aiden? Are you still here?" I call out.

"Yeah, of course. I wasn't going to leave you behind." His voice drifts out from his office.

Pushing back from my desk, I stand and stretch before moving towards the open door. I find him sitting behind his desk, looking a little disheveled. His wavy hair is rumpled, like he's been running his hands through it continuously, and he's loosened his tie to undo the top button.

"You okay?" I ask, coming to stand beside him.

He's got the application page open for the online university course I'd sent him a few days ago, suggesting it can't hurt just to look at what his options are.

"You're applying?" I ask, running my hand through his hair.

"I'm considering it," he replies, resting his head against my hip.

"I think you should do it. Applying doesn't mean you have to go. But at least you'll have your options open."

He sighs, raking his hand through his hair once again. "I don't know why I'm so resistant to this," he mumbles.

I smile. "It's hard starting over. But you've already done that, and you know you can do it. Here, I'll help." I move to grab the chair from the other side of his desk, but he pulls me down onto his lap so that I'm facing the computer. "Ooff. I'm going to squash you if I sit here."

He brings his arm around me and pulls me further back into his lap. "No you won't," he says, his voice sounding a little rough in my ear.

I turn slowly to look back at him, noting the desire in his eyes. "Why, Mister Sanderson, are you trying to seduce me?"

He smirks back, sliding his other hand slowly up my leg. "I would never dream of it, Miss Richards."

"Glad to hear it. Because it would be highly unprofessional for us to do anything naughty in the office," I reply, putting on a prim accent, even as my heart begins to beat faster in my chest with each inch he moves his hand up under my skirt.

"Terribly unprofessional." He presses his lips to the spot where my neck curves to meet my shoulder, and I shiver.

"Anyone could walk in," I murmur, although I make no move to stop the slow progression of his hand.

"Everyone has left. But be a good girl and come for me quick, just to be safe." He kisses his way up my neck while his fingers work their way between my legs, and he circles my clit over the fabric of my underwear, applying just the right amount of pressure.

I moan, muffling the sound with my hand while he picks up the pace. I'm not sure if it's the adrenaline from worrying about someone walking in on us, or just the overall affect he has on my body, but it's not long before an orgasm begins to build. I can feel him growing hard against my back the closer I get, and I love that he is so turned on by bringing me pleasure. Just as my body begins to unfurl, he pulls my face around with his other hand and kisses me hard while I cry out, muffling the sound.

"God, you're so bloody sexy," he whispers against my lips while my body quivers.

"I want you," I reply once my wits have returned to me.

"Well, if you insist." He helps me up before moving to the door and locking it, pulling the blinds closed. "Just in case. I don't want to scare any cleaners if they rock up," he says when he takes note of my raised eyebrow.

He comes back to stop in front of me, sliding his hand behind my head to hold me still while he crushes his lips to mine. I lean into his chest, opening my mouth to him when he runs his tongue along my lower lip. He walks me backwards until my butt hits his desk. Spinning me around, he kisses his way down my neck while pulling my skirt up. But he stops, letting out a frustrated sigh and resting his forehead against my shoulder.

"What's wrong?" I ask.

"I don't have a condom."

"Oh." Disappointment sets in for a moment, but I turn to look at him over my shoulder. "I'm on the pill."

He lifts his head and meets my gaze. "What are you saying?"

"I'm saying, we could still do this... if you want?"

He considers me for a moment. "Are you sure?"

I bite my lip and nod. "I've never had unprotected sex before. I'd like you to be my first. Like you've been my first with so much else."

He kisses my temple. "It will be a first for me, too." He slides my underwear down my legs, helping me step out of them in my heels. "These shoes are just the right height for this. Do you have any idea how many times I've imagined bending you over this desk?"

My heart skips a little at the possessive tone in his voice. "No. How did you imagine this? What was I doing?"

"You were giving me attitude because I'd pissed you off. So I'd bend you over and remind you that you work for me." He moves between my legs and runs his finger over my clit while pushing me down to rest my cheek against the cool desk top. My breath hitches when he slides his finger inside me. "And then I'd make you come so hard you'd see stars."

I moan when he begins moving his finger in and out, adding a second finger to stroke my inner wall. "I like this fantasy."

"Oh, it's not a fantasy, Tara. This is real life." His hand disappears and I hear him undo his fly.

The empty feeling is soon replaced by pleasure when he slides inside me. We both moan, the lack of any barrier between us making the feeling even more intense.

"Jesus. I'm not going to last long like this. You feel amazing." He thrusts, small and shallow, like he's worried that anything harder will send us both over the edge too soon.

"Oh god," I moan, moving my hands up to grip the edge of the desk above my head. "Please, fuck me, Aiden."

My words unleash something primal in him, and he begins thrusting into me hard and fast. He slips a hand around to rub my clit, and another orgasm races to the surface. As it explodes through me, he moves his hand up, bending over me from behind to grip my hands tightly and changing the angle. He hits my g-spot, and my vision blurs when a different type of orgasm follows close behind. I don't even attempt to keep quiet this time, too overcome by the pleasure rolling through me.

"Am I fucking you to your liking?" he growls into my ear, his breath hot against the back of my neck.

"Yes. Keep going," I whimper.

Using my body for his own pleasure now, he drives my hip bones into the edge of the desk. It's the most erotic experience of my life, and I absolutely love it. I can feel him growing harder inside me, moments before he moans, and his own release rockets through him.

He eventually stills, resting his head against my shoulder.

"Was it as good as you imagined?" I whisper.

He brushes a kiss to the back of my neck. "No. It was a thousand times better."

40
ALL THE WAYS YOU'RE WRONG

TARA

AFTER SEVERAL FAILED attempts to catch up, Tuesday morning rolls around and I'm sitting beside Aiden on the couch with my laptop open on the coffee table in front of us while we talk to Kylie and Seth.

"So, what are your intentions with my sister-wife?" Kylie asks, her expression full of mischief.

"Kylie," I say with a sigh.

We've been talking for about half an hour, and she has been on her best behaviour until now.

"Why does everyone say my name like that?" she asks, pretending to pout.

"Because you're a loveable pain in the ass," a voice says from behind the screen.

"Lincoln?! Get your butt where I can see you!" I demand, leaning forward with a smile when Seth's best friend and the fourth member of our European tour group appears behind them.

"Hey Miss Tara. Tara's boyfriend," he adds with a nod in Aiden's direction.

"His name is Aiden," I say with a stern look on my face.

"It's okay, I'm good with being known as Tara's boyfriend," Aiden says, squeezing my knee.

"Smooth. I like him," Lincoln says, nodding.

"Yeah, he's alright." I shoot a cheeky grin at Aiden, who just rolls his eyes before pulling me into his side to kiss my temple.

"Ugh, you guys are so fucking cute," Kylie says, pretending to gag.

"Excuse me, but did I not just walk in on you two doing unspeakable things to each other about twenty minutes ago? You are not allowed to make gagging faces over temple kisses." Lincoln wags his finger at the pair of them.

Seth's face turns a very cute shade of red, while Kylie just shrugs.

"Whatever, you guys have been gone for five days. Not my fault you didn't knock."

"Not my fault that the two of you couldn't manage to make it any further than the hall," Lincoln grumbles.

"You loved it." She reaches over to ruffle his hair, and he bats her hand away.

"While I admit that it warms my heart to see how sickly in love the pair of you are, I could have done without seeing Seth's naked ass anymore than I already have to in the locker room, thank you very much."

"You know the solution to all of this is to just knock, right?" Seth joins the conversation finally.

"I did knock!"

"Yeah, and then opened the door with your key. One would normally wait to hear the words 'come in' before just sauntering on in," Kylie shoots back.

They continue to bicker while Seth sighs, and Aiden and I start laughing at the absurdity of it all. Who needs TV when you've got the Kylie and Lincoln show right in front of you.

"Children, perhaps we should let Tara and Aiden head off to

work?" Seth says, ending all talk about voyeurism (Kylie) and having sex in public spaces (Lincoln).

It must be exhausting for the poor man to deal with the pair of them on a daily basis.

"Sadly, yes, we should probably go," I reply, patting Aiden's knee.

"Fine. Have fun at work! And Aiden, I expect a full essay on how you'll be treating my girl like the queen she is," Kylie says, pointing her finger at the screen.

"I can do that. I could write you a novel, if you'd prefer?" Aiden replies.

"Seriously, Tara, I like this guy," Lincoln adds, nodding towards Aiden. "You're allowed to date her."

I roll my eyes. "Goodbye family."

We hang up to a chorus of goodbyes and I sigh.

"You handled that all very well," I tell Aiden as we get up and start gathering our things together.

He grins at me as he opens the door for me. "Are you kidding? That was hilarious. Who's Lincoln?"

"Seth's best friend. He plays on the same team as Seth and from what I can tell, pretty much lives at their house."

"You're friends are great, Love. I'm glad you have so many people who love you."

I slide my arm around his back while we wait for the elevator. "Yeah... They are pretty awesome. Sometimes I forget just how lucky I am."

"I think they are just as lucky to have you." He turns me around to brush his lips against mine as the elevator arrives, and it takes all my resolve not to keep him there in that hallway, remaining in our little bubble together.

But sadly, we have to head into the office.

After buying our drinks, he heads up first while I linger near the busy cafe. Although it's been two months now, neither of us are interested in dealing with the office gossip circle, so we've been avoiding being seen together much outside of the office. Something I thought we'd been doing fairly well.

Until now.

"So, what's going on with you and Aiden?" Felicity appears out of nowhere, startling me while I'm scrolling through my phone.

Fumbling to keep from dropping the device, it takes me a moment to register what she'd said. Straightening up, I look over to see her smirking, not a single hair out of place on her perfect blonde head. No matter how nice my clothes are, I will never be able to come close to the perfectly put together look that she has. But I don't particularly care, because as far as I'm concerned, her ugly personality takes away the shine of her appearance.

"What do you mean, what's going on with me and Aiden?" I ask, stalling.

She tsks and rolls her eyes. "Don't play dumb. I've seen you guys arrive together every morning for weeks. And last night, when I was at the gym across the street, I saw you both leaving the building, and you were holding hands."

"I didn't realise you were so interested in my life, Felicity. What business is it of yours, anyway?" I ask, figuring denying it isn't worth it.

"I just find it really interesting that the boss's hot son shows up, and you suddenly start dressing better and actually giving a shit about your appearance. Then you get taken to Singapore even though no other assistant has ever been to any of those conferences before."

The comments on my appearance hit me hard, and I struggle not to let it show on my face, pulling my features into a glare instead. "Wow... I don't even know where to start with all the ways you're wrong there. But I don't need to justify anything to you, so you can just keep on wondering what's going on." I surprise myself with how nonchalant I seem, given that my insides feel like I've just been on a rollercoaster.

Felicity gives me a disdainful look. "Whatever. I'm on to you, Tara. You knew you would never get any further in your career, so decided to jump into bed with Aiden and sleep your way to the top instead."

I don't bother replying to her, continuing to watch her with a stony glare and wait for her to disappear back to the cave she slithered from. When she fails to get any information out of me, she spins on her heel and marches off towards Amber, who has just entered the lobby.

Once they are both out of sight, I open my phone again, noticing for the first time that my hand is shaking.

TARA

Just got cornered by Felicity. She's seen us holding hands and basically accused me of sleeping with you to get further in my career.

AIDEN

Serious?! She actually said that to you?

It's good to know he doesn't believe anything like that about me.

AIDEN

If anyone is furthering their career by sleeping their way to the top, it's me. It was my secret plan all along - get you to fall in love with me so that you'd take pity on me.

I laugh, despite myself, imagining him grinning while he typed that, trying to defuse the situation for me.

TARA

I can't believe I fell for it so easily. It's those dimples, they'll get you out of anything.

AIDEN

True, that's what Mum always told me, too.

My heart hurts a little at the mention of his Mum, and I send a silent thank you to her, wherever she is now, for raising such an amazing guy. I reply with a kiss emoji before dropping my phone back into my handbag. Figuring it's been enough time for the piranhas to have made their way upstairs, I sigh and head towards the elevators, reluctantly making my way up to the office.

Celeste greets me when I walk through reception, but there's something off about her expression. With a sinking feeling in my stomach, I realise Felicity has already started spreading the news about Aiden and me. I consider turning around and walking back out of the office, but know that would just add fuel to the fire, so I hold my head high and march towards my desk.

Damien steps out of Aiden's office a few moments later, followed by the man himself, who gives me a smile while nodding along to whatever Damien is saying.

"Hey Tara. Thanks for your help yesterday. Any chance I can get your expert eye to look over a few more for me today?" Damien gives me what I'm sure he thinks is his most charming grin.

I laugh a little. "Sure. Send through the details and I can check them out."

He pats my shoulder and heads off towards his desk, leaving Aiden and I standing together next to my desk.

"So the cat is well and truly out of the bag now. I just saw Celeste, and it was obvious Felicity had already told her about us."

Aiden winces. "I'm sorry. Do you want me to say something to her?"

I shake my head and sigh. "No. That would probably just make it worse. But it's definitely going to make keeping off their radar a whole lot harder."

"I guess all we can do is hope that some other drama comes up and they lose interest in us."

"I'm just going to ignore them and hope when they see that my career isn't suddenly skyrocketing that there's no perks coming my way," I say, dumping my bag on the desk with more force than I intended, knocking my desk phone out of its cradle with a clatter.

A few heads lift to see the source of the noise, and I cringe. All these years doing my best to keep to myself, and in the space of ten minutes, it's all coming undone.

Aiden moves to touch my arm, but stops himself when I shake my head slightly. "It's fine. Let's just get to work, shall we."

He hesitates for a moment, before nodding.

Once he heads back into his office, I sit down and turn my laptop on, silently cursing nosey-gossips and wishing I cared less about what everyone was no doubt saying about me.

41

DON'T REGRET A SINGLE MOMENT

AIDEN

AFTER A PARTICULARLY UNCOMFORTABLE day at work, Tara has been eerily quiet on our walk home. While she isn't always the chattiest, I can tell that our relationship becoming fodder for the office gossips has affected her more than she's letting on.

When we reach our building, I lead the way into the lift, hitting the button for the penthouse automatically.

"I think I need a night to myself tonight," Tara says, standing in the open door.

Sensing her unease, I nod and hit the button for my floor as well. "Okay. You know you can talk to me though, right?"

She gives me a tense smile and steps further into the lift to allow the doors to close behind her. "I know. I just need a moment to process everything."

I reach out to touch her arm, worried that if I was to try for anything more, like a hug, it will spook her. "I get that. Just know I'm here for you, okay?"

She nods and lets out a shaky breath. The lift arrives at my floor, and after giving her a quick kiss goodbye, I step out into the hall. Turning back, I give her a wave as the doors close, pushing aside the growing sense of unease.

Determined not to think about it too much, I spend the next hour cooking myself some dinner with the meagre ingredients I have in the apartment. I hadn't realised how much time I'd been spending at Tara's until now, and the loneliness I thought that I'd moved passed raises its ugly head. Deciding I need to get outside and get the endorphins flowing, I change into workout clothes and go for a run. I've slacked off a little lately - the joys of being in a new relationship I guess - and the first kilometre is tough until I find my groove.

Deciding to make it a longer one, I head back through the city, dodging commuters while my music pumps through my ear buds. It feels good to be out in the crisp spring air, and I pause for a break on the footbridge at the end of South Bank, taking a seat on one of the benches and watching the sun go down.

My phone vibrates in my pocket, and I pull it out to find a message from Tara.

TARA

> Do you think I'm only with you because you're the boss's son? Everything that Felicity said is just going round and round in my head.

I shake my head. I swear, when I see Felicity again, I'm going to be having some choice words with her.

AIDEN

> I don't think that at all, and I know you don't either. Try not to let her get in your head. That's exactly what she wants.

The little text bubble appears and disappears several times while I wait for her response. I can tell she's started to work herself up over the events of today, and I wish she hadn't pushed me away. One thing I've worked out with Tara, though, is that she needs to work through things on her own. She doesn't like to ask for help or rely on others.

TARA

I just wish we'd done a better job of keeping it private. We should have realised that people would work it out eventually.

AIDEN

We shouldn't have had to worry about hiding our relationship, though. It's none of their business. Dad is fine with it, so we just need to ride out the initial wave of interest, then I'm sure they'll find something else to talk about.

TARA

That's easy for you to say. No one is accusing you of sleeping your way to the top. I've worked so hard to get where I am, and now no one is going to take me seriously.

The unease from earlier reappears.

TARA

Maybe we should take a bit of a break. We moved so fast, right?

Yep, she's gotten in her head about everything and is spiralling. Abandoning my plans for a longer run, I get up and start running back towards our building. The urge to get there before she can talk herself into making this theoretical break a real one has me running faster than I ever have before.

When I get back, I take the lift up to her apartment and knock on the door. I can hear her moving around inside, and she opens the door a moment later. Her eyes are a little bloodshot, and I can tell she's been crying.

"I wanted to say this in person," I say, making no move to go inside. "I think we moved at the right pace for us. I don't regret a single moment between us and I would do it all over again. If you need space, I'll give it to you. But I need you to know this. I'm not going anywhere. I'm so in love with you that you're the first thing on my mind every morning and the last thing on my mind when I go to sleep. I love waking up beside you and going to sleep with my arms around you. I love dancing with you and hanging out on the couch. I love everything about our lives together. I don't give a crap about what some woman at work has to say about us, because I know the truth of who you are, and you are the most amazing woman I have ever met."

She swallows hard, gripping the door handle while watching me, her eyes glistening with more unshed tears. I step closer and lift her chin slightly so that I can brush my lips against hers in a gentle kiss. I don't push for anything more, and step back after only a few heartbeats, fixing her with an earnest look.

"I'll see you tomorrow."

I don't wait for her to reply, just head back to the lift, which is thankfully still there. Once the doors close, I sag back against the wall and run a hand through my hair, hoping I didn't just fuck things up further. But I was completely honest. I don't regret a moment of our time together, and I don't think she does either. She has so much going on in her life that it's no surprise she's feeling hesitant, but it's my job to show her how right our relationship is.

I take a shower once I'm back in my apartment, and settle on the small balcony with a beer and a book. Anything to keep my mind from running through scenarios in my head. Cause I don't know if I can handle it if she decides we shouldn't be together after all.

While I'm struggling to get into the book, my phone vibrates on the table, and I dive for it. I've become that person - the one who is obsessed with their phone and desperate to hear from the one person who can make everything better.

TARA

I love you, too. And I don't want a break. But I think I need a little time to work out how to navigate my way through this.

Relief washes over me, and I put my beer down while I try to think of the right way to respond to that. She needs to know that she doesn't have to navigate her way through this alone. One thing I've learned is that, in a healthy relationship, we lean on each other instead of trying to do everything ourselves.

AIDEN

I'll follow your lead on this, but just remember, we're a team. In every part of our lives, not just work. As soon as you're ready, I'm here.

I put the phone back down and take a deep breath, hoping my words will comfort her enough to make the right choices, not just for herself, but for us both.

42

YOU WERE AN ASSHOLE

TARA

THE NEXT MORNING I do something I have never done before in all my working life.

I take a mental health day.

Even after Aiden's incredible monologue the night before, I can't face the office today. I feel sick to my stomach at the idea, so that feels like a good enough reason to call in sick. The mere thought of having to spend another day pretending not to notice the looks on everyone's faces when they see Aiden and I just talking to each other has stirred up anxiety I'd never felt before.

I've always shied away from the spotlight, preferring to keep to myself and let people like Kylie soak up the attention. So, to suddenly find myself in the limelight is so far outside of my comfort zone that my stomach is in knots.

I message Aiden so that he doesn't worry before deciding to see Dad.

Arriving unannounced, I find Jo leaning against the wall outside his room with tears in her eyes.

"Jo? Has something happened?" I ask, my heart rate picking up.

She wipes away a tear and shakes her head. "No. Nothing new, anyway. I just needed a moment." She has dark circles under her eyes, and I wonder how long it's been since she's had a full night's sleep.

I can't even comprehend how hard it must be for her. My grandparents passed before I was born, and from what I know, she doesn't have any family here, so she's doing it all alone. Coping with a spouse who is dying while raising two preteens can't be easy.

"I'm sorry," I say, and she cocks her head to the side.

"What for?"

"I haven't asked you how you're dealing with everything. I've been so focused on my relationship with Dad, but there's so much more going on than how I'm feeling."

She lets out a long breath and gives me a watery smile. "That's to be expected, Tara. Your relationship with your father has been tough, and you had no time to prepare yourself before having this all thrust upon you. I've been managing as okay as I can. With how his health has been going the last few weeks, it won't be much longer now, and it will be a relief for him to no longer be in pain."

Her words hit me hard, and I can feel my grip on my emotions slipping a little, but force myself to keep my tears in.

"Is he awake?" I ask, nodding towards the closed door.

"No. But I know he'll want to see you, so please go in. You did well with the girls, but you still need that time alone with him."

I nod and head towards the door. I reach for the handle before stopping and turning back.

"If you ever need my help with the girls, please let me know. Even if it's just for a few hours, so you can have some time for yourself."

She smiles and nods. "Thank you Tara. I would like that very much. So would the girls."

Nodding again, I turn back to the door before taking a deep breath and going inside.

Dad is hooked up to the IV once more, and the beeping of the machine is the only sound in the room while he sleeps peacefully. His skin has developed a yellowish tinge, and from the research I've been doing on kidney disease, he's showing all the signs of his body deteriorating.

I pull out my phone and send yet another message to my sister.

TARA

Hey. I know our last conversation wasn't great, and you probably don't want to hear this, but I really think you should try to talk to Dad. They are saying it won't be much longer, and I truly believe you will regret not saying goodbye. I love you and respect whatever decision you make, but I just thought you should know.

Knowing it's the middle of the night for her, I put my phone away and hope that when she sees the message in the morning, she'll be in the headspace to make the right decision.

Sitting down in the chair closest to the bed, I take Dad's hand in mine and just watch him sleep. I refuse to feel guilty about the lost years, knowing that it won't help with processing the grief, but I'm glad I have this time with him now.

After a few minutes, I start talking. I tell him all about my life over the last twelve years, sharing funny stories that I know would make him laugh. I tell him how much it hurt not having him around as I entered adulthood, but that I forgive him for what happened. While I'd thought I'd processed these feelings already, saying the words out loud has a cathartic effect on me.

It also puts my current problems into perspective.

Who cares what anyone at work has to say about my relationship with Aiden? We both know the truth and we're not doing anything wrong. Watching someone you love slip away can serve as a reminder of how precious life truly is. As I sit here sharing these thoughts with my sleeping father, I feel the broken pieces of myself slowly merge back together.

Now I just hope that my sister gets that same chance.

I spend the rest of the day with Dad and Jo. He wakes around lunch time and we end up having a great couple of hours together, just chatting and discussing mundane things until Jo leaves, returning with Jordan and Piper after school. For the first time, it feels like spending time with family.

While I'm getting ready to leave, my phone dings, and I pull it out of my handbag, expecting to see a message from Aiden. Instead, I'm surprised to see Chris's name on the screen.

CHRIS

Hey. Have you got plans tonight?

While we're close, it's not like Chris to send me a message like this out of the blue, so once I've said goodbye to everyone and head back to my car, I dial his number.

"Hey," he says, answering after only one ring.

"Hey. Is everything okay?" I ask, arriving at the elevator just as the doors are closing.

"Yeah. Do you want to come to dinner at our place tonight? I have something I wanted to talk to you about."

Curiosity gets the better of me, and despite just wanting to go home and see Aiden, I agree to head to their place instead.

By the time I've pulled up in front of their house twenty minutes later, various scenarios have started doing the rounds in my head. It takes me a moment to register that Will's ute is parked across the street, and that just adds to my concern. Has something happened with Morgan and the baby?

"Hey," I call out as I walk in the front door.

After two and a half decades of friendship, knocking isn't something that happens anymore.

"We're in the kitchen," Morgan yells back.

She sounds normal, so I rule out problems with the baby.

Navigating my way through their lounge area that is littered with various tools and other equipment, I walk into the kitchen to find Chris and Morgan preparing dinner. Will is doing something in the ceiling, with half his body missing while he stands on a ladder.

"What's going on?" I ask, very confused.

"Will is checking stuff out so we can start renovating in the next few months," Morgan replies, and I raise an eyebrow.

"You're starting renovations now? How long will it take to finish them all? Isn't that going to be stressful with a baby?"

She shrugs. "Yeah, but once we're done with it, we'll finally have our dream home, and we'll have it completed before the tiny human starts walking, which would be even worse."

"I guess. Is that what you wanted to talk to me about?" I ask Chris.

He shakes his head. "No. Hang tight til we get dinner sorted and then we can chat about that. Why weren't you at work, anyway?"

I sigh. "I was up at the hospital."

Morgan looks up quickly. "Is everything okay with your dad?"

I shake my head, feeling my throat constrict a little with emotion. "He doesn't have much longer, apparently."

"Oh honey. I'm so sorry." She steps away from the stove to give me a hug, and I let her hold me tight for a few moments.

Once she returns to stirring whatever is in the pot, I turn to see that Will has emerged from the ceiling and is watching me with concern. Of all the people in this room, he knows the most about what our family went through after Dad left. Despite our recent issues, it's hard to forget how much he and his family supported us through it.

"I probably shouldn't ask this, but is Annelisa going to come back to see him?" Chris asks, flicking a cautious look towards Will before returning his gaze to me.

"I honestly don't know. I've told her what's going on and that I think she should speak to him. But the ball's in her court now. I know she'll regret it if she doesn't at least speak to him on the phone, though. Regardless of how she's felt about him over the years, he's still our dad."

"Annie will come around," Will says, and the three of us turn to look at him.

It's the first time he's spoken about her in front of me in three years, and hearing him use the nickname that only he used for her is like a blast from the past. The utter conviction in his tone reminds me how well he knows her. I just hope he's right.

Will doesn't stay for dinner, saying he needs to get home to his dog, which is another surprise for me, because I didn't even know he'd gotten one. I hadn't realised just how out of the loop I am on his life these days, and that makes me sad. I miss the way our friendship used to be.

Once he heads off, the others finish making dinner and usher me towards the table.

"So, enough suspense. What's going on?" I ask, stabbing a piece of broccoli with my fork.

"I've been promoted at work to senior partner, and that means my job is up for grabs. It's up to me to fill the role, and I think you'll be perfect for it."

I stare at Chris for a moment, not entirely sure I heard him properly. "What?" I ask.

He laughs. "You heard me."

"But... You can just hire me without having to talk to anyone about it?"

"I told you, I'm a senior partner now. They trust me to find someone who will be a good fit with the company, and I've spoken to them about you in the past."

I put down my fork and sit back in my chair, lost for words.

It's never occurred to me before, but Chris has always been such a champion for my career progression. And here he is, once again putting me forward for a role that would help me move my way up in the industry.

He tells me about the salary and explains what the role entails, which sounds too good to be true. Morgan watches the conversation with a smile, staying quiet, which is very unlike her.

Once he's finished talking, I consider his offer silently while he watches me closely. "Can I think about it? With everything going on, I don't want to make a drastic decision without at least weighing up all my options."

Chris nods. "Of course. I just need to know in the next week or so, though."

"I'll let you know by the end of the week."

After all the work talk is finished, we fall into easy conversation while we finish dinner. Noting the fatigue on Morgan's face, I offer to clean up before I leave, but Chris waves me off, telling me he'll sort it out, and sending his wife to have a shower. I've always been a little in awe of their relationship, and I feel a tightening in my chest when he kisses her forehead and tells her he'll bring in a hot chocolate for her to have in bed.

He walks me to my car, and after promising to be in touch to let him know about the job, I head home, my thoughts all a jumble. When I park my car, I send Aiden a message to say I'm home and to come up if he wants.

When I get out of the elevator, I'm only slightly surprised to see Will sitting on the floor beside the door with his back against the wall.

"Hi," I say, unlocking the door and looking down at him.

"Hi," he replies, getting to his feet.

"Do you want to come in?"

He nods and follows me inside.

Sensing that this conversation is going to be draining, I walk to the fridge and pull out a bottle of wine. I rarely drink, and this bottle has been sitting here since Jake and Bri's wedding weekend, but with how my last forty-eight hours have been, I don't think tea is going to cut it.

Pouring us each a glass, I stand behind the bench and watch while he takes a seat on one of the stools.

"So," I say after a few moments of silence.

"So," he echoes, finally looking at me.

"What's up?"

He lets out a breath before replying. "I wanted to check on you. I hadn't realised stuff with your dad was this serious. I've wanted to reach out for a while, but with how things have been between us, I didn't know whether you'd welcome that or not."

This is the Will that I've missed. The big brother figure who cared about my wellbeing just as much as Annelisa's.

"It's been rough - I won't lie. Aiden has been really supportive, but he lost his mother a few months ago. I worry about burdening him too much with all of this when he's still going through his own grieving process."

Will nods. "He seems like a great guy. I'm glad you found someone who will be there for you."

I don't know why, but having Will tell me he likes Aiden is comforting. It's strange how, three years on and after everything that's happened between us, I still want him to approve of the man I'm with.

"He is honestly the best man I've ever met. Present company excluded, of course." I give him a smile, and his shoulders drop a little.

"I don't think I deserve to be put in that category these days, T. I was a really shitty friend to you after everything that happened with Annie, and you were right to shut me out after how I handled it all."

I lean my hip against the bench and pick up my glass.

"True. You were an asshole. And it really fucking hurt. I lost a sister and a brother all at once, and it felt like I was being punished for something that wasn't my fault." I choke a little on my words before taking a large mouthful of wine. "But I'm trying this new thing where I don't hold grudges for things that people did in the past. So I'm willing to move on from it if you promise never to do anything like that again."

He gets to his feet and comes around the bench, wrapping me in a hug that I sink into. A tear appears in my eye, and I squeeze both eyes shut to keep myself from crying.

"I can one hundred percent promise I will never be that dickhead ever again."

"Good. Because you were, indeed, a big dickhead," I reply, my words muffled against his chest.

He laughs. "The biggest dickhead."

I hear the apartment door open and we both look over to see Aiden standing there.

"Sorry. I didn't mean to interrupt," he says, looking from Will to me, confusion written all over his face.

"Will just popped around to check on me," I say, as Will takes a step back.

"Are you okay? Did something happen at the hospital?" Aiden immediately moves forward, stopping in front of me when Will moves aside.

"I'm okay. It's just been a bit of a draining day."

"I'm going to head off," Will says, nodding towards the door.

I step around Aiden and touch Will's arm. "Thank you. I mean it. I'm glad we talked."

He gives me a small smile. "I'm glad we talked, too. I'll see you soon, okay?"

"I'd like that," I reply, and he waves goodbye to us before heading out the door.

Once we're alone, Aiden pulls me into his arms, and I allow myself to draw comfort from his embrace while I fill him in on the events of the day. By the time I'm finished speaking, the emotions have worked their way to the surface, and the tears that I've been holding back start to flow.

He wipes them away and kisses my forehead. "Come on. Let's get you to bed. I think you need a good night's sleep and we can talk about it all more in the morning."

I nod, and we start the process of getting ready for bed. Once I've had my shower, I join him on the bed, and allow myself to drift off while he holds me close, feeling safe and loved.

43
I'M DONE

TARA

"I KNOW I sound like a broken record, but you know you can talk to me about anything, right?" Aiden murmurs into my hair the next morning when I roll into his arms.

I nod, burrowing into his side and slinging my arm over his stomach. "I know. I just... I'm not used to having someone to turn to when things get rough. It's always just been me."

He runs his hand up and down my back and brushes his lips against my temple. "That's not true, though. From what you've told me, your friends have always been there for you. Look at Bri and Kylie. You were struggling, and Bri showed up to take you to buy a cat because Kylie reached out to her from half a world away. You've got so many people who love you. You just need reminding of that every now and then, and that's okay. But you're not alone."

I lift my head to look him in the eye. He fixes a beautiful smile on me, causing the butterflies in my stomach to flutter, and I marvel for about the millionth time that he always has my back. Even when I tried to run, he was just there, refusing to let my own self doubt affect what we have together.

Unable to find the words to articulate everything I'm feeling, I lean down and kiss him softly. He cups the back of my head as he kisses me back, his actions unhurried, like he has all the time in the world just to lie in bed with me like this.

Unfortunately, we need to get up or we'll be late for work, so I pull away reluctantly, placing a hand on his chest.

"Thank you," I whisper.

He reaches up to push my hair back behind my ear. "Always."

We arrive at work, and I grip Aiden's hand tightly when we exit the elevator together. I fight the urge to let go when Celeste's gaze drops to our entwined fingers, and Aiden gives my hand a gentle squeeze.

"Hi Celeste. How are you this morning?" he asks, holding her gaze.

She hesitates for a moment before replying. "Um, good. How about you guys?"

"We're great, aren't we, Tara?" He smiles at me, and I clear my throat.

"Yep. Couldn't be better."

"Oh, and Celeste? I'd appreciate it if you ask Felicity to come and see me when she gets in," he says, and her eyes go wide.

There's no mistaking his tone. He wants to have a frank discussion with the leader of the office mean girls. While I want to tell him to let it go, it's not just me that she's spreading lies about, and he has every right to step in.

Celeste nods, swallowing hard, and I allow Aiden to lead me through to my desk. He gives me a quick peck on the lips in full view of everyone before continuing on to his office. I marvel at how he can just act like he's unaffected by the weight of so many eyes on us. I wish I was even half as cool about it all, but right now, I just want to shrink down into a little ball and hide from everyone.

• • •

As the morning goes on, it's obvious that something else is going on amongst the advisers and upper management. They've all been pulled into an unscheduled meeting. Felicity hasn't appeared at all, which has me on edge, torn between relief and anxiety.

By lunch time, I've barely been able to finish a single task, and I wonder if I should just call it a day.

Aiden comes out of the meeting with a troubled look on his face, making a beeline right for me.

Alarm bells start ringing loudly in my head. "What's going on?" I ask as soon as he reaches my side.

"Darryl quit abruptly last night, so we've had to spread his clients out amongst the rest of us until his replacement can take over."

Despite the additional workload for everyone, a jolt of excitement runs through me. "Who's replacing him?"

Is this it? Is this my chance to move up into a senior role finally?

But the next words out of Aiden's mouth deflate me entirely. "They are going to train Felicity to take over."

I freeze, staring at him open mouthed while I process his words. "You can't be serious?"

Aiden sighs, raking a hand through his already messy hair. It looks like he's been running his hands through it constantly.

"Apparently she approached Dad first thing this morning when she found out and put herself forward for the role. Made a convincing argument about how there is so little opportunity for the female staff in this office to move up and that it was time there was a female adviser."

I shake my head. "But... She's not even an assistant?" I struggle to keep my voice low, anger beginning to overcome me.

"I know. I am going to talk to Dad, but it seems like it's all already been decided." His expression tells me that he's as concerned about this as I am.

Felicity swans past us on her way to the printer, a vindictive smile on her face as her eyes meet mine, and something inside me snaps.

Jumping to my feet, I stalk towards David's office. I don't care in this moment that he's my boyfriend's father, even as said boyfriend follows quickly behind me.

I knock loudly on the open door before walking in. David is sitting behind his desk, looking at something on his computer, and he glances up with a surprised expression. Aiden closes the door behind us, but I don't care who has to hear what I'm about to say.

"Why did you give Darryl's job to Felicity?" I demand, and David's eyes widen.

"How did you know about that already?" His gaze flicks from me to Aiden, who is still standing behind me.

"She deserved to know," Aiden replies without a hint of apology in his voice.

David's eyes narrow before he looks back at me. "I don't understand why this is such a concern."

"Because she literally has no experience with clients. You've promoted her over several more qualified staff without even giving us a chance to apply for the job. It was one thing to slide your son in over our heads - sorry babe -" I shoot Aiden an apologetic look before continuing, "but to completely disregard the rest of us in favour of someone who has no experience and a reputation for being a truly horrible human being to every other person in this office is something else." I'm practically breathing fire at this point, and where I'd normally be trying to reign my anger in, this time I don't hold back. "You have repeatedly overlooked everything I've brought to this company in the time I've worked here. You've refused to acknowledge the hard work I've put in and the fact that I have a genuine relationship with the clients. One thing Felicity had right was the lack of opportunity for the women in this office, but you've given the role to the wrong woman."

David stares at me, his mouth hanging open. Deflating, I realise that no matter what I say, nothing is going to change for me here. I have nothing more to give, and as Aiden takes a step closer to stand immediately behind me, I know what I need to do.

"You know what David, I quit. I'm giving you my notice. I have so much leave owing to me, because I worked my ass to the bone here, so I will be leaving effective immediately and you will pay me out for every single second of that leave. I'm done."

Despite his spluttered protest, I have made up my mind. I turn on my heel and march right back out of his office. It's obvious from the looks on my now ex-colleagues faces they heard every word. A few of the women give me nods of approval, while others simply just stare, openmouthed, while I gather any personal belongings together and throw them into my handbag.

Aiden follows behind a few moments later, his expression wary while I slam my work pass on top of my laptop before picking up my phone to message Chris.

TARA

Just basically told David to go fuck himself.
That job offer still on the table?

His response comes through almost instantly.

CHRIS

Of course. Well done. When can you start?

"I'll see you at home," I tell Aiden, who nods before kissing me on the forehead.

With every eye in the office on me, I turn and walk out without another word, unable to believe that this is how it's ending.

Good luck to them all. I know I'm moving on to bigger and better opportunities than those available to me at Sanderson and Chambers.

For the first time in a long time, I feel confident in myself.

44
DO I KNOW YOU?

AIDEN

After Tara leaves, I walk back into my Dad's office and shut the door again.

He's still sitting at his desk, and I can tell he's struggling to understand what just happened. I take a seat across from him and wait for him to speak first.

Eventually, he gathers his wits about him and fixes me with a hard look. "You had no right to tell her anything."

I shake my head. "With everything she just said, that's the first place your mind went? You didn't tell any of us in that meeting that the information was confidential, and she would have found out when Felicity started lording over everyone. She's already walking around like she's untouchable, and you just handed her exactly what she wanted. I get that you're a little terrified of her, but everything Tara said was true. I have been trying to tell you for months that Tara was a valuable asset to this company and needed to be treated better, but you disregarded my words every single time. You are a great broker, but as a boss, I'm sorry, you kind of suck." His face turns red, and he opens his mouth to speak, but I cut him off. "You know I'm right, Dad. Now you're going to see just how badly you screwed up because Tara kept so many people in this place afloat, including me. I guess this is how you'll learn, though."

Despite my shock at how quickly everything just happened, I'm incredibly proud of her for putting herself first and telling Dad exactly what he needed to hear. This is going to make family dinners decidedly uncomfortable, though.

"Well, now we'll have to find you another assistant," he grumbles.

I laugh. "Good luck with finding one as qualified as Tara. Any other completely inexperienced people you want to just slot in there?" I ask, crossing my arms and sitting back in my seat.

"Careful, Aiden. You're my son but even you have limits on what you can get away with."

"Maybe so, but someone needs to be able to tell you the truth, and that's me. I've got work I need to get done, and now I'll be having to explain to the clients that the person they trusted has gone. I'll talk to you later when you decide who will be taking Tara's job."

I head back to my office, sitting down at my desk to try and process how quickly things have changed. But instead of getting into the mountain of work I now have to tackle, I open up the application form I've been opening and closing for the last week, deciding that if Tara can take the leap with her career, I can do the same thing. Within twenty minutes, it's completed and when I hit send, I know we're both moving on to bigger and better things. As long as we're doing it together, it's exciting and I can't wait to tell her.

While I'm contemplating what to do next, Dad walks in and takes a seat across from me.

"I think we need to clear the air." I stare at him, stunned. He continues when it becomes clear that I'm not going to respond. "After your mother took you to London, all I could think about was that one day, I'd convince you to come and work with me, and we could build a relationship that way. But I don't think that's really possible, is it?"

I turn his words over in my head, trying to understand what he's getting at, but it's just not computing. "What are you saying?"

Oh God, is he about to fire me?

He sighs again. "I'm saying I've failed you as a father. I don't really know how to build a relationship with you after all our years apart. That's why I've been pushing with work, I guess. I thought that if we could share the running of this office together, maybe we could find some common ground. But it's not going to work that way, is it?"

I slowly shake my head. "No. I get why you hoped it would go that way, but insurance just isn't for me. I do want to try to build a relationship with you, but work won't be our common ground, unfortunately."

He nods. "Well, when you know what you want to do, just let me know, I guess. In the meantime, maybe we can try and have lunch together more often? Try and find that common ground somewhere else?"

I smile, still reeling from the about face, but relieved that he's at least willing to consider supporting me. "That would be good."

"Good. How about today?"

"Oh." I pause, not having expected to have to start this new venture straight away. "Um, sure."

"Let's go then. I'm buying."

He gets to his feet, and I trail after him, wondering at the speed at which that all happened.

When I finish work, Tara messages me to let me know she's up at the hospital again.

Concern floods through me and I jump in a cab, heading straight over.

I meet her outside her father's room, and it's obvious from her red eyes that things have taken a turn for the worse. I pull her into a hug, and she sobs into my chest.

"I'm sorry. I know we need to talk about everything that happened today, but then Jo called me to let me know that his organs have started to fail and I should get up here." Her words are muffled against my shirt and I rub a soothing hand up and down her back, feeling a pang in my chest as the memories of the final days with Mum come flooding back.

It's hard watching a parent slip away, and she's going to need all the support she can get right now. I'm just relieved that I can be here for her.

She steps back and gives me a shaky smile.

"What do you need right now?" I ask, placing my hands on her shoulders.

She lets out a breath while she thinks. "Could you get Jo a coffee from the cafeteria? She's close to burn out right now. Maybe take the girls with you?"

I nod. "I can do that."

Tara goes back into the room, reappearing moments later with Piper and Jordan in tow. The girls both look like they are struggling, and I figure a distraction is in order.

"You guys want ice creams?" I ask.

Piper immediately nods her head excitedly, but Jordan is a little more wary. She shrugs, but follows along while Piper takes my hand and we walk back towards the lift.

Piper chats animatedly about her day, and Jordan nods along quietly, while I lead the way to the cafeteria. They pick their ice creams and we take a seat at the table while I wait for Jo's coffee to be made.

After ten minutes, they call out my name, and I retrieve the coffee before guiding the girls back towards the lift. As I hit the button, a woman joins us, dragging a small suitcase behind her. There's something familiar about her, and Jordan peers at her for a moment, before glancing at me with wide eyes. Looking closer, I realise where I recognise her from, taking in her long red hair and features that are so similar to Tara's and the girls. I freeze, wondering if I should say something or keep quiet for the girls sake.

We all silently get in the lift, and once we arrive back on the ward, Piper and Jordan race ahead of me while I hang back. Once they're out of earshot, I turn to the woman who is looking from her phone to the room numbers.

"Annelisa?" I say, hesitating in case I'm wrong.

She gives me a startled look. "Um. Yes? Sorry, do I know you?"

I shake my head. "I'm Aiden."

Her shoulders relax and she smiles. "Ah. Hi. So those girls..." She looks ahead of us to where Piper and Jordan disappear into their father's room.

"They're your sisters, yes."

She tenses a little before nodding. "Is Tara in there?"

"Yeah. Do you want me to get her so you can speak to her first? You might need some time to prepare yourself."

She gives me a stricken look before nodding. Telling her to give me a minute, I head into the room and hand Jo her coffee. She accepts it gratefully, and I move to Tara's side. She's sitting in a chair near her father's head, and Jordan watches me closely when Tara looks up as I squeeze her shoulder.

"Can you come out into the hall for a sec? There's someone out there."

She gives me a confused look, but gets to her feet. I nod at Jordan, and the young girl sits forward, watching us walk out. As soon as Tara catches sight of Annelisa, she starts crying and throws her arms around her sister. They cling to one another, and I go back into the room to give them a moment. Relief that Annelisa made it before their father slips away floods through me, knowing that it had been weighing on Tara greatly.

"Is she coming in?" Jordan demands, and Jo gives me a questioning look.

I glance at Paul. He's asleep, and I wonder how much longer he has left.

Will Annelisa get the chance to talk to him?

"Annelisa's here," I tell Jo, before looking back at Jordan. "I don't know. But she flew all the way from London, so I'd say she will. It's just going to take her a moment."

Jordan stares sullenly at the door, and I wonder how it's all going to go once they are all in a room together.

45
GLAD YOU CAME

TARA

I HOLD Annelisa tightly while the tears pour down my face. I feel like all I've done in the last few days is cry, and it's exhausting.

"I can't believe you're here," I half sob while she returns my hug.

Pulling away, she looks me over while holding me at arms length. "I had already decided to come before I got your message. Booked the next flight and came straight from the airport." She gestures towards the suitcase beside her.

"I'm glad you reconsidered."

She nods, glancing towards the door to Dad's room. "How is he?"

I shake my head. "They're keeping him comfortable, but I'm not sure how much time he has left. He's asleep at the moment, but you should come in."

She hesitates for a moment. "I'm not sure I'm ready to face the girls yet," she says, and I sigh.

"Lis, I say this with love, but this isn't about you and what you're ready to deal with. Just... Just do it for Dad. Do it for yourself. You and I are both pretty broken, and the only way we can put ourselves back together is to be there in the last days he has left."

Her lower lip quivers a little, but she pulls herself together before nodding, steeling herself as she follows me back into the room.

Jo looks over, nodding towards Annelisa, who freezes in the doorway, her eyes locked on our father's still form. Sensing that she needs a moment, I reach back to squeeze her hand before turning back to my step-mother.

"Do you think we could give Lis a minute with Dad first?"

Jo nods towards the girls. "Of course. Girls, let's go for a walk."

Jordan looks like she's going to argue for a moment, but she relents and follows her mother out of the room. I move to follow them, but Annelisa grips my hand.

"Please stay," she pleads.

I nod and exchange glances with Aiden. He nods and follows the others out into the hall.

Once we're alone, Annelisa lets out a breath before moving closer to the bed. I can tell that she hadn't been fully prepared for how much Dad's appearance has changed, and she reaches a tentative hand forward to brush his hair away from his forehead.

"Hi Daddy," she whispers.

As if her voice has woken him from a magical sleep, his eyes flutter open, and once he's able to focus, his eyes meet hers. A smile slowly forms on his lips, and she lets out a deep, wracking sob before leaning down to hug him. With great effort, he lifts his arm to pat her on the back.

"Hi, baby girl."

A lump forms in my throat as they hold each other. Dad just lets her cry while using every ounce of his strength to stroke her hair. Eventually, he has to let his arm drop back to his side, and Annelisa finally pulls herself together.

It's so rare to see my sister show emotion openly. In fact, I'm pretty sure the last time I saw her cry like this was when Dad left. I am sure that the exhaustion from a straight day of travel isn't helping, but it's a relief to see her allowing herself to feel the grief in this moment and not bottle it all up.

"I'm so glad you came," Dad says, his voice barely more than a whisper.

"I'm sorry I didn't come earlier," she replies, wiping away the tears that are sliding down her cheeks.

"It's okay." He takes a breath that rattles deep in his chest, and my throat tightens.

Aiden pokes his head back inside and motions for me to come out.

"Your mum is here," he says quietly once I reach the door.

I nod, and follow him back into the hall. Thankfully, it's empty except for Mum. I'm not sure if the girls could handle seeing Mum after Jordan's response to Annelisa's arrival.

"Annelisa messaged me from the airport. I thought I'd better come up. How's he doing?" Mum asks, pulling me into a hug.

I struggle to compose myself, and Aiden steps up behind me, rubbing my back while I begin to sob into my mother's neck.

"They've said it won't be much longer," Aiden replies for me, and I feel Mum nod.

The grief I'm feeling is worse than the pain I'd felt when Dad left, and I'm not sure I can handle much more. So when Mum offers to go in and sit with Dad and Annelisa, I'm flooded with relief. She's better equipped for this, and I don't know if I can support Annelisa while dealing with my own pain.

I allow her to transfer me into Aiden's arms and hear the door open and close behind me.

A few moments later, Dad's nurses come by and check to make sure everything is okay. I ask them to hold off on their check-up, explaining briefly what's happening, and they nod, moving on to the next room.

When Jo reappears, Aiden gives her the latest update, and she takes a deep breath, letting it out slowly while looking down at the girls, who are gripping both her hands.

"What's going on?" Piper asks, looking between all the adults with wide eyes.

"Dad's old wife is here. And that lady in the elevator was Annelisa," Jordan says, summing it all up simply for her little sister.

"Oh… Why are they here?" The innocence on Piper's little face is heartbreaking, and I wonder how she's going to cope once Dad is gone.

"They just came to see Dad. It's okay." Jordan steps around Jo to slide an arm around Piper's shoulders, her gaze fixed on mine.

Eventually, Mum emerges from Dad's room and waves everyone inside. Seeing how crowded it is in the small room, Aiden and Mum decide to head down to the cafe to give us all space. I move to Annelisa's side while the girls look at her with wary expressions.

"Jordan, Piper. This is Annelisa," I say.

They both nod, and Piper speaks up. "Are you our big sister?" Her little voice waivers.

To my surprise, Annelisa nods. "Yes. It's really nice to meet you."

The joy on Dad's face is beautiful while he watches the four of us talk. When he eventually drifts off again, Jo gathers the girls' things together and gives my hand a squeeze.

"I need to get these two home and to bed. Will we see you tomorrow?" She looks between Annelisa and I, and we both nod.

"I need some sleep, but when I wake up in the morning, I'll come up," Annelisa says, pulling up the handle of her suitcase.

"And I quit my job today, so I'll be here as often as you need me," I chime in, and they both look at me with raised eyebrows.

"Uh, you what?" Annelisa asks.

"Yeah, it was a whole thing. I'll fill you in on the way downstairs."

With another glance back towards Dad, the three of us walk out together.

I never thought I'd see the day when my sister and I were willingly spending time with Jo, but it's funny how life throws curveballs at you. I'm just glad we were all able to give Dad his wish to see all his girls together.

I give them both the abbreviated version of what happened at work, which feels like a lifetime ago now, even though it's only been a few hours.

"And this is Aiden's father? That's going to make family time a tonne of fun," Annelisa says, shaking her head.

"Yeah. Might be a while before I join him for any dinners," I reply with a cynical laugh.

"He seems like a great guy, Tara. You've got a good one there," Jo says as we make our way to the cafeteria.

I smile when my gaze falls on where Aiden is talking to Mum, both looking at complete ease together. "Yeah... Yeah I do."

46
CAN'T ALL FIND THE ONE WHEN WE'RE TEENAGERS

TARA

THE NEXT MORNING, I arrive at Mum's house earlier than planned to pick up Annelisa. She's staying here for now, not wanting to chance running into anyone if she stays with me. Given the chances of people showing up unannounced is pretty high, it's probably for the best.

I want to talk to her before we're back at the hospital. While I was so happy to see her yesterday, we still have some tension to work out, and I'd rather not do that in front of others.

I walk inside to find Annelisa sitting in the kitchen, practically inhaling her breakfast.

"Not been able to get Vegemite in London?" I ask, admiring her skill at making a piece of toast disappear in 4 bites.

"I can but it's ridiculously expensive so I don't get it often. I'm taking a few jars back with me." She moves on to her tea, taking a sip while watching me sit down.

"So," I say, and she raises an eyebrow.

"So."

I take a breath. "About the stuff I said on our last video call..."

She puts her cup down and waits for me to continue. "I said some stuff that was probably a little too harsh."

She shakes her head. "No, you didn't. I needed to hear it, as much as it hurt like hell at the time. I did a lot of self reflection after that conversation and you were right. When I left, I was in such a shit headspace that I didn't stop to think about how any of it would affect anyone else, except maybe Will." She winces a little when she says his name. Like just the mention of the love of her life causes her physical pain. "I'm sorry that things between the two of you soured because of my actions. And for what it did to everyone else."

I watch her while she stares at the table, lost in thought. After a moment, I ask cautiously, "Lis? Why did you leave? What happened between you and Will?"

She slowly brings her gaze to mine. "Has he not told anyone?"

I shake my head. "No. He's been as tightlipped as you. Although I think Chris knows something," I reply, remembering Chris saying that Will had shared a little with him about what happened.

She sighs. "I can't tell you everything, but it wasn't because of anything Will did. Something happened, and I realised I wasn't the right person for him. I wasn't in a good place for awhile, and the way I handled it was terrible. But I wasn't thinking straight, so I just left."

"Why can't either of you just tell us what happened?" I ask, growing frustrated with the secrecy.

"Because some things just need to stay between us," she replies, her expression closing over.

I bite back my retort, wanting to point out that they are no longer an "us" because of how she broke them. Some things aren't worth saying out loud, though.

Annelisa has always kept her feelings to herself, which has long frustrated me, but I guess she's entitled to her secrets.

I nod, deciding not to push it any further. She's already told me more in this short conversation than she's opened up about in the last three years.

She continues eating her breakfast while we sit in silence for a few minutes, and I try to work out what more I can say on the subject. It still doesn't feel resolved, but I don't know how to fix it while we have so much else going on. Inspecting her closer, I realise now how much weight she's lost since I last saw her in person, and I wonder what her life in London is really like. I've always been curvier than her, but this is on a whole different level.

"When are you coming home, Lis?" I ask, eventually.

She leans her hip against the bench and sighs, the lines of fatigue on her face seeming to go deeper than just the jet lag. "I'm not."

I cross my arms. "Everyone who loves you is here. I just worry about you being all alone over there. Do you even go out? Every time I speak to you, there's another deadline you're working towards. You used to be able to balance work with everything else, but it feels like work is all you do now."

She shakes her head. "I can't come back, Tara. I fucked everything up here. I don't deserve to be happy anymore. It's just better for everyone if I stay away."

Her words are like a punch to the chest. That she is so convinced that we're better off without her is devastating, and I get up to give her a hug. She resists at first, but eventually allows herself to relax and hug me back.

"No matter what happened, Lis, you deserve to be happy. Whatever it was, I'm sure it's not as bad as you've built it up in your head."

She shakes her head but doesn't reply, and I can tell there's no convincing her. I just hope that one day, she realises that the people who love her are hurting more without her in our lives than if she came back.

"We should get going," she says, stepping back.

I nod, waiting for her to collect her handbag before leading the way out to my car.

"Where's Aiden?" she asks, settling into the passenger seat.

"I sent him to work today. I don't want to make him sit around the hospital and bring back memories of his mum constantly."

Last night, I was too emotionally drained to talk about the events of the last few days, and Aiden had been amazing, just allowing me to lie with my head on his chest without pressuring me to talk. But I know we're eventually going to have to talk it all out.

"He doesn't seem to mind, Tara. I think it's great you've found someone who seems so supportive," Annelisa says, pulling me from the memory of Aiden running his fingers through my hair in the early hours of the morning.

"He is honestly amazing, Lis. I don't know how I got so lucky, but I love him more than I ever thought possible. After all the years alone, I thought it would never be my turn."

She reaches over and squeezes my leg. "You were always meant to be with someone like him. You were never going to be the one who dated around. You just needed to find your person. We can't all find the one when we're teenagers." Her tone is wistful, and I know she's thinking of Will.

It's so obvious that they are both miserable without each other. I just have to hope that they both eventually find a way to move on. Or, even better, find their way back to each other.

47
BEST CHOICE I'VE EVER MADE

AIDEN

WHEN TARA TOLD me she was going to spend the day at the hospital again, I offered to take the rest of the week off work so I could be there for her. But she told me it was okay. I tried not to let the rejection sting, and considered just going to the hospital again after work, but decided against it.

Arriving at the office, it feels so strange knowing that Tara won't be coming back again. One of the other assistants has taken on some of her work, but no one could ever replace her. It's going to take some getting used to.

"Hey Celeste." I nod towards the young receptionist when I head through to my office.

"Hi Aiden. How's Tara?" she asks.

Not wanting to go in to details about Tara's personal life, I nod and say "she's okay."

"Can you tell her I'm sorry?"

I study her for a moment. "What do you have to be sorry for?"

"For letting Felicity get in my head and believe that Tara was just sleeping her way to the top. I should never have listened to her. I know Tara would never do anything like that."

Resisting the urge to tell her exactly what I think of Felicity, I simply nod. "I'll let her know. Thank you for apologising."

She gives me a relieved smile and I continue on my way, glad that at least one of the admin staff has realised the error of their ways.

After work, I stop at the shops on the way home to buy the ingredients for one of my mother's favourite recipes when I was growing up, a simple beef stew with vegetables. I've been feeling closer to the memory of my mother lately, and it feels like I'm sharing a bit of her with Tara by making her a meal that had brought me so much comfort growing up.

Letting myself into her apartment, I get started on the meal prep, and once she messages to tell me she's on her way home, I go in to the ensuite and run her a bubble bath.

Returning to the kitchen, I open a bottle of wine, pouring two glasses and leaving them to sit on the bench.

When she walks in the door fifteen minutes later, I can see that the emotions of the day have worn her down again. The lines of fatigue and grief on her face have become more pronounced, and she looks ready to pass out.

Moving to stand in front of her, I pull her into my arms and she sinks into the embrace, bringing her arms around to cling to me tightly.

"Something smells great," she mumbles into my chest.

"It's one of my Mum's old recipes. I thought you could use something warm and comforting tonight," I reply.

She steps back and gives me a tired smile.

Moving back to the kitchen, I hand her one of the glasses of wine and nod towards her room. "I've run you a bath, and dinner should be ready in about half an hour."

She grips the glass while running her eyes over my face, her eyes starting to glisten a little. "You ran me a bath?"

"Yeah. I used some of the bubble bath you had in there, I hope that's okay?" I ask, suddenly wondering if I've done the wrong thing.

Her lower lip wobbles and she launches herself at me. I catch her as she crashes into me, stumbling back slightly before finding my footing and holding her tight. She lets out a little sob while she squeezes me around the middle.

"You are too good to me," she says, her words muffled.

I give her a gentle squeeze. "I just thought you could use some taking care of, with everything going on."

She looks up at me, a tear rolling down her face. "I'm sorry this is all happening now. I hate that you've been dragged into all of this when you're still dealing with your own grief."

I wipe away the tear, cupping her cheeks in both hands. "Hey. I want to be here, okay? I want to hold your hand through this. I want to be the one to wipe away your tears, and hold you when you feel like it's all too much. This is part of what being in a healthy relationship is like. We can't always be happy, but we ride out the storms together."

She swallows hard, her eyes shining while she studies my face. Raising up on to her tiptoes, she presses a soft kiss to my lips, before resting her forehead against mine.

"Thank you," she whispers.

"You're welcome," I whisper back, brushing my lips against her forehead when she lowers herself back down. "I love you."

She smiles up at me. "I love you, too."

As I watch her walk into the bedroom, my heart feels like it's doubled in size, and I'm so grateful to have found her when I did.

That night, as we lie in bed, I tell her about filling in the application to finish my degree.

"I'm so proud of you," she says, stroking my cheek.

I cover her hand with mine before lifting it and kissing her palm. "I never would have had the courage to do it if you hadn't pushed me."

Her responding smile is so beautiful it hurts. "We're a team, remember? I'll always support you."

"And I'll always support you. I don't know much in this life, but I know this. The decision to sit down and talk to a stranger at a hotel bar was the best choice I've ever made. We met at the right time, when we needed each other, and I can't wait to spend the rest of my life with you." I reach up to rub my thumb over her lips before lifting my head to kiss her.

She kisses me back, and as the kiss grows and we begin to move together, shedding clothes before finding solace in one another.

It feels so right.

It feels like coming home.

EPILOGUE

4 MONTHS LATER

TARA

I POINT to my suitcase as it moves past on the conveyor belt, and Aiden steps through the crowd to retrieve it. Now that we've both got our things, we pull on some extra layers of clothing before joining Will, Jake and Bri. The five of us weave our way through the busy airport towards the Arrivals area.

Once we walk through the doors, I'm immediately set upon by a blur of brown hair and excited squeals. Stumbling backwards, I laugh while wrapping my arms around Kylie as she grips me tight.

"I can't believe you're finally here! Hi Aiden," she adds, giving him a quick squeeze before moving on to give the others the same greeting as me.

The two of them have gotten to know each other over regular video calls, but this is the first time they've seen each other since their brief introduction all those months ago.

Seth steps up beside Kylie and gives me a hug. "Welcome to Canada."

"Thanks!"

"Come on, let's get you guys home so you can start to get settled." Kylie takes my suitcase and bounces along beside me while Seth leads the way outside.

The freezing cold air hits me the minute I'm through the door, and my gaze falls to the snow piled high on the other side of the road.

When Kylie convinced us to come for a visit, she'd used seeing snow as the main draw card, and now I can't wait to see more.

The last four months have certainly been interesting. My father had held on for another two weeks, and while it's hard knowing he's gone, it's a relief to know he's no longer in pain. Since then, I've been focusing on getting settled at my new job, which has been so much better than I ever thought it could be. Having Chris's support has been great, and I wish he and Morgan were here too, but they had their little girl a few weeks ago, and have been trying to settle into life with a newborn.

Aiden moved into the apartment with me once his six-month lease ended, and we started searching for a house together, putting in an offer on our dream home last week. They accepted it two days before we left, and we were busy getting all the finances sorted before we got on a plane.

When Kylie and Seth shared the news of their engagement after a brief trip to Paris in the week between Christmas and New Year's, the rest of us jumped at the chance to come over and celebrate with them. She's planned several trips for us in areas around Calgary, excited to show us all the places she's fallen in love with since she moved here.

Deciding it's safer to go with Seth than risk death by getting in a car with Kylie behind the wheel, Aiden and I chat easily with him for the drive back to their place, which is absolutely massive.

When we get inside, I let out an excited squeal when I see who's waiting for us in the lounge room, launching myself at

Lincoln. I wrap my arms around him, and he laughs before ruffling up my hair.

"Hi Tara," he says, before introducing himself to Aiden and shaking his hand.

A golden retriever puppy comes scuttling out of the kitchen a moment later, coming to a stop at his feet.

"Who's this little guy?" I ask, bending down to scoop the puppy into my arms, where it licks my face and neck.

"That's Milo. I just got him," Lincoln replies, scratching the little dog behind the ears.

"Of course you have a golden retriever, it suits your personality perfectly," I joke, and Lincoln grins.

Kylie's cousin, Adele, is also here and once the others arrive, introductions are in order.

Aiden steps up beside me and puts his arm around my waist, brushing his lips to my temple. "When do you want to tell them?" he whispers in my ear.

We've been sitting on our secret for a few weeks, and I'd told him I didn't want to tell Kylie over video chat, so we kept the news to ourselves until we arrived.

"What are you two whispering about over there?" Kylie says, running her eyes over us.

Smiling, I pull out my phone and dial Chris, who answers on the first ring, his tired face appearing on the screen. I can see little Lucy's soft curls next to his cheek and can tell he's sitting in the chair in her nursery. After I say hi, I tell him we have an announcement and he calls Morgan in to join him.

Aiden takes the phone, holding it up so that they can see while I put my hand into my left pocket. I slide the two rings onto my finger before pulling it out again, holding my hand up for everyone to see.

A moment of stunned silence, and then Kylie lets out another squeal and hugs me again.

"You guys are engaged, too? Oh my god!"

"No, not engaged," I reply, and she pulls away to give me a confused look.

I hold my hand out to her and she looks closely at my rings. "Wait... there's two rings... I'm so confused."

Bri laughs, shaking her head as she comes to give me her own hug. "Isn't it obvious? They skipped a step. That's an engagement ring *and* a wedding ring."

Kylie's mouth drops open and looks between Aiden and I. "Wait, you guys got married?!" She glances at Aiden's hand, spying the ring he just slipped onto his own finger.

I smile. "Yeah. Neither of us wanted to make a big deal, so we just went to city hall three weeks ago. Only Mum, Jo and the girls know, cause they were our witnesses. And Lis knows, obviously. We wanted to tell everyone else together. But don't worry, this holiday is all about your engagement, Kyles."

She tsks, shaking her head. "As if I care about that. I'm just so happy for you guys."

While I stand here, surrounded by most of the important people in my life, I can't help but feel a little sad that Annelisa isn't experiencing this along with me. When she returned to London after Dad's funeral, I could tell that her determination to stay away had started to slip, and I've been slowly working on convincing her to come home. I don't know if I'll ever succeed, but I'm determined to keep trying.

After more congratulations, Kylie and Seth show us all to our rooms, and I take a moment to rest my forehead against Aiden's, stealing a little moment together before having showers and joining the others for dinner.

"How do you feel now that we've told everyone?" Aiden asks, rubbing his hand up and down my back.

I smile, giving him a soft kiss. "The happiest I've ever been. We can tell them the other news once we hit the three month mark," I reply, laying my hand gently on my stomach. I'm two months along, so not showing yet. "I love you, Mr Sanderson."

He grins. "And I love you, Mrs Sanderson." He takes my hand and guides me into a spin before dipping me backwards, and I giggle. "I'm so glad I get to spend the rest of my life dancing with you."

"And what a dance it will be."

We kiss again, and, for the thousandth time, I marvel at how lucky we both are to have found each other when we did. Sometimes, things just fall perfectly into place when everything seems to be falling apart. And I wouldn't change a second of our moments together for all the world.

IF YOU HAVE A MOMENT

Thank you for reading! I hope you enjoyed Dance With Me. Next up in The Circle of Friends is Will & Annelisa's story, Pieces of Us, out now. Read on for a preview of the what's to come.

Please take a moment to leave a rating or review on the platform you purchased from or Goodreads. Every review helps in an incredible way.

If you enjoyed this book and would like to stay up to date with all new releases and behind-the-scenes shenanigans, please sign up for my substack.

ACKNOWLEDGMENTS

When I set out to write this book, I knew I would be dealing with some pretty heavy subject matter. Tara's inner thoughts in the beginning reflected a lot of my own experiences in my late teens to late twenties, watching others have the life that I thought I wanted for myself. I thought that tapping back into those feelings would be the hardest part of writing Dance With Me.

I knew that the story would be dealing with the grief of losing a parent, as this was always the relationship that would be the most painful for both Tara and Annelisa.

What I wasn't expecting was to experience that grief first hand as I was writing those final chapters. The pain Annelisa felt when she saw her father lying sick in his hospital bed was the first time I've ever cried writing a scene, and it was because I was mourning the loss of my beloved mother-in-law, who passed away as I was writing the first draft. I thought my own cancer fight was the worst 2024 could throw at our family, but sadly, that wasn't the case, and the world is a little colder without her in it.

I truly hope that you all found a piece of yourself in these characters, and I can't wait to share Annelisa's story with you next.

And now, for the less emotional part.

Firstly - to my husband, who has been my rock throughout the last year, and the many before that as well. Thank you for carrying the load the last twelve months and I hope the next few years are far less fraught for us both.

To my beautiful daughter - thank you, as always, for being my number one fan, even though you are years away from being old enough to read any of these books.

To my beta readers and amazing friends (and sister), Melinda, Jammi-Lee and Shannon - thank you for loving these characters as much as I do, and for the incredibly helpful feedback that made their stories even better.

To my editor and dear friend, Krystal, thank you for powering through my words even while your life has been so busy! Getting closer to that lunch date I owe you once we're on the same continent again.

To my Writing Fridays ladies, Lauren, Demi, Mel and Kaitlyn, thank you for all your support this year. I'm so glad I am able to spend Friday's with you again now that I'm no longer in hibernation, and I look forward to many more unhinged library sessions together.

To my Street Team - Maddie's Bark Brigade - I hope you enjoy this one as much as you did The Winning Ticket and Chasing Horizons, and I can't wait to work with you all again! You make my little author heart so happy.

And to you, the reader. Thank you for making my author journey such an amazing experience. Without you all, this would be nothing more than a dream.

WANT A SNEAK PEEK
OF PIECES OF US?

Turn the page to read the first chapter.

1

ELSA WAS REALLY A RED HEAD

ANNELISA

I LET myself into my sister's house and take in the chaos before me.

My four-year-old niece, Brandie, has covered every inch of floor in the lounge room with blankets from the large basket where they are kept. At least, I'm assuming it was Brandie, judging by the various stuffed animals scattered around. It definitely seems more likely to have been her than Tara, her thirty-one-year-old mother and my younger sister. And I'm pretty sure Tara would kick her husband's backside if he left her lounge room looking like this. Aiden isn't always the tidiest, but I think he even he has enough self-preservation instincts not to leave the house looking like a bomb went off.

"Tara! Are you here?" I call out, navigating my way through the sea of blankets.

"In here!" Tara hollers back, and I continue on towards the kitchen.

Brandie sits at the kitchen table, colouring, and singing to herself while kicking her legs back and forth. Her deep red hair, identical to mine and Tara's, hangs down her back in waves.

Smiling, I take a seat next to her, picking up a pencil and beginning to colour in a picture of Elsa from Frozen.

"So, what are you cooking me for dinner?" I ask, turning to Tara with a toothy grin.

"I'll cook you dinner if you get those boxes out of my spare room and take them back to Mum's," she replies, not looking up from the cupcakes she's icing.

"Ugh... I guess I'll just starve," I reply, and she pauses to glare at me.

"Annelisa Richards, you take those boxes before I have to rock up with them in my car and accidentally drop one on your head while you sleep."

I raise an eyebrow. "Jeez. That's a tad violent, Tara."

She snorts. "I've had to resort to violence because asking nicely has not worked once since you got back and I had to keep asking over and over. I want people to be able to use my spare room, Lis. And at the moment, the boxes completely ruin the aesthetic. Mum brought them here when she was downsizing and promised me that you'd deal with them the next time you were in town. Well, guess what, you've been in town for a month, and I still can't see the floor in there."

"Chill. I'll take them with me. I've got Mum's car cause I had to take the rental back, so they should all fit."

She claps her hands together and holds them against her chest. "Thank god. In that case, I will cook you dinner. Also, why'd you have to take the rental back?"

I shrug, continuing to colour the picture in front of me. "It was getting expensive, and Mum wasn't using her's for awhile, so figured I'd just save some money and use hers."

"You know, you could just buy a car." Tara gives me a pointed look, which I choose to ignore.

"I still don't know if I'm sticking around, so why would I buy a car?"

She snorts again. "Come off it. We both know you're back for good, you just refuse to accept it."

"Why would I accept it when I don't know if that's what I want? Besides, I still have stuff back in London. And a room I'm paying for."

She purses her lips. "Can you honestly tell me that you'd rather go back to London, where you were miserable and lonely, than stay here where you've got your family who love you? And friends, who, if you bothered to contact any of them, would love to spend time with you again?" When I don't answer immediately, she continues. "Maybe it's time to sort through those boxes?"

I glare at her, but am saved from responding when Brandie notices what I'm doing.

"Aunty Lissa, that's the wrong colour! Elsa's hair is yellow!"

I grin while I continue colouring Elsa's hair red. "I feel like Elsa was really a redhead. I mean, she has the fire of a redhead, just like us, huh?" I nudge Brandie with my elbow and wink.

The little girl fixes me with a determined glare. "No, it's yellow. Do it right." She hands me a yellow pencil, removing the red one from my hand before returning to her own picture.

I look over at Tara with raised eyebrows while she smothers a laugh with her hand.

"What can I say? She's a woman who knows what she wants... World domination is in her future, I swear." Tara hands me a plate with a cupcake on it. "So, no avoiding it. It's time to deal with those boxes"

I sigh, wishing her sister wasn't quite so good at finding my sore spots. "I'll be taking the boxes back to Mum's and shoving them into her spare room cupboard that no one sleeps in but me."

My tone should be enough of a hint that we need to end the conversation, but I can tell that Tara isn't going to let it go. It's a well-worn conversation. Discussed to death, actually. Well, at least on Tara's side. I rarely discuss it and spend most of my time avoiding the topic when it comes up.

"You know, you might actually feel better about everything if you open those boxes..." Tara keeps pushing.

"Can we just let it go? The past is in the past... No point in opening old wounds after all this time. No good can come from it." I pick the cupcake up and rip the bottom half off before smashing it into the icing on top.

Brandie watches me, fascinated, while I eat it like a sandwich. "I wanna do that too!" She proceeds to attempt the same thing and almost loses the icing altogether before Tara rescues it.

Never have I been so grateful to have the focus off me.

"Hello?" My brother-in-law, Aiden, appears in the doorway with a stack of notepads in his arms.

"Hey, babe," Tara replies while Brandie jumps to her feet and throws her arms around Aiden's waist.

"Annelisa," Aiden says, nodding towards me.

I wave back while I finish chewing.

"How was school?" Tara asks, taking the books from Aiden's arms.

He brushes a kiss to her forehead. "Fine. I've got so much marking to do tonight, though."

Aiden's recently started working as a primary school teacher, and I have no idea how he does it. I love my niece, but I couldn't spend that much time with a large group of children and stay sane. He handles it all really well, though.

"Dinner will be ready in about half an hour, if you want to take a shower and decompress?" Tara suggests.

Aiden nods. "Yeah, that's a good idea, thanks Love. Are you staying for dinner, Lis?"

I grin. "Yep. Sorry."

He laughs, shaking his head. "Nothing to be sorry for, you're always welcome here."

"Good man."

As he walks out, he calls back over his shoulder, "Just remember to take the boxes when you leave this time!"

Tara shoots me a triumphant grin while I drop my forehead onto my arms in defeat.

"Oh, and Tara... what happened to the lounge room?" Aiden calls from the other room, and I'm saved from any further comments when Tara goes to look and loses her mind.

After staying for dinner, Aiden and Tara help me load the car with the boxes, and I roll my eyes when Tara claps her hands with glee once they are all out of the spare room.

Waving goodbye, I head back to Mum's apartment a few streets away and lug the boxes up the stairs over several trips.

When she'd finally sold the house that Tara and I grew up in, she'd bought a three bedroom apartment in an older building. It's fully renovated, but the lack of elevator makes me wonder how long she plans on staying. At sixty, her knees aren't getting any younger.

Once I get all the boxes inside, I take them to the third bedroom that I've been as an office while I've been here, and pile them in the wardrobe,. I figure, if they are in here, I don't have to look at them. Stepping back, I stare at them for a moment, my gaze fixed on the once familiar handwriting that spells out my name, before tentatively reaching out and opening the first one.

At the very top, a framed photo from seven years ago looks up at me. Taken at the wedding of two of my oldest friends, I run a finger over the image of the person sitting next to me. His beautiful face was once more familiar to me than my own, and I wonder how much it's changed since then. Do his eyes still sparkle with laughter? Or have the years worn him down like they have me?

I stare at the photo for a long time, lost in thought and drowning in memories. Memories that I swore I would never relive, knowing that it would be like ripping my heart out over and over. Seven years is a long time to nurse a broken heart...

Hastily wiping a tear away, I shove the photo back in the box and close it again.

I'll never be ready to deal with the memories inside of those boxes. Like I said to Tara, the past is in the past. There's no point in opening old wounds.